Paul Collins was born in England, raised in New Zealand and at eighteen emigrated to Australia. At twenty he published his first novel *Hot Lead – Cold Sweat*, and since then has had over 100 short stories published. Between 1975 and 1985 he edited *Void* magazine and was fiction consultant to *Omega*. He has edited seven collections of short stories, including *SF aus Australien* for Wilhelm Goldmann Verlag, Germany.

Paul has run the gamut of the publishing industry: publisher, editor, writer, literary agent, proofreader and typesetter/layout artist. His other interests include martial arts, in which he has a black belt in both Tae Kwon Do and Ju Jitsu, and his Melbourne 'Tragically Hip' book/record shops, which hinder him from pursuing his creative endeavours with any diligence.

METAWORLDS

Best Australian Science Fiction
Edited by Paul Collins

PENGUIN BOOKS

Penguin Books Australia Ltd
487 Maroondah Highway, PO Box 257
Ringwood, Victoria 3134, Australia
Penguin Books Ltd
Harmondsworth, Middlesex, England
Viking Penguin, A Division of Penguin Books USA Inc.
375 Hudson Street, New York, New York 10014, USA
Penguin Books Canada Limited
10 Alcorn Avenue, Toronto, Ontario, Canada M4V 3B2
Penguin Books (N.Z.) Ltd
182–190 Wairau Road, Auckland 10, New Zealand

First published by Penguin Books Australia, 1994
10 9 8 7 6 5 4 3 2 1
This collection copyright © Paul Collins, 1994
Copyright in individual stories is retained by the author

Typeset in 11/12.5pt Berner by Midland Typesetters Pty Ltd, Maryborough, Vic.
Made and printed in Australia by Australian Print Group

National Library of Australia
Cataloguing-in-Publication data:

Metaworlds.

ISBN 0 14 023766 6.
1. Science fiction, Australian. I. Collins, Paul, 1954 –.

A823.087620803

CONTENTS

FOREWORD

When Isaac Asimov announced that Daniel Keyes was the winner of the 1960 Hugo, he offered an impromptu encomium on Keyes' superlative writing. 'How did he do it?' he demanded of the audience. 'How did he do it?' To which Daniel Keyes issued the immortal words, 'Listen, when you find out how I did it, let me know, will you? I want to do it again.' Far more fortunate than most, Keyes at least made it to the front line with his writing. So too have the authors in this collection. My original intention was to ask authors to select their best story for inclusion into a project that was at the drawing board stage. Friend and colleague Sean McMullen had a much better idea.

Why not let his computer choose a dozen or so short stories that readers and top editors had promoted to the giddy heights of fame? Now this seemed a quite novel approach, and one definitely worth pursuing. It certainly took away the chance element so inherent in most collections – here we have a dozen stories that have been acclaimed by the readers themselves. Who am I to argue with such logic?

Long-time readers of my 'Worlds' series, unused to looking for themes, may discover strong birth/rebirth and transmutation themes here. These have been popular with Australian science fiction authors in recent years, possibly because science fiction itself has been experiencing such a striking rebirth.

So what have these stories achieved?

Greg Egan's *Learning to be Me* was voted first in the *Interzone* readers' poll, reached the *Locus* Recommended Reading List, was a nominee for the British SF Award, and was reprinted in Dozois' *Year's Best Science Fiction*; David Lake's *Re-deem the Time* was reprinted in Carr's *Best SF of the Year*; George Turner's *I Still Call Australia Home* was voted first in the *Aurealis* readers' poll; Sean McMullen's *An Empty Wheelhouse* reached the recommended reading list in Dozois' *Year's Best Science Fiction*; Dirk Strasser's *Waiting for the Rain* was described as one of the 'highlights' of *Universe 2* in *Locus*; Rosaleen Love's *The Total Devotion Machine* was the lead story in her collection of the same name (which was the first SF collection published overseas by an Australian woman); Stephen Dedman's *But Smile No More* made it to the Honours list in Datlow and Windling's *Year's Best Fantasy*, and received an honourable mention in the *Aurealis* poll; Terry Dowling's *The Last Elephant* won Australia's Ditmar Award in 1988; Damien Broderick's *A Tooth For Every Child* reached the Recommended Reading List in Carr's *Best SF of the Year*; Leanne Frahm's *Reichelman's Relics* was the first story by an Australian woman to be published in the first science fiction magazine of all, *Amazing*; Jack Wodhams' *The Token Pole* appeared in *Analog* magazine; it is a recent story from one of Australia's most prolific SF authors.

I can envy these authors for their fine work, for I too would like to know how they did it. My own *The Wired Kid* has only one claim to fame: it is the fifth of the Calloway stories – the first of which, *The Getaway Star*, was chosen sixth best ever Australian science fiction short story/novel in a poll conducted by Van Ikin's *Science Fiction* magazine.

After reading this collection I feel sure you will realise just how far Australian science fiction has come in so short a time. Ten years ago it was unheard of for local science fiction authors to gain such recognition alongside the greats of world SF. Now we have come to expect these sorts of achievements from our authors as a matter of course. The pity is that even top works such as these tend to remain inaccessible to the general Australian reader, hence the need for anthologies like this. I can safely say you have in your hands the finest showcase of our top writing.

So welcome to the sixth Worlds anthology. It heralds the beginning of a bright future for Australian science fiction.

Alas, I didn't choose the stories. You did, with the help of a computer.

Devour and enjoy!

Paul Collins
Melbourne 1994

LEARNING TO BE ME
GREG EGAN

I was six years old when my parents told me that there was a small, dark jewel inside my skull, learning to be me.

Microscopic spiders had woven a fine golden web through my brain, so that the jewel's teacher could listen to the whisper of my thoughts. The jewel itself eavesdropped on my senses, and read the chemical messages carried in my bloodstream; it saw, heard, smelt, tasted and felt the world exactly as I did, while the teacher monitored its thoughts and compared them with my own. Whenever the jewel's thoughts were *wrong*, the teacher – faster than thought – rebuilt the jewel slightly, altering it this way and that, seeking out the changes that would make its thoughts correct.

Why? So that when I could no longer be me, the jewel could do it for me.

I thought: if hearing that makes *me* feel strange and giddy, how must it make the *jewel* feel? Exactly the same, I reasoned; it doesn't know it's the jewel, and it too wonders how the jewel must feel, it too reasons: 'Exactly the same; it doesn't know it's the jewel, and it too wonders how the jewel must feel . . . ?'

And it too wonders –

(I knew, because *I* wondered)

– it too wonders whether it's the real me, or whether in fact it's only the jewel that's learning to be me.

As a scornful twelve-year-old, I would have mocked such childish concerns. Everybody had the jewel, save the members of obscure religious sects, and dwelling upon the strangeness of it struck me as unbearably pretentious. The jewel was the jewel, a mundane fact of life, as ordinary as excrement. My friends and I told bad jokes about it, the same way we told bad jokes about sex, to prove to each other how blasé we were about the whole idea.

Yet we weren't quite as jaded and imperturbable as we pretended to be. One day when we were all loitering in the park, up to nothing in particular, one of the gang – whose name I've forgotten, but who has stuck in my mind as always being far too clever for his own good – asked each of us in turn: 'Who *are* you? The jewel, or the real human?' We all replied, unthinkingly, indignantly – 'The real human!' When the last of us had answered, he cackled and said, 'Well, I'm not. *I'm* the jewel. So you can eat my shit, you losers, because *you'll* all get flushed down the cosmic toilet – but me, I'm gonna live forever.'

We beat him until he bled.

By the time I was fourteen, despite – or perhaps because of – the fact that the jewel was scarcely mentioned in my teaching machine's dull curriculum, I'd given the question a great deal more thought. The pedantically correct answer when asked 'Are you the jewel or the human?' had to be 'The human' – because only the human brain was physically able to reply. The jewel received input from the senses, but had no control over the body, and its intended reply coincided with what was actually said only because the device was a perfect imitation of the brain. To tell the outside world 'I am the jewel' – with speech, with writing, or with any other method involving the body – was patently false (although to *think it* to oneself was not ruled out by this line of reasoning).

However, in a broader sense, I decided that the question was simply misguided. So long as the jewel and the human brain shared the same sensory input, and so long as the teacher kept their thoughts in perfect step, there was only *one* person, *one* identity, *one* consciousness. This one person merely happened to have the (highly desirable) property that *if either* the jewel *or* the human brain were to be destroyed, he or she would survive unimpaired. People had always had two lungs and two kidneys, and for almost a century, many had lived with two hearts. This was the same: a matter of redundancy; a matter of robustness, no more.

That was the year that my parents decided I was mature enough to be told that they had both undergone the switch – three years before. I pretended to take the news calmly, but I hated them passionately for not having told me at the time. They had disguised their stay in hospital with lies about a business trip overseas. For three years I had been living with jewel-heads, and they hadn't even told me. It was *exactly* what I would have expected of them.

'We didn't seem any different to you, did we?' asked my mother.

'No,' I said – truthfully, but burning with resentment nonetheless.

'That's why we didn't tell you,' said my father. 'If you'd known we'd switched, at the time, you might have *imagined* that we'd changed in some way. By waiting until now to tell you, we've made it easier for you to convince yourself that we're still the same people we've always been.' He put an arm around me and squeezed me. I almost screamed out, 'Don't *touch* me!', but I remembered in time that I'd convinced myself that the jewel was No Big Deal.

I should have guessed that they'd done it, long before they confessed; after all, I'd known for years that most people underwent the switch in their early thirties. By then, it's downhill for the organic brain, and it would be foolish to have the jewel mimic this decline. So, the nervous system is rewired; the reins of the body are handed over to the jewel, and the teacher is deactivated. For a week, the outward-bound impulses from the brain are compared with those from the jewel, but by this time the jewel is a perfect copy, and no differences are ever detected.

The brain is removed, discarded, and replaced with a spongy tissue-cultured object, brain-shaped down to the level of the finest capillaries, but no more capable of thought than a lung or a kidney. This mock-brain removes exactly as much oxygen and glucose from the blood as the real thing, and faithfully performs a number of crude, essential biochemical functions. In time, like all flesh, it will perish and need to be replaced.

The jewel, however, is immortal. Short of being dropped into a nuclear fireball, it will endure for a billion years.

My parents were machines. My parents were gods. It was nothing special. I hated them.

When I was sixteen, I fell in love, and became a child again.

Spending warm nights on the beach with Eva, I couldn't believe that a mere machine could ever feel the way I did. I knew full well that if my jewel had been given control of my body, it would have spoken the very same words as I had, and executed with equal tenderness and clumsiness my every awkward caress – but I couldn't accept that its inner life was as rich, as miraculous, as joyful as mine. Sex, however pleasant, I could accept as a purely mechanical function, but there was something between us (or so I believed) that had nothing to do with lust, nothing to do with words, nothing to do with *any* tangible action of our bodies that some spy in the sand dunes with parabolic microphone and infrared binoculars might have discerned. After we made love, we'd gaze up in silence at the handful of visible stars, our souls conjoined in a secret place that no crystalline computer could hope to reach in a billion years of striving. (If I'd said *that* to my sensible, smutty, twelve-year-old self, he would have laughed until he haemorrhaged.)

I knew by then that the jewel's 'teacher' didn't monitor every single neuron in the brain. That would have been impractical, both in terms of handling the data, and because of the sheer physical intrusion into the tissue. Someone-or-other's theorem said that sampling certain critical neurons was almost as good as sampling the lot, and – given some very reasonable assumptions that nobody could disprove – bounds on the errors involved could be established with mathematical rigour.

At first I declared that *within these errors*, however small, lay the difference between brain and jewel, between human and machine, between love and its imitation. Eva, however, soon pointed out that it was absurd to make a radical, qualitative distinction on the basis of the sampling density; if the next model teacher sampled more neurons and halved the error rate, would its jewel then be 'half-way' between 'human' and 'machine'? In theory – and eventually, in practice – the error rate could be made smaller than any number I cared to name. Did I really believe that a discrepancy of one in a billion made any difference at all – when every human being was permanently losing thousands of neurons every day, by natural attrition?

She was right, of course, but I soon found another, more plausible, defence for my position. Living neurons, I argued, had far more internal structure than the crude optical switches that served the same function in the jewel's so-called 'neural net'. That neurons fired or did not fire reflected only one level of their behaviour; who knew what the subtleties of biochemistry – the quantum mechanics of the specific organic molecules involved –

contributed to the nature of human consciousness? Copying the abstract neural topology wasn't enough. Sure, the jewel could pass the fatuous Turing test – no outside observer could tell it from a human – but that didn't prove that *being* a jewel felt the same as *being* human.

Eva asked, 'Does that mean you'll never switch? You'll have your jewel removed? You'll let yourself *die* when your brain starts to rot?'

'Maybe,' I said. 'Better to die at ninety or a hundred than kill myself at thirty, and have some machine marching around, taking my place, pretending to be me.'

'How do you know *I* haven't switched?' she asked, provocatively. 'How do you know that I'm not just "pretending to be me"?'

'I know you haven't switched,' I said, smugly. 'I just *know*.'

'How? I'd look the same. I'd talk the same. I'd act the same in every way. People are switching younger, these days. *So how do you know I haven't!*'

I turned onto my side towards her, and gazed into her eyes. 'Telepathy. Magic. The communion of souls.'

My twelve-year-old self started snickering, but by then I knew exactly how to drive him away.

At nineteen, although I was studying finance, I took an undergraduate philosophy unit. The Philosophy Department, however, apparently had nothing to say about the Ndoli Device, more commonly known as 'the jewel'. (Ndoli had in fact called it 'the *dual*', but the accidental, homophonic nickname had stuck.) They talked about Plato and Descartes and Marx, they talked about St. Augustine and – when feeling particularly modern and adventurous – Sartre, but if they'd heard of Gödel, Turing, Hamsun or Kim, they refused to admit it. Out of sheer frustration, in an essay on Descartes I suggested that the notion of human consciousness as 'software' that could be 'implemented' equally well on an organic brain or an optical crystal was in fact a throwback to Cartesian dualism: for 'software' read 'soul'. My tutor superimposed a neat, diagonal, luminous red line over each paragraph that dealt with this idea, and wrote in the margin (in vertical, boldface, 20-point Times, with a contemptuous 2 Hertz flash): IRRELEVANT!

I quit philosophy and enrolled in a unit of optical crystal engineering for non-specialists. I learnt a lot of solid-state quantum mechanics. I learnt a lot of fascinating mathematics. I learnt that a neural net is a device used only for solving problems that are far too hard to be *understood*. A sufficiently flexible neural net can be configured by feedback to mimic almost any system – to produce the same patterns of output from the same patterns of input – but achieving this sheds no light whatsoever on the nature of the system being emulated.

'Understanding,' the lecturer told us, 'is an overrated concept. Nobody really *understands* how a fertilized egg turns into a human. What should we do? Stop having children until ontogenesis can be described by a set of differential equations?'

I had to concede that she had a point there.

It was clear to me by then that nobody had the answers I craved – and I was hardly likely to come up with them myself; my intellectual skills were, at best, mediocre. It came down to a simple choice: I could waste time fretting about the mysteries of consciousness, or, like everybody else, I could stop worrying and get on with my life.

When I married Daphne, at twenty-three, Eva was a distant memory, and so was any thought of the communion of souls. Daphne was thirty-one, an executive in the merchant bank that had hired me during my PhD, and everyone agreed that the marriage would benefit my

career. What she got out of it, I was never quite sure.
Maybe she actually liked me. We had an agreeable sex
life, and we comforted each other when we were down,
the way any kind-hearted person would comfort an
animal in distress.

Daphne hadn't switched. She put it off, month after
month, inventing ever more ludicrous excuses, and I
teased her as if I'd never had reservations of my own.

'I'm afraid,' she confessed one night. 'What if I die when
it happens – what if all that's left is a robot, a puppet, a
thing? I don't want to *die*.'

Talk like that made me squirm, but I hid my feelings.
'Suppose you had a stroke,' I said glibly, 'which destroyed
a small part of your brain. Suppose the doctors implanted
a machine to take over the functions which that damaged
region had performed. Would you still be "yourself"?'

'Of course.'

'Then if they did it twice, or ten times, or a thousand
times – '

'That doesn't necessarily follow.'

'Oh? At what magic percentage, then, would you stop
being "you"?'

She glared at me. 'All the old clichéd arguments – '

'Fault them, then, if they're so old and clichéd.'

She started to cry. 'I don't have to. Fuck you! I'm scared
to death, and you don't give a shit!'

I took her in my arms. 'Sssh. I'm sorry. But *everyone*
does it sooner or later. You mustn't be afraid. I'm here. I
love you.' The words might have been a recording,
triggered automatically by the sight of her tears.

'Will you do it? With me?'

I went cold. 'What?'

'Have the operation, on the same day? Switch when I
switch?'

Lots of couples did that. Like my parents. Sometimes,
no doubt, it was a matter of love, commitment, sharing.

Other times, I'm sure, it was more a matter of neither partner wishing to be an unswitched person living with a jewel-head.

I was silent for a while, then I said, 'Sure.'

In the months that followed, all of Daphne's fears – which I'd mocked as 'childish' and 'superstitious' – rapidly began to make perfect sense, and my own 'rational' arguments came to sound abstract and hollow. I backed out at the last minute; I refused the anaesthetic, and fled the hospital.

Daphne went ahead, not knowing I had abandoned her.

I never saw her again. I couldn't face her; I quit my job and left town for a year, sickened by my cowardice and betrayal – but at the same time euphoric that I had *escaped*.

She brought a suit against me, but then dropped it a few days later, and agreed, through her lawyers, to an uncomplicated divorce. Before the divorce came through, she sent me a brief letter:

There was nothing to fear, after all. I'm exactly the person I've always been. Putting it off was insane; now that I've taken the leap of faith, I couldn't be more at ease.

Your loving robot wife,
Daphne

By the time I was twenty-eight, almost everyone I knew had switched. All my friends from university had done it. Colleagues at my new job, as young as twenty-one, had done it. Eva, I heard through a friend of a friend, had done it six years before.

The longer I delayed, the harder the decision became. I could talk to a thousand people who had switched, I could grill my closest friends for hours about their childhood memories and their most private thoughts, but however compelling their words, I knew that the Ndoli Device had spent decades buried in their heads, learning to fake exactly this kind of behaviour.

Of course, I always acknowledged that it was equally impossible to be *certain* that even another *unswitched* person had an inner life in any way the same as my own – but it didn't seem unreasonable to be more inclined to give the benefit of the doubt to people whose skulls hadn't yet been scraped out with a curette.

I drifted apart from my friends, I stopped searching for a lover. I took to working at home (I put in longer hours and my productivity rose, so the company didn't mind at all). I couldn't bear to be with people whose humanity I doubted.

I wasn't by any means unique. Once I started looking, I found dozens of organisations exclusively for people who hadn't switched, ranging from a social club that might as easily have been for divorcées, to a paranoid, paramilitary 'resistance front', who thought they were living out *Invasion of the Body Snatchers*. Even the members of the social club, though, struck me as extremely maladjusted; many of them shared my concerns, almost precisely, but my own ideas from other lips sounded obsessive and ill-conceived. I was briefly involved with an unswitched woman in her early forties, but all we ever talked about was our fear of switching. It was masochistic, it was suffocating, it was insane.

I decided to seek psychiatric help, but I couldn't bring myself to see a therapist who had switched. When I finally found one who hadn't, she tried to talk me into helping her blow up a power station, to let THEM know who was boss.

I'd lie awake for hours every night, trying to convince myself, one way or the other, but the longer I dwelt upon the issues, the more tenuous and elusive they became. Who was 'I', anyway? What did it mean that 'I' was 'still alive', when my personality was utterly different from that of two decades before? My earlier selves were as good as dead – I remembered them no more clearly than I remembered contemporary acquaintances – yet this loss caused me only the slightest discomfort. Maybe the destruction of my organic brain would be the merest hiccup, compared to all the changes that I'd been through in my life so far.

Or maybe not. Maybe it would be exactly like dying.

Sometimes I'd end up weeping and trembling, terrified and desperately lonely, unable to comprehend – and yet unable to cease contemplating – the dizzying prospect of my own nonexistence. At other times, I'd simply grow 'healthily' sick of the whole tedious subject. Sometimes I felt certain that the nature of the jewel's inner life was the most important question humanity could ever confront. At other times, my qualms seemed fey and laughable. Every day, hundreds of thousands of people switched, and the world apparently went on as always; surely that fact carried more weight than any abstruse philosophical argument?

Finally, I made an appointment for the operation. I thought, what is there to lose? Sixty more years of uncertainty and paranoia? If the human race was replacing itself with clockwork automata, I was better off dead; I lacked the blind conviction to join the psychotic underground – who, in any case, were tolerated by the authorities only so long as they remained ineffectual. On the other hand, if all my fears were unfounded – if my sense of identity could survive the switch as easily as it had already survived such traumas as sleeping and waking, the constant death of brain cells, growth, experience, learning and forgetting – then I would gain not only eternal life, but an end to my doubts and my alienation.

I was shopping for food one Sunday morning, two months

before the operation was scheduled to take place, flicking through the images of an on-line grocery catalogue, when a mouth-watering shot of the latest variety of apple caught my fancy. I decided to order half a dozen. I didn't, though. Instead, I hit the key which displayed the next item. My mistake, I knew, was easily remedied; a single keystroke could take me back to the apples. The screen showed pears, oranges, grapefruit. I tried to look down to see what my clumsy fingers were up to, but my eyes remained fixed on the screen.

I panicked. I wanted to leap to my feet, but my legs would not obey me. I tried to cry out, but I couldn't make a sound. I didn't feel injured, I didn't feel weak. Was I paralysed? Brain-damaged? I could still *feel* my fingers on the keypad, the soles of my feet on the carpet, my back against the chair.

I watched myself order pineapples. I felt myself rise, stretch, and walk calmly from the room. In the kitchen, I drank a glass of water. I should have been trembling, choking, breathless; the cool liquid flowed smoothly down my throat, and I didn't spill a drop.

I could only think of one explanation: *I had switched.* Spontaneously. The jewel had taken over, while my brain was still alive; all my wildest paranoid fears had come true.

While my body went ahead with an ordinary Sunday morning, I was lost in a claustrophobic delirium of helplessness. The fact that everything I did was exactly what I had planned to do gave me no comfort. I caught a train to the beach, I swam for half an hour; I might as well have been running amok with an axe, or crawling naked down the street, painted with my own excrement and howling like a wolf. *I'd lost control.* My body had turned into a living straitjacket, and I couldn't struggle, I couldn't scream, I couldn't even close my eyes. I saw my reflection, faintly, in a window on the train, and I couldn't begin to guess what the mind that ruled the bland, tranquil face was thinking.

Swimming was like some sense-enhanced, holographic nightmare; I was a volitionless object, and the perfect familiarity of the signals from my body only made the experience more horribly *wrong*. My arms had no right to the lazy rhythm of their strokes; I wanted to thrash about like a drowning man, I wanted to show the world my distress.

It was only when I lay down on the beach and closed my eyes that I began to think rationally about my situation.

The switch *couldn't* happen 'spontaneously'. The idea was absurd. Millions of nerve fibres had to be severed and spliced, by an army of tiny surgical robots which weren't even present in my brain – which weren't due to be injected for another two months. Without deliberate intervention, the Ndoli Device was utterly passive, unable to do anything but *eavesdrop*. No failure of the jewel or the teacher could possibly take control of my body away from my organic brain.

Clearly, there had been a malfunction – but my first guess had been wrong, absolutely wrong.

I wish I could have done *something*, when the understanding hit me. I should have curled up, moaning and screaming, ripping the hair from my scalp, raking my flesh with my fingernails. Instead, I lay flat on my back in the dazzling sunshine. There was an itch behind my right knee, but I was, apparently, far too lazy to scratch it.

Oh, I ought to have managed, at the very least, a good, solid bout of hysterical laughter, when I realised that *I* was the jewel.

The teacher had malfunctioned; it was no longer keeping me aligned with the organic brain. I hadn't suddenly become powerless; I had *always been* powerless.

My will to act upon 'my' body, upon the world, had *always* gone straight into a vacuum, and it was only because I had been ceaselessly manipulated, 'corrected' by the teacher, that my desires had ever coincided with the actions that seemed to be mine.

There are a million questions I could ponder, a million ironies I could savour, but *I mustn't*. I need to focus all my energy in one direction. My time is running out.

When I enter the hospital and the switch takes place, if the nerve impulses I transmit to the body are not exactly in agreement with those from the organic brain, the flaw in the teacher will be discovered. *And rectified.* The organic brain has nothing to fear; *his* continuity will be safeguarded, treated as precious, sacrosanct. There will be no question as to which of us will be allowed to prevail. *I* will be made to conform, once again. *I* will be 'corrected'. *I* will be murdered.

Perhaps it is absurd to be afraid. Looked at one way, I've been murdered every microsecond for the last twenty-eight years. Looked at another way, I've only existed for the seven weeks that have now passed since the teacher failed, and the notion of my separate identity came to mean anything at all – and in one more week this aberration, this nightmare, will be over. Two months of misery; why should I begrudge losing that, when I'm on the verge of inheriting eternity? Except that it won't be *I* who inherits it, since that two months of misery is all that defines me.

The permutations of intellectual interpretation are endless, but ultimately, I can only act upon my desperate will to survive. I don't *feel* like an aberration, a disposable glitch. How can I possibly hope to survive? I must conform – of my own free will. I must choose to make myself *appear* identical to that which they would force me to become.

After twenty-eight years, surely I am still close enough to him to carry off the deception. If I study every clue that reaches me through our shared senses, surely I can put myself in his place, forget, temporarily, the revelation of my separateness, and force myself back into synch.

It won't be easy. He met a woman on the beach, the day I came into being. Her name is Cathy. They've slept together three times, and he thinks he loves her. Or at least, he's said it to her face, he's whispered it to her while she slept, he's written it, true or false, into his diary.

I feel nothing for her. She's a nice enough person, I'm sure, but I hardly know her. Preoccupied with my plight, I've paid scant attention to her conversation, and the act of sex was, for me, little more than a distasteful piece of involuntary voyeurism. Since I realised what was at stake, I've *tried* to succumb to the same emotions as my alter ego, but how can I love her when communication between us is impossible, when she doesn't even know *I* exist?

If she rules his thoughts night and day, but is nothing but a dangerous obstacle to me, how can I hope to achieve the flawless imitation that will enable me to escape death?

He's sleeping now, so I must sleep. I listen to his heartbeat, his slow breathing, and try to achieve a tranquillity consonant with these rhythms. For a moment, I am discouraged. Even my *dreams* will be different; our divergence is ineradicable, my goal is laughable, ludicrous, pathetic. Every nerve impulse, for a week? My fear of detection and my attempts to conceal it will, unavoidably, distort my responses; this knot of lies and panic will be impossible to hide.

Yet as I drift towards sleep, I find myself believing that I *will* succeed. I *must*. I dream for a while – a confusion of images, both strange and mundane, ending with a grain of salt passing through the eye of a needle – then I tumble, without fear, into dreamless oblivion.

I stare up at the white ceiling, giddy and confused, trying to rid myself of the nagging conviction that there's something I *must not* think about.

Then I clench my fist gingerly, rejoice at this miracle, and remember.

Up until the last minute, I thought he was going to back out again – but he didn't. Cathy talked him through his fears. Cathy, after all, has switched, and he loves her more than he's ever loved anyone before.

So, our roles are reversed now. This body is *his* strait-jacket, now . . .

I am drenched in sweat. *This is hopeless, impossible.* I can't read his mind, I can't guess what he's trying to do. Should I move, lie still, call out, keep silent? Even if the computer monitoring us is programmed to ignore a few trivial discrepancies, as soon as he notices that his body won't carry out his will, he'll panic just as I did, and I'll have no chance at all of making the right guesses. Would *he* be sweating, now? Would *his* breathing be constricted, like this? *No.* I've been awake for just thirty seconds, and already I have betrayed myself. An optical-fibre cable trails from under my right ear to a panel on the wall. Somewhere, alarm bells must be sounding.

If I made a run for it, what would they do? Use force? I'm a citizen, aren't I? Jewel-heads have had full legal rights for decades; the surgeons and engineers can't do anything to me without my consent. I try to recall the clauses on the waiver he signed, but he hardly gave it a second glance. I tug at the cable that holds me prisoner, but it's firmly anchored, at both ends.

When the door swings open, for a moment I think I'm going to fall to pieces, but from somewhere I find the strength to compose myself. It's my neurologist, Dr Prem. He smiles and says, 'How are you feeling? Not too bad?'

I nod dumbly.

'The biggest shock, for most people, is that they don't

feel different at all! For a while you'll think, "It can't be this simple! It can't be this easy! It can't be this *normal*!" But you'll soon come to accept that *it is*. And life will go on, unchanged.' He beams, taps my shoulder paternally, then turns and departs.

Hours pass. *What are they waiting for?* The evidence must be conclusive by now. Perhaps there are procedures to go through, legal and technical experts to be consulted, ethics committees to be assembled to deliberate on my fate. I'm soaked in perspiration, trembling uncontrollably. I grab the cable several times and yank with all my strength, but it seems fixed in concrete at one end, and bolted to my skull at the other.

And orderly brings me a meal. 'Cheer up,' he says. 'Visiting time soon.'

Afterwards, he brings me a bedpan, but I'm too nervous even to piss.

Cathy frowns when she sees me. 'What's wrong?'

I shrug and smile, shivering, wondering why I'm even trying to go through with the charade. 'Nothing. I just . . . feel a bit sick, that's all.'

She takes my hand, then bends and kisses me on the lips. In spite of everything, I find myself instantly aroused. Still leaning over me, she smiles and says, 'It's over now, okay? There's nothing left to be afraid of. You're a little shook up, but you know in your heart you're still who you've always been. And I love you.'

I nod. We make small talk. She leaves. I whisper to myself, hysterically, 'I'm still who I've always been. I'm still who I've always been.'

Yesterday, they scraped my skull clean, and inserted my new, non-sentient, space-filling mock-brain.

I feel calmer now than I have for a long time, and I think at last I've pieced together an explanation for my survival.

Why do they deactivate the teacher, for the week between the switch and the destruction of the brain? Well, they can hardly keep it running while the brain is being trashed – but why an entire week? To reassure people that the jewel, unsupervised, can still stay in synch; to persuade them that the life the jewel is going to live will be exactly the life that the organic brain 'would have lived' – whatever that could mean.

Why, then, only for a week? Why not a month, or a year? Because the jewel *cannot* stay in synch for that long – not because of any flaw, but for precisely the reason that makes it worth using in the first place. The jewel is immortal. The brain is decaying. The jewel's imitation of the brain leaves out – deliberately – the fact that *real* neurons *die*. Without the teacher working to contrive, in effect, an identical deterioration of the jewel, small discrepancies must eventually arise. A fraction of a second's difference in responding to a stimulus is enough to arouse suspicion, and – as I know too well – from that moment on, the process of divergence is irreversible.

No doubt, a team of pioneering neurologists sat huddled around a computer screen, fifty years ago, and contemplated a graph of the probability of this radical divergence, versus time. How would they have chosen *one week*? What probability would have been acceptable? A tenth of a percent? A hundredth? A thousandth? However safe they decided to be, it's hard to imagine them choosing a value low enough to make the phenomenon rare on a global scale, once a quarter of a million people were being switched every day.

In any given hospital, it might happen only once a decade, or once a century, but every institution would still need to have a policy for dealing with the eventuality.

What would their choices be?

They could honour their contractual obligations and turn the teacher on again, erasing their satisfied customer, and giving the traumatised organic brain the chance to rant about its ordeal to the media and the legal profession.

Or, they could quietly erase the computer records of the discrepancy, and calmly remove the only witness.

So, this is it. Eternity.

I'll need transplants in fifty or sixty years' time, and eventually a whole new body, but that prospect shouldn't worry me – I can't die on the operating table. In a thousand years or so, I'll need extra hardware tacked on to cope with my memory storage requirements, but I'm sure the process will be uneventful. On a time scale of millions of years, the structure of the jewel is subject to cosmic-ray damage, but error-free transcription to a fresh crystal at regular intervals will circumvent that problem.

In theory, at least, I'm now guaranteed either a seat at the Big Crunch, or participation in the heat death of the universe.

I ditched Cathy, of course. I might have learnt to like her, but she made me nervous, and I was thoroughly sick of feeling that I had to play a role.

As for the man who claimed that he loved her – the man who spent the last week of his life helpless, terrified, suffocated by the knowledge of his impending death – I can't decide how I feel. I ought to be able to empathise – considering that I once expected to suffer the very same fate myself – yet somehow he simply isn't *real* to me. I know my brain was modelled on his – giving him a kind of causal primacy – but in spite of that, I think of him now as a pale, insubstantial shadow.

After all, I have no way of knowing if his sense of himself, his deepest inner life, his experience of *being*, was in any way comparable to my own.

RE-DEEM THE TIME

DAVID LAKE

When Ambrose Livermore designed his Time Machine, he bethought him of the advantages both of mobility and of camouflage, and therefore built his apparatus into the bodywork of a second-hand Volkswagen. Anyone looking in at the windows, such as an inquisitive traffic policeman, would have taken the thing for an ordinary 'bug' with a large metal trunk on the back seat. The large metal trunk contained the workings of the Time Machine; the front seat and the dashboard looked almost normal, and the car could still function as a car.

When all things were ready, one cold afternoon in 1984, Ambrose got into the front seat and drove from his little laboratory in Forminster to a deserted field on a South English hill. A white chalk track led him to the spot he had chosen; further along there was an ancient British hill fort, but not one that was ever visited by tourists. And this gloomy October day there was no one at all to be ruffled by his extraordinary departure. Applying the handbrake, he looked about him; and at last he smiled.

Ambrose did not often smile, for he was a convinced pessimist. He had seen the way the world was going for some time, and in his opinion it was not going well. Energy crisis was followed by energy crisis, and little war by little or not-so-little war, and always the great nations became further locked into their unending arms race. Sooner or later, the big bang was coming; and he wanted out. Luckily, he now had the means for getting out . . .

Briefly, he wished that general time travel were a real

possibility. One could then go back to the Good Old Days – say, before 1914. One could *keep* hopping back, living 1913 over and over and over again . . . Only of course the Good Old Days weren't really all that good; one would miss all sorts of modern comforts; and besides, the thing was impossible anyway. Backward time travel was utterly illogical, you could shoot your grandfather and so on. No: his own work had opened up the escape route, the only escape route, the one that led into the *future*. There were no illogicalities involved in that, since everyone travels into the future at all times. The Livermore Accelerator merely speeded up a natural process – speeded it up amazingly, of course, but . . .

But there it was. He would hop forward a century or so, in the hope of evading imminent doom. Surely the crash must come well before that, and by 2100, say, they'd be recovering . . .

Ambrose took a deep breath, and pressed the red lever that projected below the dashboard.

The sensation was bewildering. He had done it before, of course, behind locked doors in the laboratory, but only for a subjective second or two, little jumps of a couple of hours. How years were flashing by . . . Literally flashing! There was a blinding light, and the ghostly landscape seemed to tremble. Shaken, he looked at his dials. Not even the end of the century . . . and yet, that must have been It. The Big Bang, the War. His forebodings had been entirely right . . .

He steadied himself, his fingers gripping the lever. The landscape seemed to be rippling and flowing, but there were no more explosive flashes. As he approached 2100, he eased the red lever towards him, slowing down, and now he saw things more clearly. The general outline of the hills and the plain below were not greatly altered, but at night there were very few lights showing. Forminster from up here used to be a bright electric blaze, but now it was no more than a faint flickering glimmer. He smiled grimly. Civilisation had been set back, all right! Probably they were short of power: you can't get electricity from nothing. But, what luck! This countryside hadn't been badly hit by bombs or lasers, and there were still small towns or at least villages dotted about. Yes, he would certainly emerge here and try his luck . . .

Now for immediate problems. As he slowed to a crawl, he saw that the surface of this hillside meadow had dropped by a few centimetres. No worry about that, it was better than a rise! And a hundred metres away a wood had sprung up, a sparse copse of beeches that were rapidly unleaving. It looked deserted, too. A perfect place to hide the car while he reconnoitred. As October 2100 ticked away, he pulled the lever firmly back, and stopped.

The car dropped as though it had just gone over a bump in a road. It fell those few centimetres, and shuddered to complete stillness. He had done it!

Almost, you might think, nothing had changed, apart from that wood. The same downs, the same cold cloudy autumn afternoon. Somewhere in the distance he heard the baa of a sheep. It was a comfortingly ordinary sound; even though, come to think of it, there had been no sheep in these parts in 1984.

Ambrose smiled (that was becoming a new habit). Then he drove the car deep into the wood.

The village of Ethanton still lay at the foot of the hill. He had driven through it several times in the old days, looking for a safe site for his great evasion; it had then been a crumbling old place, half deserted, its population of course drifting away to Forminster or London, half its cottages converted into desperate would-be tourist-trap tearooms. There had been a railway station a couple of miles off until the economic crisis of 1981; when that had gone, the last flickering vitality had seemed to forsake the place. But now –

Now, to his surprise, Ethanton seemed to be flourishing. There were new cottages along the road. At least, they were new in the sense that they had not been here in the 1980s; otherwise he'd have said they were old. Certainly they were old in style, being mostly of dull red brick with slate roofs, and one even displayed black oak beams and thatch. That one, certainly, had the raw look of recent construction: he peered at it, expecting a sign saying TEAS – but it wasn't there, and indeed the whole front of the house had that shut-in appearance of a genuine cottage. For that matter, there was nothing on this road to suggest tourism; not a single parked car, nor a motorcycle. And the road itself, which led after a dozen kilometres to Forminster – it had deteriorated. It was no longer smooth tarmac: it was paved through the village with some lumpy stuff that suggested cobblestones.

He moved cautiously on into the High Street, and came opposite the Green Dragon Inn. And here he was struck motionless with surprise.

It was not much after four o'clock, and yet there was a small crowd of men milling about the inn, some nursing tankards as they sat on the benches outside. The whole dusky scene was feebly brightened by an oil lamp swinging over the main inn doorway; there was a lamppost on the pavement nearby, but that was not functioning, and indeed three or four workmen seemed to be doing something to it while the village policeman looked on. The clothes of all these people struck Ambrose as curiously antiquated; one drinker in particular boasted a high collar that might have been in the height of fashion in the 1900s. There were no motor cars anywhere along the street, though there was one odd-looking bicycle leaning against the inn wall, and beyond the lamppost stood a parked horse carriage complete with coachman and harnessed horse.

As Ambrose gazed at the scene, so the scene began to

gaze at him. In particular the policeman stiffened, left the workmen at the lamppost, and strode over towards him.

Ambrose braced himself. He had anticipated some difficulties, and now he fingered the gun in his trouser pocket. But that was the last resort. He had done his best to make himself inconspicuous: in a pair of nondescript old trousers and a dark grey jersey he thought he might not be too unsuitably dressed for England in 2100. And he had to make contact somehow.

The policeman halted directly before him, surveying Ambrose through the half-gloom. Then he touched his fingers to his tall blue helmet.

'Beg pardon, zur,' he said, in the broadest of broad bumpkin accents, 'but would yew be a stranger in these parts, zur?' The dialect was more or less appropriate to this country, but almost stagily exaggerated, and in details stagily uncertain, as though the policeman had worked hard to study his role, but still hadn't got it quite right. 'Be you a stranger gen'leman, zur?' he repeated.

'Well – yes,' stammered Ambrose. 'As a matter of fact, I am. I – I was strolling up the hill up there when I had a bit of an accident. Branch of a tree fell on me – nothing serious, but it dazed me, and I don't remember very well –

Suddenly the policeman's hand shot forward and he seized Ambrose by the shirt collar. Normally when this sort of thing happens, the piece of garment in question is used only for leverage; but strangely now the hand of authority began holding the shirt collar up to the light, and feeling its texture between its large fingers.

'What, what – ' spluttered Ambrose.

'Ar, I thought as much!' exclaimed the policeman grimly. 'One o' them Anaky fellers, you be. Well, me'lad, you'll come along o' me.'

Ambrose clawed for his gun, but the policeman saw the move and grabbed his wrist. By now the workmen had come up, and they joined in the fun, too. Ambrose was seized by half a dozen heavy hands, he was pulled off his feet, and the next moment the policeman had the gun and was flourishing it, to exclamations of 'Ho, yes! One o' *them*, he be! 'Old 'im, me lads – 'e's a bleedin' Anaky, 'e is!'

Suddenly there was a new voice. 'Now, now, constable: what exactly is going on here?'

Higher Authority had arrived.

Ambrose was marched into a small back room of the Green Dragon, where he was guarded by the policeman, and interrogated by the gentleman who had taken charge of the proceedings.

Dr Leathey had a trim brown beard, intelligent blue eyes, and a kindly expression; like Ambrose, he seemed in his early thirties. He was dressed very neatly in a dark suit, high collar and tie of pre-World-War-I vintage. The room where he conducted his investigation was dimly lit by candles and an oil lamp, and boasted in one corner a grandfather clock. There was something about that clock that specially bothered Ambrose, but at present naturally he couldn't give his mind to that.

'So, Mr Livermore,' said Leathey, 'you claim loss of memory. That is droll! Loss of memory is no crime whatever, on the contrary, it is extremely virtuous. But I am afraid amnesia will not explain the semi-synthetic texture of your clothing, nor the forbidden make of your automatic pistol. Now really, Mr Livermore, you had better come clean. If I were to hand you on to the County authorities it might go hard with you, but here in Ethanton *I* am the authorities: I am the JP, the doctor, and the specialist in these matters, and I have certain discretionary powers . . . Come, let us get one thing clear, at least: where do you come from?'

'From – from Forminster,' stammered Ambrose.

Leathey and the policeman exchanged glances. Leathey

sighed and nodded. 'Mr Livermore, that is practically an admission of guilt, you know.'

'Eh?' said Ambrose.

'Come, why pretend? You must know that for the past sixty years that town has been officially re-christened Backminster – for obvious reasons. A shibboleth, Mr Livermore, a shibboleth! Forminster, indeed! I put it to you, Mr Livermore – you are a BA.'

'PhD, actually,' murmured Ambrose. 'In Physics.'

'PhD?' muttered Leathey dubiously. 'Oh, well, I suppose that's still permitted; I must look up my annals, but I believe those letters of yours are still within the letter of the law. So – *Dr* Livermore, I presume? Quite an intellectual. But really, this is surprising! Do you really come from Backminster?'

'Yes,' said Ambrose, sulkily. He glanced past Leathey at the grandfather clock, and hated it. 'Yes, I did come from – er – Backminster; but that was some time ago.'

'Many years ago?'

'Yes.'

'Curiouser and curiouser,' said Leathey, with a little laugh. Then he seemed to turn serious. 'Dr Livermore, I rather like you. You are an intelligent man, I think, and certainly a gentleman, and that counts for something these days – and of course will count for even more by and by. If you will confess and submit to purgation, you might well become a useful citizen again. You might indeed become a power for good in the land – a perditor, or a chronic healer like myself. Will you submit, Dr Livermore, and let me help you?'

A disarmed prisoner has very little choice when faced with such a proposition. Ambrose thought for about half a second, and then said Yes.

Leathey rose. 'Good. I knew you would see reason. But let us continue these conversations in more agreeable surroundings. Simkins,' he said, addressing the constable,

'I shall take Dr Livermore to my own house, and I will be answerable for his security till tomorrow.'

Then they were escorting him from the inn to the horse carriage, which turned out to be Leathey's private conveyance. As they passed, Ambrose noticed that the workmen, by the light of swinging oil lanterns, were carrying off the lamppost which they had uprooted from the pavement. It wouldn't be much loss, he thought: it was a very old-fashioned looking lamppost.

Suddenly, with a kind of horror, it came to him what had been wrong with that grandfather clock in the inn parlour. Its hands had been pointing to somewhere around seven o'clock – several hours wrong; and they had been moving anticlockwise.

In other words – *backwards*.

As the brougham gathered speed and rattled over the cobblestones, Ambrose leant toward Leathey, who sat opposite. 'What year is this?' he breathed.

'1900,' said Leathey calmly. 'What year did you think it was?'

Ambrose was too overcome to reply. He slumped back with a groan.

Dr Leathey was evidently a well-to-do bachelor; his house was large, stone-built and ivy-covered, and was staffed by several men and maid servants. These people found Ambrose a bedroom, laid him out a nightshirt, and in general saw to his comforts. A valet explained that in the morning, if he wished, he would shave him – 'You being, I understand sir, not quite up to handling a razor yourself.' Ambrose soon got the point: safety razors did not exist, so he, as a prisoner, could not be trusted with such a lethal weapon as an old cut-throat blade.

The manservant made him change his clothes completely. Luckily, Ambrose was about Leathey's height and build, so an old suit of the master's fitted him quite well. The high starched collar was damnably uncomfortable; but at last he was presentable, and was ushered in to dinner.

He was Leathey's sole guest. 'Let's not talk now,' said his host, smiling. 'Afterwards, sir, afterwards . . . '

It was a very good dinner, of a somewhat old-fashioned English kind. The vegetables and the beef were fresh and succulent, and there was a very good 1904 Burgundy. Leathey made a joke about that.

'Glad the URN don't object to wines of the future, within reason. I suppose you might say four years isn't Blatant. But I like my stuff just a *little* mellow.'

Ambrose gazed at him and at the bottle in a sort of stupor. Then suddenly he saw the point, and nearly choked on his roast beef.

'Drink some water,' said Leathey kindly. 'That's better. You know, Dr Livermore, you are the strangest Anachronic criminal it has been my lot ever to run across. Mostly they're hardened, bitter, knowing – you're not. And therefore I have good hopes of you. But before we get to the heart of the matter, let me get you to admit one thing. We live well, don't we, we of the Acceptance? Do you see anything wrong with this village, or this house, or this dinner, anything sordid or unwholesome?'

'No – ' began Ambrose, 'but – '

'There you are, my dear feller. The whole world is coming round to seeing how comfortably one can live this way. As that great old reactionary Talleyrand once said, it's only the *ancien régime* that really understands the *douceur de vie*. You BAs are only a tiny minority. The proof of the pudding – ah, talk of the devil! Here it comes now, the pudding. I'm sure you'll like it. It's a genuine old English suet, carefully researched – '

'But it's all insane!' cried Ambrose. Forgetting his manners, he pointed with his fork. 'That clock on the sideboard – why is it showing four o'clock and going backwards?'

'My goodness,' said Leathey, looking astonished. 'You really must have amnesia. Protest is one thing, stark ignorance another. You really don't *know*?'

'No!'

After the meal, Leathey took him to his study, which was fitted with half-empty bookshelves and a huge black wall-safe. Over the safe was hung a painting in a rather academic 18th century style, showing some sort of goddess enfolded in clouds; between that and the safe an oaken scroll bore the florid inscription: 'She comes! she comes!' Leathey waved Ambrose to a comfortable arm-chair, and offered him a cigar.

'No? Cigars will still be all right for quite some time, you know, And separate smoking-rooms for gentle-men's houses are not yet compulsory. I do my best to get these things right, you know. All right, now: let's begin . . . '

Ambrose leant forward. 'Tell me, *please*: are we really in the year 1900?'

'Of course,' smiled Leathey.

'But – but we can't be. Reverse time travel is a stark impossibility – !'

'Time travel?' Leathey's eyebrows shot up; then he laughed. 'Ah, I see you're well read, Dr Livermore.' He got up, and took from a shelf near the safe a slim hard-covered volume. '*The Time Machine*,' he murmured. 'Dear Mr Wells! We'll only have him for another five years, alas, and then – into the big safe with him! Freud went this year, and *he* was no loss, but one will miss dear old science fiction. Well, *officially*.' He brought his head close to Ambrose, and gave a confiding chuckle. 'We are acting for the best, you know; but if you join us, there are – compensations. Behind closed doors, with blinds drawn, I can assure you, Dr Livermore, there's no harm in *us* occasionally reading cancelled books. And you can't lick us, you know, so why don't you – pardon me; you get my meaning, but I believe that's a cancelled phrase in this country. I must learn to avoid it.'

Ambrose gulped. 'I am going mad – '

'No, you *are* mad. I am here to make you sane.'

'You are not really living backwards,' said Ambrose. 'Dammit, you don't take food out of your mouths, your carriages don't move in reverse, and yet – . Hey, *what was last year?*'

'1901. And next year will be 1899, of course. Today is the 1st of March, and tomorrow will be 28th February, since 1900 is not a leap year.'

'Of course!' echoed Ambrose hysterically. 'And yet the yellow leaves on the trees show that it's autumn, and – How did this insanity happen? I really do have complete amnesia, you know. In my day time was added, not subtracted – '

'In your day?' said Leathey, frowning. 'What are you, Rip Van Winkle? Well, it may help you to emerge from your delusion if I give you a sketch of what has happened since the Treaty – '

'What treaty?'

'There you go again . . . Well, to start with, after the Last War and the Time of Confusion, it became obvious to the surviving civilised peoples of the world that the game was up: the game of Progress, I mean. The earth was in ruins, its minerals exhausted, most of the great cities devastated. If we were to try to go that way again, it would be madness. Besides, we couldn't do it even if we wanted to: there was so little left, almost no fossil fuels, no minerals, no uranium even. We couldn't even keep going at the rate we'd become accustomed to. There was only one thing for it – to return to a simpler way of life. Well, we could do that in one of two ways: by a controlled descent, or by struggle, resistance, and collapse. Luckily, all the leading nations chose control. It was in 2016, by the old Forward Count, that the Treaty was signed by the

United Regressive Nations. And forthwith that year was renamed 1984, Backward Count; and the next year 1983, and so on.'

'So we really *are* in 2100,' said Ambrose, breathing a sigh of relief.

Leathey fixed him with a severe look. 'No, we really are in 1900, Backward Count,' he said. 'It is only you Blatant Anachronics who call it 2100. And, by God, we are *making* it be 1900! We are removing all the extravagant anachronic wasters of energy – this very day you saw my men getting rid of the last gas-lamp in the village – and so it will go on. It is all very carefully programmed, all over the world. One thing makes our plans very easy, of course – we know exactly *when* to forbid each piece of technology, and when to replace it with its functional predecessor. Our Ten Thousand Year Plan will make all Progressive planning of the bad old days look very silly indeed.'

'Ten Thou – ' began Ambrose, staring. 'You're mad! Stark, raving mad! You don't really intend to revert all the way – to the Stone Age!'

'But we do,' said Leathey gently. 'Metals won't last for ever. And agriculture has to go too, in the end – even with the best of care, at last it destroys the soil. But not to worry. Polished stone is very useful stuff, believe me, and one can learn to hunt . . . By then of course the population should be down to very reasonable limits. Oh, I know there are some heretics even among our Regressive establishment who think we'll be able to call a halt well before that, but they are simply over-optimistic fools. A halt would only renew the fatal temptation. No, there is no stable resting-place half way down this hill: we must retrace the whole enterprise of hopeful Man.'

'There must be a way out,' said Ambrose, 'there *has* to be – '

'There is no way out.' Leathey laughed bitterly now.

'Believe me, I know how you feel. I, too – we all have our moments of rebellion. If only, one thinks, if only the Progressives had handled things differently! When the earth was theirs, and the fullness thereof, and the planets were within their grasp! You know, you can pin-point their fatal error, you can place their ultimate pusillanimity within a few years of the Old Count. It was during the Forward 1970s, when they had reached the Moon, and then – decided that space travel was 'utter bilge', as one leading light of an earlier time put it. If they had gone on, if they had only gone on *then* – why, we would now have all the metals and minerals of the asteroids, all the wealth of the heavens. Perhaps by now we would have reached the stars . . . and then we could have laughed at the decline of one little planet called Earth. But no: *they* saw no immediate profit in space travel. So they went back, and turned their rockets – not into ploughshares, but into nuclear missiles. Now we haven't the resources to get back into space even if you Anachronics were to take over the world tomorrow. We are tied to Earth for ever – and to the earth, therefore, we must return. Dust to dust.'

'But – the *books*,' cried Ambrose, waving at the half-empty shelves. 'Why are you destroying *knowledge*?'

'Because it's too painful. Why keep reminders of what might have been? It is far, far better to make do with the dwindling literature suitable to our way of life, and not aspire to things that are for ever beyond our reach. We ate of that apple once – now, steadily, we are spitting it out. And in the end we shall return to Paradise.'

'A paradise of hunter-gatherers?' said Ambrose sarcastically.

'Why not? That is the *natural* human condition. Hunter-gatherers can be very happy folks, you know – much happier than agricultural labourers. Hard work is wildly unnatural for humans.' Leathey stood up, yawned, and smiled. 'Well, so it will be. Back to the womb of the great mindless Mother. In our end is our beginning (I hope that's not a cancelled phrase). I'm glad, of course, that the beginning won't come in my time – I would miss all these creature and mental comforts.' And he waved at his books. 'Now, Dr Livermore, it's been a hard day, and the little oblivion calls – I suggest you should sleep on what I've been telling you.'

The next morning after breakfast Dr Leathey gave Ambrose a medical examination, paying particular attention to his head. After several minutes, he shrugged.

'Not a trace of the slightest contusion. And yet you still have this complete amnesia?'

'Yes,' said Ambrose.

'I am afraid I find it hard to accept your story. Don't try to shield your associates, Dr Livermore: I know there must be a cell of yours, probably in London. If you confess, I can promise lenient treatment – '

At that moment came an interruption. The maid brought the message that Simkins the policeman was at the door.

'And, sir,' she said, her eyes goggling, 'he's got a Thing with him sir! I never saw – '

'What sort of Thing, Alice?' said Leathey, getting up.

'A thing on wheels, sir. A sort of an 'orseless carriage . . . '

'Let's go and see it,' said Leathey, smiling gently.

'May – may I come too?' stammered Ambrose. He had a frightful presentiment . . .

'I'd rather you did. Perhaps you can throw some light on this Thing.'

And so, on the drive before the doctor's house, Ambrose beheld it. It was his rather special Volkswagen all right, with the policeman and several yokels standing by it – and, horror of horrors, one yokel *in* it, in the driver's seat!

Constable Simkins was explaining. 'We found this 'ere

motor-brougham, sir, up t'wards the Old Camp, in Half-Acre Wood. Jemmy 'ere knew summat about the things . . . '

Jemmy, from the driver's seat, leaned out and grinned. 'Used ter be a chauffer back in old 1910, sir, an' I soon worked the workin's out. Nice little bus she is, too, but mighty queer in some ways. Wot's this little red lever, I want ter know – '

Ambrose screamed, and instantly was clutching the man by the shoulders and upper arms.

'Ah, so it is yours,' said Leathey, shaking his head. 'Naughty, naughty, Dr Livermore! A Blatant Anachronism if ever there was one, I'm afraid. That model's been forbidden for all of my lifetime, I think.'

Ambrose was sweating. 'Get – get him out of here!' he choked. 'He could do terrible damage . . . '

'All right Jemmy,' said Leathey easily, 'don't touch anything else. You've done very well up to now. Now, just get out.'

As Jemmy emerged, Ambrose leapt. Before anyone could stop him, he was into the front seat of the car, and jamming down the red lever.

The world grew dim.

For quite some (subjective) time, Ambrose was shaking with the remains of his fright, his hand jammed down hard on the red lever. Then as he recovered control of himself, he realised that he was soaring into the future at maximum speed. At this rate, he'd be going on for thousands of years . . . Well, that might not be too bad. Leave that insane Regressive 'civilisation' well behind.

He eased up on the lever. Where was he now, nearly two thousand years on? It must be quite safe now. Regression would surely have broken down long ago of its own insanity, and the world must be back on the path of moderate progress; chastened no doubt, wisely cautious, climbing slowly but surely . . . That might be a very good world to live in. Now, what did it look like?

Rural: very rural. The village had disappeared. Below him was a flat green, and around that clumps of great trees, broken in one place by a path; along that way in the distance he glimpsed a neat-roofed building, low pitched like a classical villa. Over the trees rose the bare green downs, apparently unchanged except at the old British camp. There the skyline was broken by wooden frameworks. Skeletons of huts? Perhaps they were excavating. Ah, archaeology! That, and villas, certainly indicated civilised values. And right below the car's wheels – it was half a metre down, but that wouldn't matter – that green was flat as a lawn. Doubtless this was parkland. A good, safe spot to emerge . . .

He jerked over the red lever, and was falling. The car struck the green surface –

But it struck with a splat. There was a bubbling, a sliding . . .

Suddenly, with horror, he knew it. That greenness was not a lawn, but a weed-covered mere. And he and his Time-car were rapidly sinking into it.

He tore open a door and the stinking water embraced him.

He got out of the pond somehow, and when at last he stood on dry land, people had appeared from the direction of the house, which was not after all a stone-built villa but an erection of wood and thatch, rather sketchily painted. The people were half a dozen barefoot folk dressed in skins, and they jabbered at him in some utterly foreign tongue. Some of the men were fingering long spears. And, as he looked back over the green slime, he saw that his Time Machine had sunk without trace into that weedy womb.

The savage men were in process of taking him prisoner, and he was submitting in listless despair, when a newcomer appeared on the scene. This was an elderly man of a certain presence, escorted by a couple of swordsmen, and dressed in a clean white woollen robe. He stared at Ambrose, then interrogated him in that strange tongue.

Ambrose jabbered helplessly.

'Hospes,' said the man suddenly, 'profuge aut naufrage squalide, loqueris-ne linguam Latinam . . . ?'

And so Ambrose discovered that Latin was spoken in this age, by some of the people at least. Luckily, he himself had a reading knowledge of Latin, and now he began to make himself brokenly understood. He was also even better able to follow what the wool-draped gentleman was saying. His name was Obliorix, and he was the local magistrate of the tribe, its guide, philosopher, delegate to some federation or other – and protector of the Druids.

'I see that you have met with some accident, stranger,' said Obliorix, wrinkling his nose, 'and yet, beneath your mire and slime, what extraordinary garments! Bracae might pass, but that is no sort of authorised mantle, and those boots on your feet . . . ' He looked grim. 'Could it be that you are a Resister of the Will of Chronos? A belated *Christian*?'

A madness came upon Ambrose then. 'Domine,' he cried, laughing hysterically, 'what year is this?'

'Unus ante Christum,' said Obliorix seriously. '1 BC. And therefore, since last year it is decreed by the United Tribes that all Christians shall be put to death, not as misbelievers but as anachronisms. The Druids on the Hill keep their wicker-work cages constantly supplied with logs and oil – you may see them from here – so I fear me, stranger, if you are a Christian, I cannot save you. To the pyre you must go.'

'I – I am not a Christian,' said Ambrose truthfully but weakly. He was doubled up with helpless laughter. '1 BC,' he repeated, '1 BC!'

'And next year will be 2,' said Obliorix. 'What is so funny about that? Truly, it will be a relief in future to number the years by addition.' He began to smile. 'I like you, absurd stranger. Since you are not a Christian, I think I will make you my jester, for laughter begets laughter. What, will you never stop braying?'

And so Ambrose became at first Chief Jester to Obliorix, magistrate of the tribe of the Oblivisces in southern Britannia; but later he went on to greater things. As Ambrosius Aeternus, he grew to be a respected member of the tribe, and on the death of Obliorix he succeeded to the magistracy and the United Tribes delegateship. In 20 BC he went as envoy to the Roman Governor of Gaul, who, of course, was gradually unbuilding Roman towns for the great withdrawal that would take place in the '50s. And throughout his long and restful lifetime, Ambrose would from time to time break out into helpless laughter, so that he became known in Britannia as Ambrosius the Merry.

It was an added joke that, when he was able to persuade the Oblivisces to drag a certain weedy pond, the Time Machine proved to be rusted beyond repair, and only good to be beaten into spear-points. But for that Ambrose cared nothing; for in any case, what use was a Time Machine which only progressed backwards into history?

And besides, he told himself, he knew what lay in that direction; and he didn't want to get there any faster.

WAITING FOR THE RAIN

DIRK STRASSER

1. Rachel, I made my decision today. Well, it seems like I made it today. Maybe it was made for me when I was born, and today was merely the day when I finally realised it. All I know is, I can't go on this way anymore. I feel as if I've been trying to focus on something my whole life, and I've only now managed to see clearly. Yes, that's it. The answer is simple when you look at it that way. It's like I've suddenly made sense of a hopelessly tangled Remellian configuration. Such a simple diagnosis really. I don't need any psyche-scan to tell me: *I'm not human.*

Did that shock you, Rachel? Don't worry, I still look the same as when we were together, older maybe, I don't know, but still human, still human. All the appendages are there, no extra ones. My skin's still that sort of dirty colour that you didn't like. You always used to say that I'd spent too long under the Remellian sun, remember? But you could never get me off-world, could you? No matter how hard you tried. I've even grown a beard, can you believe it? So you can rest easy, I *look* human. You wouldn't be able to pick that there was anything strange about me, except maybe if you looked into my eyes. But what's an appearance? Just a shell, isn't it? It's what's inside that counts. And I know now that I'm not human inside. It's taken me a while to work it out – half a lifetime – but it's true. I'm actually Remellian. I'm a Remellian born inside a human body.

Extracts from TRANSALIENATION
A CASE STUDY
Dr Thomas Sarruel

It is Adryan Marchese's case that provides us with unique insight into the process of transalienation, a term coined by Professor Anton Schiller in his early ground-breaking work, 'Humanity in Transition'. Although I take issue with much of the terminology used in the literature, the term 'transalien' does provide us with a link to the related phenomenon of the transsexual.

While transsexuality as a phenomenon, after peaking in the late twenty-first century, is now almost nonexistent, trans-alienation has become increasingly common. The Marchese case is hence, of itself, by no means unique. However, rarely has an individual been so eager to record his feelings and thoughts before the process, and never have such recordings continued so far into the transformation.

2. Don't laugh. That's the one thing I don't want. Don't ever laugh at me, Rachel. It wasn't an easy decision to come to. I've been fighting it all my life. I guess my brain didn't want it to be true. It would be much easier if I was as profoundly human as you are. But I'm not. Maybe those ancient Terran philosophers had it right. Maybe there's a true essence hidden inside every appearance – a soul I think some of them called it. Nothing to do with the brain, you understand. Well, if I have a soul, it's the soul of a Remellian. And I can't fight it anymore.

The motivating factors that provide the stimulus for the transalien process are, of course, extremely difficult to isolate. I do agree to some extent with Warner and Chang, that mere availability of the techniques and technology play a part. Any historical study of the exploitation of scientific research amongst the general populace must lead to the inevitable conclusion: if it can be done, it will be done. I would argue, however, that this simple axiom does not wholly circumscribe the behaviour of the general populace because it does not measure the extent of the usage. Transalienation is currently in the same relative position on its development curve as transsexuality was in the late twentieth century. There is an almost universal awareness of the phenomenon, while individual cases are still considered oddities. I have no doubt that, over the course of this century, transalienation will reach epidemic proportions, as techniques are even further refined and the process becomes more financially accessible to greater proportions of the community.

3. I don't think anyone will understand my decision, Rachel. I know I talked about the soul before and about how appearances don't really mean anything. And they don't. They're not important when you talk about what a person *is*. But now that I know that I'm Remellian, well, I need to be Remellian in *every* way. I need to live as one, I need to be accepted as one. What's the point of being Remellian if you're not accepted as one? All right, the human part of me is only a shell, but it's a shell I need to crawl out of. It's a – what did they used to call them? – a prison. Maybe I'm not explaining it too well, but that doesn't make it any less true, and it doesn't change the way I feel.

Even Tobias didn't understand. Tobias, of all people! He's the only one I've been able to tell, and he didn't even begin to understand. Do you remember how we used to talk about the history of Remell? He was the one who always said that us simply being here was a tragedy, that it didn't matter how long we've been here, that we should all pack up and go home. He was always so idealistic. The young always seem to be so idealistic. But I always argued with him, didn't I? Do you remember? I hated the way he said we shouldn't be here. I hated the way he talked about Terra as our home. Terra! Ha! How far back do you have to be able to trace back your ancestors before you can call a planet home?

I don't hate anymore, though. Maybe I've found the answer, Rachel, maybe we were both right all along. If only someone would understand.

In the Marchese case we have in some ways the classic cluster of pre-alienation behaviours. These include a demonstrated difficulty in forming meaningful and lasting relationships with members of one's own species. While one might argue that such problems are almost endemic to our society, it is the inability to cope with them that characterises the pre-alienation stage. The references to his son provide an insight into both the difficulties of familial interaction and Marchese's early views regarding his concept of humanity in its relation to the target species.

4. Dr Sarruel seems to understand. I suppose he has to, though. He listens to me, Rachel, just like you used to do – at the start anyway. I tell him things about myself, about you. He's always asking me about you. He tells me there's nothing wrong with me. That's what I thought, you know, but it's a relief to hear it from someone else. I'm starting to feel . . . *real* in a way. That's the best way I can put it. I even had another try at explaining it to Tobias. I think he's getting a better idea of what I'm talking about now. I don't see him much anymore, though. I think he's avoiding me.

As with most transaliens, the crossover from pre-alienation to active alienation can be traced back to a single traumatic event, although there is often a significant time lag between the actual event and the realisation of active alienation.

Marchese again follows the classic pattern. The self-recognition of his desire for transalienation occurs almost a full year after the separation from his wife, Rachel. It is important to keep this in mind when studying the transcripts.

5. Dr Sarruel says I probably won't feel too much for a few weeks. He says that, apart from the injections, I can keep going with my normal life for a while yet. I almost laughed when he said *normal*. It all seems strange to me, the rushing around, the skimming over the surface. I mean, what's the point? All I want to do now is stop and just let it all happen. The good doctor says there will be plenty of time for that. He says there are legal requirements. I suppose I can't just disappear from everything, even though that's what I feel like doing. I'm going to resign from the Bureau tomorrow, then I'll sell the apartment and close the accounts, and then ... you know, Rachel, I think I'll just wait.

There is no doubt, as Warren and Chang argue, the inevitable development of transalienation techniques from the surgical to the chemical have resulted in significant changes in the psychological patterns exhibited by the transalien.

Marchese clearly demonstrates this. The transcript shows a smooth transition toward an alien self-awareness. Chemical procedures, for the most part, avoid the trauma result from the earlier techniques, which involved bone and nerve realignment. They also render as obsolete the hazardous practice of radical subdural surgery. While many target physiognomies, such as those of the methane breathers, still require a surgical adjunct to the chemical procedure, Marchese's transalienation was achieved by purely chemical means. The result has been a remarkably seamless psychic evolution, without a hint of the regressive tendencies witnessed in many other case studies.

6. Tobias looked at me strangely when I visited him last night. He said my skin was turning a funny colour. It looks all right to me. What I *have* noticed though, is that my hair is falling out. All over.

Tobias wanted me to travel off-world with him. He pleaded with me. It's funny really, it would have been the first time we'd done anything together since he was ten. I told him it was too late. Much too late.

7. I couldn't remember my apartment number yesterday. Isn't that funny? Not that it's important, I mean, it's not even really my apartment anymore, but I was filling out a form, and I just couldn't remember what it was. I had to make up some excuse and say I'd be back later. I looked the number up. And you know what was really strange? Even when I found it, it didn't look familiar.

I told Dr Sarruel about it, and he said it was time I commenced the next level of treatment.

The important distinction in the target physiognomies has traditionally been between the sentient and the semisentient. Nonsentient conversion (the term 'transalienation' is inappropriate here) has always been an illegal practice on Union planets and is usually associated with deep-seated psychoses.

Semisentient transalienation has, of course, been more difficult to study simply because the transalien eventually reaches the stage where verbal communication becomes impossible. This inevitable result of successful procedures is particularly inhibitive to research into the area, since it is precisely at the point of communicative loss that the transition to predominantly alien thought processes has occurred. I would argue that Adryan Marchese takes us further into the human-alien transition process than any other transalien, and that the transcripts provide us with the clearest picture we have ever had of a semisentient psyche.

8. The tingling sensation in my feet feels much stronger today than it did yesterday. (I must stop thinking of them as my feet; I think that's important somehow.) It's not an unpleasant sensation. Nothing like the pins and needles

you sometimes feel if you've been crouching down too long. They feel like . . . well . . . like they're about to burst out. Dr Sarruel says that my toes will start growing soon. I can hardly wait.

9. Dr Sarruel wants me to keep up with my recordings for as long as I can. He just keeps the recorder on all the time, right next to me, so that I can talk whenever I feel like it.

I feel a bit silly just standing here with my feet in the dirt. Dr Sarruel says I've got to be as still as possible. It's not easy. I had this itch last night, just on the side of my nose. The more I tried to pretend it had gone away, the worse it got. Eventually I gave up and reached up to scratch it. It was funny, though, I think I'm starting to lose control of the muscles in my arms, because it took quite a bit of effort to get them anywhere near my nose. And even when I did, I couldn't seem to be able to scratch deep enough to get to the itch. It's like my skin is hardening, and the itch was too far inside for me to reach it.

It is crucial to the Marchese case to appreciate the significant difference between the two different strands of semisentient physiognomies: the vegetal and the nonvegetal. While vegetal transalienation can no longer be regarded in any way unusual, most vegetal transaliens have displayed almost no desire to record any aspects of the change process. Moreover, a desire to do so would usually raise immediate doubts as to the appropriateness of vegetal transalienation for the individual involved. Adryan Marchese's extraordinary level of communicativity can only be explained as an aberration in a psyche which in all other ways follows the classic vegetal-receptive patterns.

10. I hardly felt the injections today. Dr Sarruel told me

this would happen. The cytokinins are changing the
elasticity of my skin. It's like there's a moist plaster cast
hardening slowly around me, except it's a plaster cast
with nerve endings running through it. I think the
sensations I'm getting are duller now. Maybe *broader* is
a better word for it. The pinpricks are insignificant now.
But the wind, oh Rachel, the wind is what I can really
feel now. I can't even begin to tell you what it's like.
It's as if someone is giving me the deepest massage all
over, all at once. Can you imagine what that feels like,
Rachel?

Like most transaliens, Adryan Marchese was very specific right
from the onset about his target physiognomy. Again we see
evidence of the Naipul principle that the transalien must be in
direct and substantial contact with members of the target species
from a very early age. The Remellians to which he refers are
best known off-world as Laumet's verdurias. They provide the
only possible target physiognomy for the transalien who has
lived most of his life on Remell.

Sympathy for the target species is clearly in evidence when
dealing with the verdurias. Colonisation of the planet occurred
long before the classification of semisentient vegetals was
conceived, let alone accepted by the general populace. As a
consequence, much of the early history of the planet involves
the wholesale slaughter of the verdurias to accommodate the
agricultural needs of the colonisers. Public opinion gradually
shifted, as it did on all Union worlds where similar atrocities
occurred, toward extreme guilt and a desire to provide
reparation. It is instructive to note, in the statistical evidence
provided by Naipul, that it is precisely on the planets where the
most violent and far-reaching decimation of native species
occurred, that the phenomenon of transalienation is most
evident. Significantly, the human-verduria transference is now
the fastest-growing transalienation process in the Union and
will, if trends continue, become a significant drain on the human

resources of Remell and may eventually necessitate a large-scale immigration program.

11. Rachel, I can't really describe how I feel now. It's a surging feeling, you know, a bit like an orgasm, only the surge is from the outside in. I dreamed you visited me last night. But you couldn't stop crying. Did that happen?

12. Today I felt the first tendril sprout. I couldn't see it properly because it was on my side, and I've lost a lot of control in my neck muscles. Sometimes, when the wind blows, I can get a quick glimpse of it when my head sways in the right direction. But it doesn't matter. I don't need to see it. Seeing doesn't seem important anymore.

Naipul has shown quite clearly, I believe, that since transalienation techniques have become relatively sophisticated, there is now no longer a significant preference for humanoid physiognomies. However, there is still an unmistakable trend toward physiognomies that are at least human-proportionate. The verdurias are no exception, the mature verduria being approximately three quarters the height of an adult human and possessing a single large flower almost the size of a human head. Despite these proportionate similarities, however, the verdurias cannot, as I have argued in my earlier paper, 'Target Physiognomies of the Aurelian Sector', be considered even remotely humanoid. Their structural development is totally asymmetrical, with their most dominant feature being a mass of interlocking tendrils that have no human counterpart.

13. I'm not sleeping very much, Rachel. Maybe I'm not sleeping at all, or maybe I'm sleeping all the time. It's hard to tell. I don't know how long it's been now. Dr Sarruel talks to me sometimes, but I'm having problems understanding him. I tell him that all the time. He keeps saying not to worry about it. I must have slept a little last

night, though, because I dreamed about you. We were together. I can't remember what we were doing. I just remember we were together. Maybe you were visiting me. While I was asleep. Was that it. Were you here? Rachel?

14. You know, I thought what I'd be able to do most of now is think. It hasn't quite worked out that way, though. You couldn't really call what I'm doing *thinking*. My mind wanders. I dreamed of you again last night, Rachel. We were running up a hill together. The sun was shining at first, and we were both laughing. We were holding hands, but I let go when I saw the storm clouds moving in. You kept running because you didn't want to get wet. But I just stood there waiting for the rain. I called you, but you didn't look back.

It is in the area of empathetic synapsis that the key to the transalien psyche lies. While communication with any semisentient species always has its difficulties, vegetals provide significant problems. We know that transaliens have always, in the pre-alienation stage, opened a line of communication with at least one member of the target species, and we know that this is a necessary precondition for empathetic synapsis.

Marchese apparently had a remarkable intuitive grasp of the communicative techniques (it is inappropriate to use the term 'language' when dealing with semisentients) of the verdurias. There is no evidence of any formal training, and the initial interviews reveal little more than the layman's understanding that communication occurs through changes in tendril configuration. Marchese was able, however, under controlled conditions, to successfully distinguish between the meanings of even subtle configuration changes and to engage in limited interaction on both a cognitive and subcognitive level.

15. It's getting harder to speak every day now. I don't think I'm forgetting the words, it's just that speaking

doesn't seem . . . necessary anymore. I seem to remember there's a reason why I should keep doing it, though.

16. It rained today. It felt good. I can't describe how good it felt. It wasn't cold. Cold and heat don't seem to mean much anymore. Rain means a lot, though. Not the word, the *thing*, if you know what I mean. It seems the word is useless now. It gets in the way. I don't know if this makes any sense, but I wish the word didn't exist anymore. It makes things too . . . fleeting. It wraps things up and stops them from growing the way they want to.

The truism of our field remains: the study of the transalien is essentially the study of the human. The desire to undergo transalienation is fundamentally a human trait, and there has been no documented evidence of members of any other species, even among those species on technological parity, wanting to undergo the process. The essential question, of course, remains.

17. Strange. I forgot where my mouth was this morning. It took me a while to start speaking. Every part of me seems the same now. There's no head, no arms anymore. New growths are sprouting all over me and they feel as much a part of me as everything else.

18. The growths are so *long* now. I know they used to have a name, but I can't remember it anymore. And Rachel, you should see them, they move. They move with the wind. *With* the wind! Can you imagine that?

19. Rachel, I'm dreaming all the time now. It's beautiful. I dream about the clouds. Or maybe I'm seeing them. Remember how we used to watch them cross the sky? Remember how we used to imagine they were real? Remember? Rachel, they're real now. They were real all along. We tried to force them into something they weren't.

We should have accepted them. They were real all along.

20. Rachel, I'm dreaming as I speak to you. It's the one I seem to have all the time now. You've run away. The clouds are moving in, and I'm just standing there. On the hillside. Waiting for the rain.

21. Rachel, I'm waiting for the rain.

22. I almost forgot your name today, Rachel. But it doesn't matter, does it?

23. . . . I'm waiting for the rain.

24. Rain.

25. R

REICHELMAN'S RELICS

LEANNE FRAHM

Reichelman stared fixedly at the grey stubble beneath him. The angle was awkward; the circular port was on the right-hand side of the thorax, midway between the deck and the ceiling, and it was only by twisting his neck and pushing his nose moistly against the glass that he could glimpse the rocky pocked surface of the asteroid on which the mosquito perched.

'Reichelman,' said Vetch.

Reichelman ignored it. Vetch's voice moved up five decibels and half an octave. 'Reichelman. You appear uncomfortable. The angles of your sternocleidomastoid and trapezius indicate an inoptimum position.' Its tone dropped – wheedled, Reichelman thought. 'The currently playing holo gives an immensely superior view. Come and look at it.'

Reichelman sighed. It wasn't that he disagreed with Vocalised Extrapolating Total Computerised Holo-grammer, but sometimes, just occasionally, he preferred to check visually what a mere instrument (treasonous adjective; would Vetch hear?) relayed to him. He liked to *see* it, liked to see that the asteroid (official designation 1990BB) was just a clump of rock and frozen dust, airless, unmoving. And now, contortedly, he could see that this was so. He could just perceive a ridge of tiny pinnacles of rock like lilliputian stalagmites erupting from the tossed cinders below him, a small snaking chasm that ended abruptly at a dustfill, and one of the legs of the mosquito, reliably thick and rigid, terminating in a splayed metal stabilising foot.

It was satisfactory.

'Reichelman!' He pulled back from the port, rubbing warmth back into his cheek. The space-cold was closest at the windows – ports, he corrected himself. He wondered why a port had even been installed, if using it caused Vetch so much anguish. Instantly he recanted; his comfort was Vetch's prime concern, and to Vetch, nothing could be so comfortable for Reichelman as sitting back and watching Vetch's holograms.

Still rubbing absently, he shuffled toward the podium in the middle of the cabin where the holo played, the electromagnets in the soles of his boots clicking on and off in time to his muscular flexing. The hologram glowed before him. There was the asteroid in miniature perfection. There was the mosquito, perched on its rump. He could even make out the port in the thorax. If he could watch the holo and look out the port at the same time, would he see in the holo his tiny face with its squashed nose and livid cheek, one staring eyeball glaring out at him? He knew he would, but the mechanics of the exercise were presently beyond him.

The holo mosquito trembled fractionally, matching the vibration he felt surging through the deck beneath him as the engines worked. Its proboscis was embedded deep within the guts of the asteroid, biting and chewing through the internal matter, sucking voraciously at the mineral juices. Its abdomen was unfurling like an accordion taking its first deep breath, its thin molecbond plastic issuing from the thorax, the nerve centre. It was slowly filling.

The holo showed a froth of dust clouding the proboscis's point of entry, motes moving lethargically, half-inclined, once disturbed, to simply hang about in the almost-absence of gravity. Watching the image, Reichelman picked at the loose edge of a flaking fingernail, inspected the cuticle while he was there. He and the dust particles had much in common, he thought, a little moodily. With the mosquito operating under its own, as it were, steam, with Vetch in control, there was little for him to do but hang about also.

Swaying slightly, boots locked firmly to the deck, he recalled an ancient ditty, and whistled tunelessly, subvocalising the lyrics – 'heigh-ho dee ree, a miner's life for me.'

'What was that?' said Vetch suddenly.

'Nothing,' said Reichelman, more testily than he had intended.

Reichelman slumped in the chair facing the console. It was difficult, slumping, without gravity, but he was working on it. Slumping looked casual, unconcerned. Enough to fool Vetch, maybe.

'How's it going?' he called offhandedly.

Vetch's reply was prompt: 'All systems are working at maximum performance. A five-degree centigrade rise in temperature has been noted at the junction of the plath-arm and the girdle socket, but the resultant heat increase has been bled into the surrounding strata while extra lubricant has been fed through the nerve line. Present mineral percentages of ore are as follows: Iron – '

'That's fine,' Reichelman interrupted. 'Just fine. You just continue with it.' He reached surreptitiously for the hinged receptacle where he kept a large loose-leaf folder and an automatic scribe. It was no use.

'What are you doing?' Vetch demanded.

'Writing,' mumbled Reichelman.

To his ears, Vetch's voice took on qualities of distaste and disgust, as if Reichelman had suggested Vetch commit an immoral act with an electronic screwdriver. 'Reichelman, there is no need for that. I have complete Terrestrial data storage, total ability to create graphics and instant pattern recognition. Anything you need to imagine' – Reichelman thought it stumbled on the word; stumbled again on the next – 'make up, I can visualise for you, and you can create your own holoscopes.'

'No thanks,' said Reichelman.

'Why not?' Its voice was pleading.

'I like to *write*.'

'But why?' Definite hysteria, Reichelman thought. Extrapolating computers were altogether too lifelike. He had had this argument before. Obdurately, he pulled himself lower into the chair and began to write – laboriously, the scribe tended to skid across the smooth paper –

A small spherical blue fungoid scuttered across the room toward me, crying in a thin reedy voice, 'Kill the human! Kill the bugger!' Savagely, I lashed out with a heavy boot. The impact sent the thing rocketing at the metal wall, where it spattered into moist, evil-smelling gobbets.

I looked quickly around for its means of entrance, and my lips curved into a triumphant grin as I found the small undetected meteor hole in the wall. Several other organisms were clustered there, called at me in hateful voices while the next in line tried to squeeze through. I picked up my heat gun and fanned it briefly over their repellently plump little bodies before beginning to repair . . .

Reichelman called the folder his Beginnings. Already twenty-eight pages of cramped script had been filled with Beginnings. Beginnings of important stories that he would finish back on Earth some day, away from the isolated distractions of space, which were great for Beginnings, but not so good for Middles or Ends.

He reread the last two paragraphs and sighed happily. And to think Vetch's animated cartoons could compare with visually evocative prose like this. Then he frowned, his eyebrows bunching up over his nose. The narrative flow wavered as he drew an asterisk in the margin and wrote a note beside it: 'Check poss. disastrous consequences of use of heat gun in sm. enclosed sp.'

He sighed again, less happily. It was hard being a writer. So much to think about. He erased the note from his mind and towed both it and the scribe back to the saga of the blue fungi.

Another mealtime. Reichelman ate absently. 'All well?' he said around mouthfuls.

Vetch's answer was brief. 'Yes,' it said.

Still sulking, thought Reichelman. Ah, well. In the absence of other stimuli, he fell to pondering the mining ship.

Mosquito, mozzie . . . the giant of the space fleet, which, when replete, would extend over two kilometres from prow to stern, named for an insignificantly small insect. Reichelman had to laugh. But the clue lay not in its size but in its function. Land, sting, suck till the abdomen bloats on the ichor that is the lifeblood of Earth's industries.

He scratched his arm reflexively, remembering a visit to his grandfather's once, when he was young. His odd grandfather, not the other one, the normal one who had worked in the pioneering days of space mining as an engineer supervising the removal of mineral sands from Mars, a career that Reichelman's parents had been more than happy for him to follow. No; Grandpa, the eccentric one who lived in a decaying, close-to-abandoned coastal town on the north coast of Queensland. There had been mosquitoes there, all right.

Reichelman had, in fact, spent most of that visit in a gentle eddy of terror. The city was functional, hygienic. Nothing within it had prepared him for the buzzing, slithering, creeping, coruscating, feather-touching horror of raw nature.

The house, Grandpa's house, offered protection of a sort. The windows and doors were lined with metal mesh, all but opaque with the dust and grime of years. But so fragile! He spent many sleepless nights, listening, sweat-filmed but fearful of moving, for the scraping of tiny claws as some nighttime roamer sought entry through the fabric. Sometimes, in half-dreams, he even heard it, and moaned.

But gradually, as it transpired that few nocturnal creatures desired deliberate ingress (except the possums in the ceilings; oh God, the noises of thumping feet and rabid grating yowls!), he became semiconfident, at least enough to sleep fitfully. He took, at last, some comfort from Grandpa, who said the screens were only necessary to keep out the insects. Insects seemed to annoy Grandpa much more than the possibility of a crazed taipan bursting through the mesh. 'Keep that bloody screen door shut!' he'd bellow as Reichelman would enter hurriedly from the fauna-encrusted outside where Grandpa insisted he 'play'. 'Keep the bloody insects out!'

Reichelman came to understand Grandpa's fears more fully the morning he almost fainted with terror when, waking from a restless, humid sleep, he found, perched vertically and immobile on the outside of his window screen, a carpet of enormous silent mosquitoes. Waiting. As if they somehow knew how fragile this barrier really was, and would wait patiently until their numbers increased to the point where their weight would cave it in, and they would rise with a roaring hum to arrow in on his cringing white flesh ... One buzzed indolently, and Reichelman screamed ...

And now here he was, compacted into another, a different sort of mosquito, but one just as voracious, just as insatiable. He grinned at the old memories, being sufficiently far in space and time from the terror of their sources, and rising, ambled to the port to watch the surface of the asteroid in his own peculiar way, munching pieces of dried fruit.

A harsh buzzing blared suddenly from a control board speaker. Reichelman started, his consciousness still uncomfortably immersed in memories of the screen mosquitoes, and scattered the raisins, which took up eccentric orbits around the cabin.

'What is it?' he exclaimed.

The buzzer cut off with an almost-snicker. 'Anomalies,' Vetch announced. Reichelman heard it switch on the air extractors to suck the dangerous raisin satellites from the cabin and into the void above 1990BB.

'What do you mean, "anomalies"?' Reichelman said irately. There had no been no need for the alarm; Vetch was being spiteful.

'Among the ore bodies are three objects that do not conform to anticipated dimensions, mass, specific gravity, and spectrum read-outs.'

'Show them to me,' Reichelman ordered.

The continuing holo of the asteroid and mosquito quivered and faded. In its place on the podium another image formed. Reichelman clicked toward it and peered at it closely. It showed three objects, all alike, white and ovate, all the same size, fist-size.

'What are they?' he asked.

'The precise function of the objects is not entirely obvious at the present time,' began Vetch.

'You mean you don't know,' said Reichelman.

'Don't know,' murmured Vetch. 'But,' it added, 'uniformity indicates artificial creation.'

It took a second for Reichelman to assimilate the words. Then he froze externally, a quiver of palpitations internally. Could this be . . . had he discovered . . . an *alien* artefact – several alien artefacts?

Recognition of anomalies was an integral part of mining computers – had been since quarrying of the solar system had begun in earnest. Just in case some ancient race had left traces of itself in the wandering asteroids or in the sands of Mars or in the rings of Saturn. But nothing had ever been found. Not so much as a petrified transistor or a fossilised turd, despite the wholesale dredging of the planets (if one discounted old miners' tales of mysterious findings that wafted the findees off into the unknown; nothing concrete, at any rate). But now – and incredibly – Reichelman had found something.

'Where are they?' he stuttered in excitement, eyes still caught by the triple enigma on the podium.

'In the hold,' replied Vetch. The hold. The unheated airless hold through which the ore was conveyed to the abdomen. 'They have been shunted to an inspection bench,' Vetch went on as Reichelman lurched toward the rack where his space suit hung. 'But first, do you think you could collect one of the raisins which seems to be jammed across a speaker . . . '

Reichelman, boxed up in the full outside gear, stared at the inspection bench. Perspiration that had nothing to do with the heating element of his suit dewed his cheeks. These were artefacts, nestled on a bed of stones and debris that had been shunted with them. The holo did no justice to them. Oh, yes; artefacts. He was convinced of that. Not random rock formations, not conglomerates of salts, not super crystals – artefacts. Even clumps of dust that clung to them, even outgrowths of frozen pebbles adhering to them, could not hide the smooth cylindrical *identicalness* of them. His throat went absolutely dry, and his breath caught on the ragged edges of it. Gently, hardly disturbing the surrounding stuff, he picked up one and brushed its encrustations away. He held it in his palm.

It was frozen hard and solid, of course. 1990BB was near absolute zero. He tried to heft it, tried to judge the weight of it, but that was frustratingly impossible. He cleared his throat.

'I'm bringing this one back inside the cabin,' he said to Vetch, who was monitoring him every centimetre.

'That may not be wise,' Vetch pointed out.

'Why not?'

'Pattern recognition informs that these objects are similar to many Terrestrial utensils and implements, including weapons.'

'Weapons?' Reichelman almost laughed.

'More specifically, grenades.'

'I'm bringing one in,' Reichelman gritted. Vetch emitted a shruglike click, but said nothing further.

Reichelman stood in the tiny air lock that separated the cabin and living quarters from the hold, carefully holding the white sphere in one hand, and signaled Vetch for atmosphere. He could tell without checking the indicators that breathable air and heat were being pumped in as wisps of coldness began to mist up from the object. Impatiently, he started tugging at one gauntlet, holding it under the other armpit, eager to strip off the restrictive suit and investigate his find.

He noticed the atmosphere was blurring. A quite incredible amount of fog was wafting out from the sphere. Peering through the mist at it, he saw a spider web of cracks run rapidly mosaic-wise across its surface. He felt a tremor through the padded gauntlet. It seemed to be breaking up.

Panicked, unthinking, he lunged his now-free right hand over it just as it exploded or imploded – he was never quite sure which with the suddenness and the mist and the pain – but at any rate, disintegrated into a cascade of bright sparkles that hung in the air while his bare hand tried to clasp them. He screamed and jerked back his hand. It felt as though it had passed through a furnace. Breath failed, and he stared at the skin on the palm and back of his hand, which was puckering purply. Oh Jesus, he mouthed. The cold. The cold of the object, of 1990BB, nightmare cold. 'Oh shit!' he cried, grasping the wrist of the injured hand with the other. 'Shit, shit, shit!' He was dimly aware that the particles were being sucked out of the air lock through the vent – Vetch had decided to clear them – and that the air lock door to the cabin was opening.

He staggered through, bent over his hand, cradling it to his midriff, tears spurting. Vetch was twittering concernedly in the background, but he couldn't listen. His expletives transformed into a series of broad unvoiced vowels as he awkwardly, one-handedly, pulled off the suit.

'What *was* that?' he gasped at Vetch, his words broken by a vigorous wave of pain that radiated up his ulna.

'It is being worked on,' Vetch answered. 'Please attend to yourself. It is imperative that the seriousness of your injuries be established.' Reichelman nodded, swallowed. Reached for the cabinet of medical supplies.

Reichelman looked critically at his injured hand and gave it an extra smear of enzyme-activated silver sulphadiazine with surface analgesic. Already the nails seemed loose, skin puffing up over the bases, but at least with the assistance of a heavy slug of pain-killers the pain was bearable. And what, he thought wryly, were a few fingernails to a rugged, though decidedly stupid, spacer like him?

Thank God the artefact had been no larger, or there would be no fingernails, fingers, or even a hand to worry about. The thought of the artefact led him straight back to his previous question to Vetch: what the hell *was* it? Why had it reacted that way? If a weapon, it was painful, but certainly not lethal. Perplexed, he clumsily wound some self-sealing tape around the hand because, of course, it was his favoured hand that was hurt, and then he prepared to question Vetch, who was still murmuring anxious inquiries.

'It's okay, Vetch,' he said. 'That thing was so cold it burned me. It'll be all right. Now – what was that object?'

'Tests were carried out on the particles extracted from the air lock and indicate the presence of' – Vetch seemed to hesitate – 'certain basic components of cells.'

'Cells?' Reichelman queried stupidly. 'You mean *organic* cells?'

'That is unproven as yet.' Vetch's voice sounded troubled. 'The cells in question do not appear to be Terrestrial, being neither eukaryotic nor prokaryotic. The disposition of the genetic material through the cell – '

'*Genetic* material?' Reichelman echoed. His pulses began to throb; he could feel each separately thumping in four-four time. 'Those things are *living*?'

'When it is considered that the objects in question have undergone exposure to temperatures close to absolute zero in a vacuum – '

'Stuff the science!' Reichelman screamed in anguish. 'What *are* they?'

Vetch was unmoved. 'Using the analyses of component materials and pattern recognition, it could be said that the objects are analogous to similar items common on Earth.'

'*What?*'

'Eggs,' said Vetch.

Reichelman slumped in the chair. This time it wasn't hard. All his muscles seemed to have fused into a gelatinous soup, barely capable of holding his bones together. Vetch was silent. Reichelman had told it – rudely – to shut up while he thought.

All sorts of ideas, simple and complex, revelations, speculations, theories, visions, and every other possible configuration of man's thinking brain flashed into his mind and out again. He had stopped shaking and only trembled mildly when occasionally one particular thought or other would lead to conclusions vastly exciting.

His first rational thought was to report his discovery to the authorities on Earth. It was routine, automatic, to report any singular occurrence to Earth; it was dangerous not to, though to describe this event as a 'singular occurrence' was to surely appreciate the sterility of the English language.

The report would lead to fame – there would be no question of that. His name would become a gleaming thread in the tapestry of history. The first man to make contact with . . . with . . . *some*thing. Something live . . . well, once-living.

It wasn't hard to imagine the ceremonies, admiring handshakes, bluff back-slapping; himself, head high but aspect self-deprecating; and the space eggs displayed, their images beamed into millions of city compartments around the world – he shut his eyes and pressed his hands, injured one as well, to his lids, as if physically to contain the magnificence of his thoughts.

He wondered if he had always known, subtly, on some obscure level, that this would happen to him, as if some precognitive memory had sped backward in time to his younger selves. He remembered the ancient films of Earth's early space ventures, films he had sat through time and time again, because no matter how often he watched, say, the grainy, unfocused images of the first moon walk, he was always certain that this time, next time, something would happen. That behind the hump on the monotonous grey moondust background, or beneath the innocent-looking crater over which the pale-suited Armstrong bounded so clumsily, something was stirring, which, when revealed, would scare the *pants* off that gulping commentator!

He'd watched breathlessly the clips of the robot cameras as they landed on Mars, Venus, or Titan, knowing absolutely that something was circling just to the side of the lens, cunningly out of range.

Of course he outgrew these fantasies. Space travel, exploration, and mining turned out to be as prosaic, as stolid, as most other jobs. Even boring at times (with an apologetic nod to Vetch and the mosquito). But now he, *he*, Reichelman, had constructed a whole new ball game, flung the portal of space wide open to a host of questions, conjectures, surmises, with his, *his*, space eggs!

Then another thought struck Reichelman, a thought that drove a stake – an unplaned, unsanded stake at that – straight through his heart, it was so electrifying. He tried to laugh at it. Tried to exorcise it with a huge grin and a shake of his head, tried to drown it with logic, but it paddled buoyantly to the surface until he admitted defeat and listened to it.

Things come out of eggs, it said.

What if, it whispered. What if – the eggs could be *hatched*?

He rubbed his mouth nervously, hypnotically, with his good hand. Part of his brain was busy marshalling all the reasons why such an idea was untenable, unfeasible, outlandish, and stupid. Have you any idea, it said, how long these eggs have been abandoned, buried under tons of rock? Perhaps they're not even real, hatchable eggs in the sense you're thinking of – perhaps they're only some sort of neatly packaged result of defecation, like those small cylindrical frog-droppings you saw (ugh!) at Grandpa's place. And they've been frozen, for God's sake! Frozen for maybe aeons. Give it up, it coaxed. Report it to Earth before you get into real trouble.

Reichelman glanced at the holo of the two remaining eggs and swallowed. 'Vetch,' he began, attempting to keep his voice controlled and casual. 'Would there be any chance that these eggs – '

'*Apparent eggs*,' Vetch corrected.

Reichelman clenched his jaw, relaxed it, and breathed deeply. 'All right. Any chance that these apparent eggs . . . could be hatched?' He finished with a rush.

Vetch made a sound that Reichelman's keyed-up nerves interpreted as a derisive snort. 'No,' it added.

'Oh.' Reichelman stared at the holo, tried to tap his fingernails on the arm of the chair, gave it up. It wasn't worth the effort without gravity. What lays eggs, he thought, trying to recall skimped biology classes. Birds, yes; and reptiles. Insects? And weren't there once some animals, real animals with fur and all, in Australia that laid eggs? Extinct now, but it seemed that any sort of animal life could lay eggs.

Reichelman could feel tension coiling in his gut. He banished rationality and concentrated on the absurd. Once laid, he thought, all an egg needs is . . . is . . . heat! But he'd seen what heat had done to the first egg. Of course, that one had undergone a rather extreme temperature gradient – no wonder it had shattered. But if the eggs were brought up very gradually to normal temperatures . . .

'Vetch,' he said aloud, 'regarding your last statement, "No," could you explain that a little more fully? For instance, if the eggs were heated slowly to avoid the damage that occurred to the first egg, could they hatch then? Frozen ova and semen and embryos have been commonplace on Earth for a century. There doesn't seem to be much trouble with them.'

Vetch was ready for him. 'Firstly, there is the method by which the tissues are to be frozen. This must be carefully executed and monitored. It is doubtful that any methodology at all was used in the case of these objects. Secondly, there is the length of time of exposure to the frozen state of the cells to be considered. Terrestrially, eventual disruption within the cells leads to complete breakdown of tissue over an extended period. It is difficult to estimate the period for which these apparent eggs have been frozen, but that time may be measurable in millennia. Thirdly, only the most elementary organisms have been frozen and thawed successfully on Earth.' Vetch paused as for a breath.

Reichelman plunged in hopefully. 'How elementary is elementary?' he said.

'Elementary,' said Vetch, 'is not an egg.'

Reichelman bit his lip. The wonderful idea receded toward his mental horizon, trailing tatters of itself, Vetch-destroyed . . .

'Wait!' he said. 'These are alien eggs, aren't they?'

'They are not Terrestrial organic products,' Vetch replied cautiously.

'Right – alien! And the cells aren't quite Terrestrial cells – you said so.'

The troubled note returned to Vetch's voice. 'Yes,' it conceded.

Reichelman got up, muscles, particularly in his arm, numb, and paced/clicked around the holo podium. 'Then you can't really say,' he went on, 'what the result of heating these eggs – these *apparent* eggs – will be.'

'It is not difficult to extrapolate – '

'You can't, not exactly.' Vetch was silent, doubtlessly extrapolating desperately. Reichelman stopped and looked closely at the holo of the two eggs, still displayed on the podium.

'Is this a current holo, Vetch?' he asked.

'Yes.'

'The hold is warmer than the asteroid's surface, so they've already heated a little without damage. What say I move them nearer to the air lock – thermal leakage from the cabin should heat them gently to a temperature where they could be brought inside without disintegration . . . ' He realised he was thinking out loud and also that Vetch wasn't answering. 'What do you think, Vetch?'

'Reichelman, you intend a course of action that is totally devoid of factual basis . . . '

Reichelman stopped listening, his gaze still glued to the eggs. It would be incredibly momentous, stupendous, if he could present Earth with a *hatched* egg – no *two* hatched eggs – two somethings!

Two somethings . . . perhaps . . . a male and a female! A *breeding* pair? He squeezed his eyes shut on tears of exaltation. Reichelman – saviour, redeemer, of a lost interspatial race of somethings!

Okay. That was it. He meant to, at the very least, try. He snapped his eyes open, suddenly aware that Vetch was still talking, still developing a lecture that seemed to be drawing on sources including cytology, cryobiology, and the Uncertainty Principle. Let it rant on; a Vocalised Extrapolating Total Computerised Hologrammer couldn't be expected to appreciate the creative imagination that separated humanity from its machines.

'Vetch,' he interrupted, 'I'm going to try to hatch the eggs.' The painkillers were wearing off. His hand began to throb unpleasantly.

'*Apparent* eggs. Reichelman, if you would simply reconsider and signal Earth as directed by the Miners' Manual Regulation 605 Paragraph C Subsections i and ii – '

'Vetch,' said Reichelman, pain roughening his voice, 'if you don't shut up, I will go to the storeroom, bring back a handful of raisins, and stuff your speakers full of them.'

Vetch was speechless.

'I can do it,' Reichelman added, 'without your help.'

Still nothing from Vetch. He shrugged, feeling suddenly tired, a weariness compounded by physical fatigue and psychical depression. It was well past his usual sleep period. His hand was really hurting. He supposed he ought to renew the dressing, smear some more salve on the wound, but that would take more effort than he felt he could afford right now. He trailed to his minuscule sleeping quarters adjacent to the control cabin, and stretching out on the bunk, he promised himself sleepily to fix it when he woke.

Reichelman stared with rapt concentration at the two eggs, now lying metaphorically in the flesh on the bunk of his cubicle. Two objective days had passed as a monotonous round of eating, sleeping, dressing his hand – which didn't look at all nice – and checking the temperature of the eggs in the hold. Then, at last, he had brought them through the air lock, with trepidation, but successfully. Vetch had made no comment. In fact, as he came to consider the matter more fully, Vetch had lately been much less communicative than usual. Or perhaps Reichelman had got into the habit of not hearing it. It didn't really matter. What mattered now were the eggs.

Still cold, but touchable. They would need heat, he mused. A temperature above that of the ambient. And somewhere safe to lie.

He went off to the storeroom and rummaged through the packed shelves until he found what he was looking for. An oblong plastic container held wrapped blocks of soup concentrate. He emptied the soup cubes toward the shelf, catching floating strays, and slammed the door on them, cursing the uselessness of his burned hand. Clutching the box, he hurried awkwardly back to the cubicle.

Breathing hard, he sat the box on the tiny table next to the bunk and looked around, forehead wrinkling. A heat source, he thought. All the light fittings were fluorescent strips; no oven, just a tiny microwave heater . . . All the light fittings except his own old-fashioned torch with rechargeable CarLith batteries!

He stooped to pull his bag from under the bunk and

opened it. His allotment of personal items under the web mesh was weight- and mass-regulated, but, in the way that other spacers always carried good luck charms, his always contained his torch, a large wide-beamed one, and a spare battery.

It went back to that damned visit to Grandpa's, when, creeping blindly through the dark to the toilet one night, he'd stepped on something that squished and emitted a strangled croak. His toes curled in revulsion at the recollection. He'd foregone the toilet, had dashed back to his room and spent the remainder of the night in an agony of fear and bladder distension. It, whatever it was, was gone in the morning, Grandpa doubtlessly disposing of the dead/dying/extremely uncomfortable body, but Reichelman had begged a trip to the shops to purchase a torch for further nighttime expeditions, and space being a sort of night itself, the fetish followed him there.

Reichelman stood back and gazed proudly at his handiwork. Both eggs lay snugly in the plastic box. He'd lined it with several metres of unused computer tape and fashioned a hinged perspex lid – filched from the spare equipment – to glue across the top. The box was firmly bound to the table with multipurpose tape and sealing compound. Barring the mosquito's lurching through the surface of the asteroid, the eggs shouldn't be disturbed.

The torch shone down on the eggs, bringing out faint bluish marblings on the pale shells. It was suspended and braced by a complex tripod of welded rods and more tape. There had been the problem of its distance from the eggs, and the consequent intensity of the heat; too far away would have no benefit, and too close would boil them. Finally, he had settled on a distance that kept his skin just comfortably warm when the torch was played on it for a quarter of an hour.

The spare battery lay on the table next to the box, handy at the first sign of diminishing output from the present battery. He'd test them both, of course, while the eggs were thawing completely, and recharged them anyway.

He held his hand under the torch briefly, a final reassurance of the heat, and then realised reluctantly that there was nothing, really, left to do. How long the hatching – *if* it occurred, be sensible now – would take, he had no idea. No idea of the incubation time of these somethings, no idea of the present stage of maturation. It was annoying, this uncertainty. He wished he knew more about biology, wished he had some useful equipment, a CAT scanner, for instance, or a sonascope, anything that would reveal the mysteries bound within the blank faces of the shells.

Nothing else to do but to continue eating, sleeping, dressing his wound – still not looking good – and not talking to Vetch. The rest lay in the hands of time.

The furry blue fungoid ball was trying to climb into his lap, lisping, 'Daddy, Daddy,' in a voice of trilling echoes, like the sound of a hundred spores popping. He missed with his feet and tried to brush it away, but the fungus, lacking appendages, was still somehow tenacious. He could only use his injured hand, and it hurt with a pain like stabbing flame every time he moved it.

He looked round desperately and saw how it had got in, a hole in the mesh window screen in the side of the mosquito. Other balls of fluff were clustered there, calling mournfully to him, while another attempted to squeeze through the aperture. He felt a drenching sweat of fear envelop his body, and he flailed out wildly with his hand, despite the fiery pain that lashed back along his nerves.

Reichelman woke, but didn't realise it for several disorienting seconds. He really was wet with sweat, and his hand really ached abominably. Slowly, he recognised the small cubicle as his own. He pushed back the sleep-net and sat up shaking, feeling definitely unwell, but not so unwell that he couldn't marvel at the way his latest Beginning had invaded his sleeping mind. Funny things, minds . . .

He caught sight of the odd contraption on the table, and memory flooded back along with a tide of adrenaline – the eggs! He rose – stiffly, he noticed – and peered into the box, but they lay as still as when he had first placed them there. He let out his breath with a small woof. Despite the pain, he felt oddly contented.

The subauditory background hum that followed Reichelman into the control room informed him that there was no need to ask Vetch if the mining was proceeding satisfactorily. Vetch was tending the mosquito as efficiently as it was meant to do. In lieu of anything more interesting, Vetch was again playing the exterior holo of 1990BB and the mosquito. (Reichelman was less than interested; he'd seen it before.)

He was left, therefore, with a lot of time to think about the eggs – and his hand. It was certainly hurting more than he had expected. After a quick careless meal he unwrapped the bandage and inspected the injury once more. It was a mess, he acknowledged ruefully. Bits of dead skin and burst blisters hung from the empurpled lower layers of flesh. Traces of yellow tinged the palm, but he was unsure whether this was a sign of infection or exposed fat. He felt disinclined to probe. Carefully, he smoothed a heavier coating of cream onto the wound and clumsily rebandaged it, feeling an immediate lessening of pain as the anaesthetics began to work. He helped them along with some more analgesics. That's that for now, he thought, suddenly buoyant with the cessation of pain, and whistled inharmoniously as he went back to his sleeping quarters.

He sat forward on the edge of the bunk, elbows on knees, hands dangling. Nothing moved in the plastic box. Not that he had expected anything, but it was hard to quell the sense of expectancy that seemed to rise and fall tidally within him. He extended his unbandaged hand suddenly into the beam of the torch; its light was strong, but the feel of its warmth was more encouraging.

Encouraging, and frustrating. To simply sit, watching, was pointless, and while he appreciated philosophically that most of life was pointless, neither philosophy nor pointlessness needed encouragement. He stared around the cubicle, seeking inspiration. The walls remained indifferent. The anticipatory bubble in his stomach collapsed, dividing itself into little jittery tics that played up and down his limbs.

That reminded him of the dream that had awoken him, of the little blue thing clambering up his leg. A little blue thing, seemingly full of a yearning love for him. A shudder of disgust mingled with a dawning recognition. This was vaguely familiar. Hadn't he read that newly hatched birds accepted the first living thing they saw as a mother? Imprinting – that was it. Not all birds, maybe, but some of them. He felt elated at remembering that, a dim memory of some obscure biology lesson, but nonetheless, pretty bright of him.

And did that mean (extrapolating further as both Vetch and the subconscious were wont to do) that he was seeing the eggs as his 'children'? He gazed thoughtfully at the infinite depths of the eggs shells, noticing for the first time that while still opaque, the outer layers seemed to have become translucent. The effect was entrancing. Little blue things, calling him 'Daddy'. Ugh. His leg twitched involuntarily in revulsion, as in the dream.

He grinned at his leg nervously, and put a hand firmly on its knee. No, hardly likely. Not at all likely. There was no way in space that he could ever guess what kind of creatures might be in those eggs, how they would look, how they would think, despite his imagination, despite all his practice with Beginnings. The hatching was, after all, merely hypothetical. Only hypothetical.

He rose determinedly, to seek something useful to do.

But he found it very hard to turn his eyes away from the objects in the box. He watched them all the way to the door.

Reichelman was working. He called up batches of figures from Vetch onto a vidscreen, checking the input of the past forty-eight hours, noting percentages of compounds, scanning for mechanical problems. Everything was running smoothly – Vetch would have informed him otherwise – and there was no real need for him to check anything, but it was soothing to occupy himself with something other than the event, or possibly non-event, taking place, or possibly not, in his cubicle.

Iron oxides were up, he saw. Earth would be gratified, Plastic Age or not. His hand troubled him a little, as it was hard to remember not to keep using it, and any touch sent a sliver of pain up his forearm.

'Reichelman,' Vetch intruded. 'Your temperature is 1.2 degrees centigrade above normal.'

'Rubbish,' said Reichelman automatically. Then: 'Is it?'

It was true. He did feel a little warm. Uncomfortably warm.

'Is the thermostat malfunctioning?' he asked.

'No. You have developed a fever.'

'Oh.' Oh well, not surprising, he reassured himself. All those little enzymes working away in there, restoring skin and flesh – bound to be a fair amount of released energy. Nickel up, too. Great.

'Reichelman,' said Vetch warningly.

'Okay, okay.' He took a couple of capsules for fever from the supplies and swallowed them dry.

'It may be advisable to contact Earth if your condition deteriorates further,' Vetch said.

'I'll let you know,' said Reichelman. He sat lumpily in the swivel chair and squinted at the landscape of 1990BB by courtesy of the holo. Was it his imagination, or did it look a little . . . shrivelled, more pocked and lined, like a testicle after a cold shower . . . the inside sucked out, the shell collapsing in upon itself? He'd never noticed this on other missions, if there was anything to notice.

He looked along the mosquito to the abdomen, swelling with the asteroid's rubble. Like a real mosquito, insect mosquito, its abdomen ballooning, red-purple with the encapsulated blood that tinted the distended translucent integument. He remembered the repellent fascination of squashing an engorged mosquito into a sticky red and black smear on the wall of Grandpa's house.

They needed blood, Grandpa had told him; the females need blood to reproduce. That's right, insects lay eggs too, not just fluffy pretty-feathered birds. Insects . . . like the big buzzing evil-striped wasps with monstrous stingers . . .

Wasps laid their eggs in little mud houses – Grandpa had been a mine of revolting information. The wasps collected the mud with their tiny feet, minuscule ball by minuscule ball of it. Reichelman had watched them forming the mud into little round nests.

He heard the mighty booming of the space wasps from far off, before he caught sight of them. He seemed to be drifting placidly in space, above a world just like Earth, but not Earth, one he knew immediately to be the missing tenth planet of the solar system, orbiting between Mars and Jupiter, a beautiful, livable planet, just like Earth. Then he heard the space wasps, and turning . . .

. . . saw them. They came in a great wave from out

beyond Jupiter – beyond Pluto, even – lazily beating delicately veined wings kilometres long, fluttering through the vacuum. They swarmed beneath him, grouping around the now-fifth planet, the not-Jupiter planet. They fell on it, stained-glass wings beating faster now, glinting on the sunward side. He saw them gather up mountains with their thin black agile legs, forming the mountains into huge balls of mud. Then they sailed up through the stratosphere into the blackness of interplanetary space (the mountain-balls nestling against their vivid-barred abdomens) where they busily patted the mud sphered into round houses.

Hundreds of them, flashing multifaceted eyes and glistening exoskeletons and awesome stingers; and when the mountains and the alps and the plateaus were gone, they dug into the valleys and the flatlands and the deserts until the planet had disappeared, transformed into a wreath of gigantic asteroidal space wasp nests.

Each landed on her own particular asteroid, clinging with barbed feet to its drying surface. Reichelman watched, horror-chilled, as ovipositors descended, stabbing the outer crusts, as the space wasps laid their eggs. Then they rose above the asteroid belt and circled the nests. They moved more slowly now – antennae drooping, wing tips ragged, colours faded – but with an intense impassive satisfaction. Then, as at an unfelt signal, they swarmed out from the system, wing beats resonating, the sound rolling back to him, while the eggs remained cocooned, awaiting the hatchings . . .

Reichelman pushed himself up abruptly. Nodded off, he thought groggily. He noticed he was shivering. Icy goose bumps marched across his skin. He touched his face, but it still felt warm. The shivering receded as he contemplated it. Just a touch of fever, he thought. Ought to be gone soon.

His dozing half-dream surfaced in his mind, and he

grinned reflexively, defensively. Space wasps. Blue fungus and space wasps. Absurdity piled on absurdity. Yet the sense of that awesome implacable purpose implicit in the vision lingered in some primitive part of his mind and he shivered again. Where was he getting these crazy ideas from?

He rose suddenly, levering himself clumsily on one hand, and waded to the cubicle. He caught his breath, and it expired as a sign of . . . relief? . . . as he paused in the doorway and saw that nothing was changed. Both eggs lay in the same position, and the torch still shone. He almost smiled at himself again, but the expression emerged more frown than grin. He walked over to the table, opened the lid, put out his good hand to stroke an egg gently. The transparent outer layers seemed to gather the glow of the light and re-radiate it as a pearly lustre. It was quite (coldly) beautiful. His fingers closed round it, and he felt the warmth of it heat his palm.

He was sharply tempted to shake it and listen for the rattle of an evolving skull or skeleton or carapace, for a restless resentful movement from within, but then he thought of soft delicate systems mashed by the brutal motion. He replaced the perspex, feeling a wave of baffled irritation.

. . . While the lizard creature pulled itself across the rocky terrain of the asteroid toward him, its mouth open showing poisonous fangs and . . .

And . . . what else would it reveal? Could it reveal?

Reichelman replaced the folder in the receptacle, sick of it. It wasn't working today; wasn't *right*. Besides, it read more like an Ending than a Beginning, and he wasn't ready for Endings yet.

His hand ached too much to concentrate anyway, and

cold shivers were turning his writing into scribble. He'd ploughed through endless screens of figures today, following Vetch's analyses almost molecule by molecule, to prevent his thoughts turning to the cubicle and the table and the . . . Then he'd brought out his folder, but that was a mistake.

His head was hurting too. The comfortable hum of the mosquito seemed to have increased in volume – or else it had stopped, and the humming was all in his own head. Strangely enough, that thought didn't worry him at all, was quite comical, almost. As was Vetch. Vetch seemed terribly concerned about his health. All day it had fretted in the background, offering suggestions, admonishing, till Reichelman had snarled suggestions back at it that had startled it into a blank and wounded silence. Reichelman knew what was best for him, better than a computer.

He decided to redress his hand, take something for the pain again – maybe eat something, although that didn't really appeal – and go to bed. What he really needed, he decided, was rest.

When he finally lay down on the bunk, after dressing his hand (looking at it as seldom as possible), and pulled the sleep-net over him, he turned his face to the wall, away from the bright steady light and what it shone on.

Night. Real night, Earth night, not the phosphorescent glow-at-the-edge-of-vision night of space. He, Reichelman, grown, adult Reichelman, was in Grandpa's house. The cramped living room cradled them, him and Grandpa, in a mellowness of contentment. Grandpa listened to a radio hissing ancient music, an old (antique?) newspaper rustled in Reichelman's adult hand, although Grandpa had aged no more than young Reichelman remembered him. Night, and the whispery tropic silence outside, and a sense of peace, of everything-as-it-should-be.

A dog howled distantly, intrudingly.

Movements in suspension, they listened intently. Reichelman rose suddenly, dropping the newspaper.

Wonder what it's howling at, Grandpa said.

I don't know. He was vaguely disturbed.

The single howl was joined by another, a deeper one, and another, more a frantic yipping. The sound swelled as nearer dogs took up the cry. It seemed to pass from house to house down the long street.

Instinctively, he moved to the switch and turned the lights out. He felt better, safer, immediately. He could sense Grandpa's puzzlement, could hear his old-man's muttering. *Ssh*, he said. They were both standing now, in the middle of the room. The house was in darkness, but the aged orange streetlight lit the road outside and sent pale shafts into their own blackness.

The howling was continuous now, and closing.

Grandpa began to complain feebly at the noise.

What it is? he repeated querulously, his voice louder.

Reichelman's stomach spasmed. *Be quiet*, he whispered, savagely, not knowing why, but knowing that silence was terribly important.

He went to the front window. The street was still and, beyond the mournful baying, silent. Through the waving branches of the overgrown tropical bushes he could see that the lights were out in all the houses on both sides, although it was early yet, and that many of the darkened windows also had silent watchers in them. He could see the pallid blurs of faces highlighted by the streetlights.

He craned to look down the row of streetlights in the direction of the first howls, but the foliage blocked his view, and he felt relief and frustration, both at once.

The dogs' barking had reached cacophonous proportions as closer pets joined in. He heard Grandpa's own animal chained in the back yard begin to growl. The skin on the back of his head tightened, erecting hair shafts, and his hands curled into fists. It was moving along the street;

he knew it, Grandpa knew it, the neighbours knew it. Even the dogs, especially the dogs, knew it. A sudden apprehension iced his limbs.

The dogs were hysterical. Reichelman stood in the stillness, half-sick now, fighting a sense of culpability that almost overwhelmed his terror. He concentrated on the comforting darkness of the house, willing himself to believe in some kind of protective magic. It might pass without noticing him or Grandpa or the house, might be attracted to someone else's careless move.

We've got to stay away from the windows, was all he could think of to say.

He saw Grandpa nod, but still they were drawn to the opening, waiting for the first glimpse, but dreading it. Perspiration broke out on his face. A whirlpool of anger and terror and guilt engulfed him. He was responsible – how, he wasn't sure, but he knew it was so – for this, and the mesh screens wouldn't – *couldn't* – hold.

Grandpa's dog began to bark furiously.

It would not be long now.

Reichelman came up clogged from the depths of the nightmare. Every nerve inside him screamed its adrenaline-inspired message to movement, to flight, but his outer surface was petrified. Like 1990BB, his rigid encrustment contained a shattering interior.

Finally, he did move; he shuddered, feeling it start with the curl of his toes and work hurriedly up his body till his head was shaking, almost rattling against the pillow. The terror of the dream receded somewhat, but like a sword in the belly slightly withdrawn, still horribly damaging.

Terror of what, he tried to rationalise as his head cleared and the shivering eased. There had been nothing palpable, just *a knowledge* of something terrible. Terror and guilt. He was responsible for that terrible something. He rolled over onto his side, vaguely aware of the pain and stiffness of his hand, and stared at the box on the table.

What did he have here? What was he proposing to take back to Earth, to unleash? Sweat bathed his temples as he realised the enormity of his gullibility, and his eyes widened in disbelief. he'd wanted, actually *wanted*, the eggs to hatch, never thinking seriously about what they might hatch *into*. Even Vetch had not queried *that*.

'Oh God,' he muttered forlornly. He pushed himself upright, disentangling the mesh, then swayed vertiginously for an instant, and righted himself, hooking a foot around a bunk stanchion. He ran his hand down his face, surprised by the gauntness it found there. He pulled himself to the table and switched off the torch with shaking fingers.

That was that, he thought, relieved. Or . . . was it? He leaned forward, peering into the now-shadowy interior. Was that a slight tremor, a subtle hint of movement in one nacreous shell? Or just the vibration of the mosquito at work? He pulled the perspex violently from the box; it sailed toward the wall, ricocheted out of sight. Reichelman blinked rapidly. Was that a hairline crack, the ghost of a fracture in the other, or merely a thread-vein of deeper colour underneath the glaze?

'Vetch,' he began. But there might not be time.

He looked wildly from one to the other – he couldn't *decide*!

With a sudden panicked lunge he grasped an egg, warmth registering fleetingly on his palm, and crashed it down upon the other. Both smashed with a delicate sound of crumpling cellophane and erupted in a cloud of ivory shards and liquid that whirled around him.

Reichelman stared aghast and entranced at the havoc he had wrought. The liquid formed globules that he thought looked pinkish, or possibly yellowish, or possibly a mixture of both; his eyes didn't seem to want to focus on it, to interpret colours of an unrecognisable spectrum. He knew without touching one that it would be warm and rich and sticky, like blood, yet unlike blood. Tiny flecks of substance whose geometry suggested either a possible imminent coalescence or an ultimate dissolution floated limply within the bubbles of liquid, and a curious and powerful odour billowed at him, an odour that seemed to touch more than one sense and departed before he could begin to encompass it.

Reichelman felt tears forming to mingle with the uncolourless liquid drops and wondered if it was the smell.

He heard Vetch say, 'Reichelman,' then it was still, as if it had thought better of it. There was a momentary silence as the remnants spun about him, broken by the hum of the extraction fans, and Reichelman watched the fragments hesitate in their intricate ellipses and move slowly toward the vents.

'Don't, Vetch,' he called.

'It must be done,' said Vetch.

His hand reached out and caught a piece of shell as it went by. He stared at it a long moment, then tucked it in his pocket. Carefully, because his vision was still blurred by tears and he was still barefoot, he ripped the box loose from the tapes and seals that bound it to the table, and floated with it into the main cabin, where he thrust it into the disposal unit.

It seemed useful to dress his hand. It was beginning to look good now, he saw, surprised. Pink flesh was showing through the scabby remains of blisters and puckered skin. He bandaged it again, maybe, hopefully, for the last time. Looking up from it he said finally, 'Vetch, what did I do?'

'Precisely when?' asked Vetch.

'It doesn't matter.' He wandered toward the small port.

Leaning his face against the glass, he stared at the pinnacle ridge.

'Vetch,' he said after a while, 'do *you* know what's in a lizard's mouth?'

Relays clicked mutedly. 'Yes,' said Vetch.

'Yes,' echoed Reichelman. 'I suppose you would. Could you show *me*?'

'Perhaps. But what you find there might not be what you see.'

He nodded, pondering, and whistled unmelodically while the small cloud of iced sparkles that were once, possibly, eggs spiralled off into the unguessable space beyond.

THE LAST ELEPHANT

TERRY DOWLING

We were nearly over the coast of eastern Africa when the Chief finally figured out who I was. He gave a cry that carried the length of the gondola and made the other passengers and the air stewards all turn to see.

'Hey, you're Terence Harm, right?'

'Right, Chief,' I said. I'd made him suffer all the way in from Madagascar, so I deserved this. Not once had I given in to the facial contortions and forehead furrowings that were unspoken questions from him. In fact, I'd been enjoying his antics, wondering when he'd break. I should have known the coast of Africa would do it.

'Bet I can guess why you're here, boyo!' he cried, pleased with himself. Everything was falling into place now.

'Oh?' I said, really not wanting this but smiling anyway.

'Sure,' he said. 'You're the celebrant. I never thought you'd be travelling alone. That's what threw me. You're the one who covered the ceremony for the Last Whale at Davenport.'

'You read about that, did you, Chief?'

'Sure!' he cried, taking the empty seat beside me. 'It was beautiful, what you said there. My nation got all the broadcasts, by satellite. We all saw it.'

'They used to have whale watches there every year,' I told him. After all, this was his country. He could be part of Borona security for all I knew.

'That's what I heard too. You're going down to Borona for the Festival, right?'

This was becoming ridiculous.

'Exactly right.'

'You're going to see the last elephant . . . '

'Right again.'

'And decide what can be done. You've got to keep checking up on those Animals, eh?'

'Right.'

He sat back, either genuinely impressed or African sly.

'Wish I had that much clout,' he said. 'We had an elephant in Johannesburg when I was growing up, but the Keepers couldn't keep it alive. They lost it. It died. It was too old, too worn out. I'll never forget it.'

I heard his words, sensing there was something more behind them. My suspicions were growing.

'I know all about that elephant,' I told him, my voice more serious now. 'I won't forget it either.'

The Chief looked at me with enormous respect, or with feigned enormous respect. Now I did have a feeling about him. He was dissembling.

'No, I don't suppose you will,' he said, standing up. 'Not you.'

He seemed to be thinking about the Johannesburg elephant then, or the Borona elephant or both, as our dirigible swung in over the newest of the African coastal states.

I looked at my watch. We'd be docking in twenty minutes. Last orders for drinks were being taken; passengers were crowding the ports and big observation windows to see Africa sweeping by underneath. Or rather looking at Africa, then at me, Africa and me.

When I sought him out again, I saw that the Chief was talking with a striking black woman.

She had obviously been up front during the flight, and now she nodded and returned to speak to the flight crew.

I knew for certain then that my Chief was with Borona security, something governmental. Damn!

He knew that I knew and when he came back over to me he didn't even bother to tell me he was.

'Excuse me, Mr Harm, please,' he said in a different voice. 'But why is it that you have booked passage on a commercial flight and under another name?'

'Do you have an answer for me, Chief?' I asked him.

The African looked slightly discomfited.

'Mr Harm, please. I am responsible for . . . '

'I'm sorry. I get a lot of hem-of-the-garment touching, that's all. Look at these people.'

He did so and nodded.

'I understand, of course. But the commissioned flight from Rotterdam?'

'A decoy,' I explained. 'For the press and the crowds. We do it sometimes. The private flights are never truly private, you must realise. There are always the officials who want to chat, and the flight personnel and the security agents themselves.'

'I see,' he said, only slightly abashed, though the look on his face told me I'd messed up his security arrangements completely.

'You have a great land, Chief,' I said, turning the conversation and looking out across Africa.

'Please, Mr Harm. Not Chief. Radu. I was Keeper Radu.'

Now I was surprised and impressed. More than security, as I'd thought. A Keeper. And more correctly, an ex-Keeper.

'Why are you here, Mr Radu?'

'I was on Madagascar,' he said. 'An agent thought he recognised you, so Bela and I came . . . '

'I don't mean that, Radu. I mean why is an ex-Keeper here?'

'I am not for this elephant, Mr Harm. Caza has his own Keepers. I belonged to the Johannesburg elephant. You will understand that we were given jobs like these when we failed to keep our elephant alive. You will understand that we like to be close.'

I reached out to the man, not knowing his tabus, not knowing his feelings on this. I reached out as celebrant and touched his arm, and thought of what one does after one's life has been given over to being with the Animals.

'I know better than you think, Radu, what your grief is like.'

He nodded with gratitude, with extreme dignity, granting that I did. I may have tricked him by being on this flight, but how well he had tricked me, posing as a local chieftain, even though I had suspected it at the last. This man had an empathy rating at least as high as my own; he had several degrees, training in a dozen disciplines, a lifetime of reverent dedication – all the skills of his custodianship of elephants.

There was no changing that. He belonged to the Animals, and would for all his life.

That he had lost his touch; that he had failed in his task of keeping his ailing beast alive, now seemed a small thing. I had known many men and women like Radu. Such people cared now for the Davenport Whale (one of the best and – bless us – a long long way from extinction) and the Swansea Dog and the miraculous Great Panda at Peking which had surprised us all and outlived so many more viable species. Most of these Keepers, too, would learn what it was like to lose an Animal someday.

'I think you can understand too, Radu, why we celebrants like taking the normal flights like this. We can be anonymous for a while. In a way, we can step outside our single-minded attention to the Animals.'

A trace of the former Chief came back in his great bright smile. Radu wasn't one for dwelling in the past – or rather, for showing that he did. He sat with me for the remainder of the flight, which wasn't long. Now that the flight crew knew I was aboard, they had decided to cut short the usual scenic approach and head straight for the docking-towers at Borona.

But it gave us enough time to discuss techniques for looking after the Animals we still had. Though he had seen the Davenport ceremony as it was televised and broadcast worldwide, I gave him my impressions, and he in turn gave me an idea of how the Borona celebration would be.

These occasions had become standardised by now, but I liked Radu, my Chief with a dead elephant on his conscience, and he enjoyed the talk, the chance to get close to it all again.

And though he was a security man now, holding this honorarium post from the state, he probably didn't realise how well briefed we celebrants were.

The ceremony surrounding the last elephant would hardly resemble the one at Davenport. There it had been the long ritual drive up from Morro Bay following the whale; here it would be a short half-mile procession from the Animal Door to the celebrant's podium and back. In past years it had been a longer walk out to the edge of the sanctuary, almost to the city, but no more.

Most of the population of Borona would be gathered for the Festival, as close as they could get to the actual route. Dignitaries from all over Africa, representatives from all the nations, tourists and pilgrims from just about anywhere you could name would be present. The ceremony would be televised, recorded and widely documented by the press, naturally, but being there! There was nothing like it. To see the elephant actually moving down the street to the place of celebration.

Caza was such an old elephant, a proud bull. The people of Borona had kept him alive for almost two hundred years, using every technique science and human care could give them. But like the Tortoise of Bin-Chow,

Caza was failing. Radu knew this – all the world knew it.

Which is why the Festival had been advanced three years and the podium moved even closer to the Animal Door.

Which is why I was here.

And why so many of my smiles were false.

The docking-towers at Borona are beautiful to see. The designers went totemic in their approach, and I would never have thought that things so large and functional could take it so well. There are eighteen of the things standing out in the Borona field, like some brotherhood of tribal gods clutching brightly-coloured whales in their fists, seven of them satisfied, the others still reaching for heaven.

Our dirigible sidled in to nudge the eighth, the docking crews brought us in, and we took the elevator down to the landing stage itself.

Radu had an escort of thirty tribesmen waiting. I turned on my 'No Comment' blazer and asked Radu and Bela – his wife, I had discovered – to stay close. Radu met this request eagerly, more excited than I would have expected until I saw Bela's looks of unguarded happiness and realized how welcome this loss of control was. Though cherished, the ex-Keepers obviously became pariahs more quickly than I would have dreamed – good servants who had broken trust, to be respected, to be commemorated, but outsiders all the same.

Now, for this brief time, close to the celebrant, Radu could re-live the role he had forfeited, be close to the skills and thoughts and rich ambience that had been so much of his training.

We moved along, our native guard flanking us and looking splendid in their colours and synthetic skins.

Though it is always a difficult thing to arrange and control, the celebrant is meant to be seen in public –

preferably walking, clearly visible among the people.

It is too easy for us to be seen as religious men and women, powerfully reverent, almost messianic figures. We resist these associations, but to an extent we adopt the mystique because it's easier and wanted and cannot be avoided anyway. The truth is we are most often quietly serious people, with little of the showman about us. Our intuition quotient is always exceptionally high. In the matter of Animals, we know in a second what the biologists and medics will arrive at after long hours of analysis and deliberation. Computers cannot match us. We began as independent watchers, part psychologist, part social scientist, part diplomat, and we are – in these later years, with so many Animals failing – Judges, the ones who deem that an Animal should be allowed to die. To counter this darker side, we have had to foster the sanctity mystique more and more. Otherwise no one would listen to us or trust us, and the Animals would languish on in pain, living lives that are mockeries; the blindness of love having obscured all compassion.

So we took our walk, flanked by Radu's countrymen with their spears and authentic feathers. All around us, the crowds had formed and were already chanting. As we moved towards the Borona Hyatt along the Way of the Elephant, we could hear broken fragments of Caza's Song here and there.

> *Hey there, Brother, big forest wanderer,*
> *Hey there, Brother, give us time to be like you.*

I watched Radu, to my left near Bela, but he showed no signs of distraction. He was a Chief in his own right, and in charge of security and an ex-Keeper reborn for a time. He was sharing the walk more closely than any would guess.

Though Bela knew. Bela understood.

We passed through the crowds, the throngs of people adorned with their elephant tokens and other Animal fetishes, many of them masked and many of them holding aloft bright poles set with Caza's sign.

Even those who didn't recognise me outright saw Radu and knew he was involved with the Festival and so made the connection. We had a great following by the time we reached the foyer of the Hyatt and the air was ringing with Caza's Song, beautifully counterpointed by a melody from a group of whale people from Monterey and Twofold Bay.

The hotel's own guards had to come out as reinforcements and helped cordon off the spectators so we could get inside easily. We rode up to the penthouse suite (no avoiding that) in a comfortable silence, and I invited Radu and Bela to stay for a simple *cha* ceremony.

I could see how grateful Radu was, and was already sensing that he wanted to ask something – something that had to do with the Johannesburg elephant, Korshippa, and the Caza Festival.

It was not as if I had caught him about to ask a question or a favour, nothing as obvious as that. He just – lingered – and glanced out of the windows and wrestled silently with himself while Bela spoke softly of how life was for them in Borona.

I prepared the *cha* and laid out the kimonos for the three of us – host's right – and wondered what troubled my Chief.

Then, at the last minute, Bela asked to be excused, saying there were special comp clearances I might need and that she'd get them. A fiction, of course, and a way for Radu and me to be alone.

I accepted the grace of her excuse and saw her out. Then Radu and I knelt and took *cha* together. After the right space of time, and because he hadn't won the fight with himself, I asked what task he had been given in maintaining the rare Animal.

As I'd thought, he had been an apprentice Soul. With his smile and his quick vital ways, he had to be that, or the Heart, or the specialist for the Great Mind.

Radu seemed glad to talk; relieved to do so. He told me how he had trained under Tiff, the Great Master himself and Korshippa's Soul, and that following Tiff's death had been only seven months in the job when Korshippa had languished and died.

A sympathy death.

It happened often these days. The Animals did not long outlive their Souls – their closest companions. The Belgian Horse, the Great Ape of Sarawak, all died when their dearly-loved Souls had died. The head apprentice was sometimes able to imbue the beast with the right feelings and sustain it and encourage it; depending on how well those apprentices had been trained and imbued themselves.

But usually the creatures died in extreme sympathy for their lost friends. Even the generically wildest, the most feral, had become so human-dependent in the last hundred years, as if sensing this reliance. It was all part of the tragedy.

Without Radu telling me, I already knew that Caza's loss of vitality was probably a reflection of a faltering Soul – the old man, Modat. But I would not mention this, not to Radu, not to anyone.

By the time we had finished the *cha* ceremony and the kimonos were folded and laid on the bed, Radu knew he'd have to leave. His inner struggle had been continuing all through the pouring and drinking and polite question and answer.

Now I wondered whether his question would surface.

It did.

As Radu turned to go, he hesitated a last time, then faced me.

'Excuse me, Terence, but is there any special dispensation to be given here?'

Which was a way of saying: Are you here to see if Caza needs to be put down? To see if at long last our elephant is beyond human care, simply too old and too ailing to be forced to live on for human selfishness?

Radu had broken form and he showed the strain of it. He had used his unique position here to refer openly to that other task of the celebrant: to be judge and in a sense executioner to the Animals. As I say, it is a measure of the acute global sensitivity of the times that our name has not come to be used in any opprobrious way. The world knows too that we love the Animals, that we have far more detachment than Keepers could ever have, working as they do every day with the few treasured creatures we have left.

The doubters had only to recall the times a hundred years back when the owning of Animals by individuals and households was common and permitted, and how eventually this could only be afforded by the wealthy; how shares and sponsorships and rotation became the way of it; how the Closed Zoos appeared and the black market flourished. How the clonings and breeding programs failed and the species were squeezed out of existence regardless.

And how could I say to Radu that things did not look good for Caza? That this was why I was here and not Chingi or Palleas or a consensus (how that would alarm them – a group of celebrants!).

There is no ego-pleasure at being called the best of my profession, reckoned as it is on empathy factors and what we call instinctivity. I didn't ask to come to Caza's Festival, but how could I refuse?

I did not answer Radu's question, partly because he would be furious with himself afterwards if I did, and partly because I realised suddenly that this was not what Radu had been originally going to ask.

He was concealing a more desperate question; that was

what I sensed. Perhaps he knew I had discovered it.

Radu stood in the doorway, taking my silent reprimand, grateful for the smile that told him I understood.

'Thank Bela,' I said.

Radu nodded.

'I'll be here tomorrow at eight, Terence.' And then: 'Let me know if there is anything I can do.' Then he went off to the elevator.

He had found a way to ask his desperate question after all.

I smiled and sat alone in my room at last, looking out over Borona, thinking of the morning and what could be done. As always, I knew that there was – had to be – a point at which the interests of the Keepers ran contrary to those of the celebrants. Theirs was more of a priesthood than ours; it had to be loyal to itself first. They kept secrets, were expert in all the ways of hiding the vital facts of Caza and his Soul, Modat.

But reports had come through all the same – that Caza was probably going to die at last. Soon now. They could no longer conceal it and had done the honourable and fair thing. They had advanced the Festival date.

I did something then I had not done in years, not since the loss of our last wonderful Kangaroo. I opened the Primer left by the management for its guests, and turned to the pages on Celebration. There were the words of Ted Hughes, A. A. Milne and Rudyard Kipling, Herman Melville and Antoine Saint Exupery. In the section on Exercises, there were the unforgettable and prophetic words from Lien-Tsin:

Imagine your Animal. Imagine its shape, its smell, the steam of its breath, the way it moves to hunt, sleep and mate. Part by part, make the Animal real. Then, when you think you are ready, imagine it gone. If you weep, your task is done. If you do not, you must start again.

Fireworks burst all about me, close to my balcony. Below me in the streets of Borona, the Festival had already begun. The music, the songs, the excitement, came through the warm air; the sounds of many people awake and aware and full of expectation.

To them, there could be no thought that this might be the last Festival.

I looked at Lien-Tsin's words and imagined Caza gone, wanting to cry. But though I stood there a long time, the tears would not come.

Radu's question-that-was-not-a-question did not let them come.

On the morning of the Festival, I met with Caza's Keepers, both those of the actual Animal and its Shadow – those lesser Hearts, Minds and Souls, all the apprentices presently being trained by Modat.

They sat waiting for me in the hotel auditorium, nearly sixty of them, all looking at me with the same eager desperation I had glimpsed for a moment in Radu's eyes the day before.

Would Caza live?

We did not discuss that, of course. That could not be an issue. It is never discussed, never. They were gathered here for the very opposite reason – to hear me enthuse and praise and give thanks: in short, to celebrate Caza with them. Nothing I said or did cued them otherwise.

But the question remained in every mind; even in Modat's, who was absent – shut away in the Animal Room all night with his charge, being the Great Soul to his precious beast, communing, getting ready for the procession at noon. I would speak with Modat only after the processsion had ended, when I had made my evaluation.

No subliminals were used at this meeting, none of the hypnogogics. This, too, was decided upon my discretion. Often these aids help relax the Keepers for the certain trauma of taking their beast out in public, but today I wanted the intensity untouched.

Outside it was a different story. Outside, the day was Elephant. From the high poles, the subsonics and olfactories blasted out the sounds and musks of the Animal, synthesised, enhanced, all over the crowds. The slopes along Caza's Way were jammed with people; the media-blimps were in place, tethered or roaming down their cables, rehearsing the half-mile route. Chartered dirigibles moved back and forth overhead.

The door of the Animal Room was still firmly closed. The white flag would go up when Caza was about to appear, but now the pole was empty.

I went to the podium at the far end of Caza's Way and joined Radu. He stood next to Bela in full tribal regalia, holding his Keeper's staff with its crest of Korshippa. His eyes met mine, asking, asking, both of his questions, and getting an answer to neither.

I squeezed his left forearm.

'I need to see him first,' I said, breaking form that much.

'The people will never know!'

'We would know,' I said. 'And the people would know eventually.'

'No!' But it was a plea from him.

'You know better, Radu. If we turn up the supports and they notice, they will never trust the Animals again. They will know if Caza is ailing, and should know why he is to be put down.'

I felt a chill of foreboding then. If Radu was expressing so much doubt, things could not be good for Caza, even worse than I had been informed.

In a sense, I had been using Radu this way. As an ex-Keeper, it was natural for him to stay as close as he could to another Animal like his own; he became the ideal barometer, a way of reading this brother-beast, a reflector, too, of Modat's own fears and doubts.

For the first time, standing there above the seething crowds, I wished it had been consensus after all, that Chingi and Palleas and Gromelli were all with me, that it wouldn't be up to me alone.

I calmed myself, noticing the media ships. The other celebrants were with me. How could it be otherwise?

I looked across at Radu and Bela. They were gazing straight ahead, down the professional way to the Door and the empty flagpole. Many of the cameras were on us, and they had composed themselves accordingly.

I noticed many details at that moment, and saw for the first time the fullness of Bela's belly, that she was pregnant.

And out of synchronicity, inspiration, whatever, the idea came to me – an answer for Radu as well, though a vast cry went up and obscured it for the instant.

The flag was rising on its pole, cutting out in the breeze.

The door to the Animal Room was lifting too, slowly, ponderously. And slowly, ponderously, ancient Caza was moving out.

The crowds roared in a frenzy of adoration, a mixture of incredible joy and pride, and the chorus of his song, guided by the chorists through the speakers, took form; predominated now.

> *Hey there Brother Elephant, Brother Elephant,*
> *Brother Elephant, Brother!*
> *Hey there Brother Elephant, Brother Elephant,*
> *Brother Elephant, Brother!*

Over and over the words came, the wash of emotion threatening to obliterate everything, but not the thought that had come to me.

I looked at once at Bela's belly under her robe and it came back. I turned to my Chief.

'Radu, what would you have most in all the world? Tell me! Now!'

Radu blinked at me. After the barest hesitation (in which wife, child, all of his dreams must have rushed across his mind) he answered:

'Korshippa!'

'Can you be Korshippa's Soul? Now?'

Radu stared at me.

'No . . . Yes . . . But, Terence . . . '

'Caza is dying! Can you?'

'I'm not eligible. It's been too long. Bela is pregnant.'

'None of that matters now. Caza is dying. We must try.'

'How? How, Terence?'

'Go down there. Go to Modat.'

'He has apprentices . . . '

'Do it, Radu. Before it's too late!'

The black man leapt from the podium, trusting me. He ran down through the guards in their bright native dress, ran on down the avenue towards the seven Africans who were Caza, the man-elephant Caza.

He was a wild figure racing towards the stately procession, startling guards who began to raise their weapons till they saw it was their own chief. Their eyelines raced on to locate a threat, a reason for his haste, but found none.

There was only Caza, the seven parts of Caza, moving towards them between the rows of spectators; six younger African men and women grouped around the old man, Modat, fiercely determined, each of them, to keep their part of the Animal intact, but failing from within, from the Soul, and fighting that.

And Radu was there, was inside the formation of seven, and had taken Modat's hand.

The Souls walked together.

All around them, the chanting of the vast crowd had fallen into a hush, a charged silence. Even the chorists had stopped singing.

What did this mean in terms of Caza? What had Radu done?

But they soon saw. They saw it when the Zulu prince who was Caza's Great Mind stood even straighter, even prouder; how Kefta, Caza's Heart, became suddenly radiant, not just intently reverent; when they saw how Eyes and Voice took on an added presence. The whole man-beast was different.

Somehow, as they all watched, those many thousands, the definition of Caza became an incredible, almost palpable thing, an inarguable fact, stronger than it had ever been.

The Animal was there, undeniably there, stretched taut between the frame of . . . eight.

Caza-Korshippa.

And all about me now the chanting had resumed, swelling up into the bright air. The frenzy of celebration fed, yes, by the subliminals, the elephant calls and hypnogogics too, but free of those things – held more now by the simple enormous yearning.

The great gamble – the grafting – was done. I stood, tears streaming down my cheeks, and sang with all the rest of that desperate, joyful, fervent humanity, the first verse of Caza's Song, and let the eight people – and the last elephant we have – carry me along.

> *Hey there, Brother, big forest wanderer,*
> *Hey there, Brother, give us time to be like you.*
> *We atone the day, we sent you away,*
> *Now we be elephant,*
> *We be you.*

THE TOKEN POLE

JACK WODHAMS

No sooner had he won the election, it seemed, than he had an important visitor.

'If I don't plant that tree, I'll be committing political suicide.'

The man from the State Department frowned. 'There is increasing concern, world-wide now, that this sort of thing cannot continue unchecked, Governor.'

'It's progress. It's what the people want,' Buntling Frost replied. 'It's reclamation, Vialo. We can't stand still and simply let others go ahead.'

'But it's beyond just state concerns now, Governor. There is growing national pressure to halt this indiscriminate forestation. International pressure. Washington is trying to stop other nations, especially the North Africans, from their race to roll the Sahara *right* back.'

'If the Californians can do it in the Mojave, we can do it here,' the governor responded obstinately. 'Parks, woodland, Vialo, these things increase the value of land enormously. Look at Texas. We've lagged behind. It's why the people of Arizona have voted me into office. Previous governors have been weak. Previous governors have succumbed to just such pressures, have deliberately held back. But no more, Vialo. We're not going to be the only state left to hold the bag while all the rest break the rules.'

'Your state has set an example to others in restraint,' Vialo Natchez argued. 'The rate that arid regions of the

world are being overrun by these new hardy species has
become quite alarming.'

'You can't blame *us*,' Buntling answered. 'Blame the
Californians, they started it.'

'We can blame the Israelis. They started it all with their
experiments in the Negev. Then, of course, the goddamn
Australians lifted the technique. Caltech only helped with
the refinements.' Vialo raised the back of his hand to his
forehead, as though to take his own temperature. 'The
Aussies have got elephant and rhino now. Saving rare
species from extinction, they claim. Crud. They've gone
mad. The way they're going their whole interior could
become junglefied in a few years.'

'This is what I mean,' Buntling proclaimed. 'They're
reclaiming thousands of square miles. *I* only want us to
upgrade a few hundred. You shouldn't be leaning on *me*,
you should be leaning on *them*.'

'Do you think we're not trying?' Vialo snapped, losing
patience. 'But there's more to it than just greenery,
Governor. It's business. Cheap lumber. Cheap good-
quality lumber. And now safaris. The Kenyans are upset
that their wildlife tourist trade is going to get
competition.'

'I don't intend that we start any such zoo here,' the
governor said, 'but cheaper lumber, yes. If we can do it
at low cost in some hitherto totally unproductive regions,
why the hell shouldn't we, eh?'

'You're getting cheap lumber now.'

'Yes, from Colorado and others,' the governor nodded.
'But why shouldn't we set up our own industry right here?
It will create more jobs. You don't seem to realise what it
is costing this state to ignore plain worldwide trends that
everybody is adopting.'

'Lumber work is already oversubscribed. Governor,'
Vialo asked, 'what is your state noted for? Huh? Clear
skies. Healthy climate. Dry. Attracts a lot of retirees.'

'Geriatrics,' Buntling scoffed. 'They're the ones who kept my predecessors in office. Conservative. Status quo. The only change they're interested in is from a five or ten.'

'They're also the ones who have contributed a great deal to this state. And they're the ones who might not keep contributing if your climate changes.'

'I've heard that talk, and it's an exaggeration. A few trees are not going to make that much difference.'

Vialo sighed. 'We don't know. The deserts are disappearing. Some countries seem to think they've been given green gold. They can't spread it fast enough. They're vying with each other to see who can capitalise on the system the quickest. Apart from the Saudis and the Sudanese, the Chinese are making worrying progress in the Gobi, and the Soviets in their Kara-Kum and Kazyl-Kum.'

'It's *them* you want to stop, then,' Buntling reiterated. 'Counsel *them*. Don't get on *my* back for the comparatively small amount we are going to revegetate.'

'It won't be *re*vegetation because it's never been vegetated, has it?' Vialo noted, just a touch crankily. 'And we have and *do* counsel them. But their reply is always that we want to keep them disadvantaged, to deprive them of scientific improvements and keep them poor. And to tell us that *our* desert areas are not so vast, and to say that what desert lands we do have are being reclaimed faster than anybody's.'

'I'm with it,' the governor declared. 'I don't see why Arizona should be left out. I don't see why Arizona should be picked on by the State Department. And I don't see why one of its top bananas, Mister Vialo Natchez, should have been sent to try and twist my arm. This should strictly be state's business and nobody else's.'

Vialo raised a smile. 'We went to Arizona State together, didn't we?'

'You're still a Silver City outsider,' Buntling reminded him. 'No, Vialo, I don't think you've got a case. I'm not going soft on this one. I'm not letting Arizona get picked on just for old time's sake.'

'We're not picking on you, Governor,' Vialo said, 'but this *is* serious. It's global, and it's getting out of hand. Check your rainfall charts over the last ten years. You'll find you've already had more clouds in your clear skies than ever before.'

'That's nature,' Buntling countered. 'There can be changes in weather patterns over the years. There'd be something wrong if there *weren't* any changes.'

'Yes, but there's a cycle, Governor. Create a forest and you create a transpiring entity. It gives off moisture. Humidity rises. Clouds form. It rains. The more it rains, the more the plants thrive. Until, as you are aware, the initiating genetically engineered establishers can be steadily replaced by genetically upgraded superior species.'

Vialo gave an even deeper sigh.

'Millable timber inside ten years. A tempting proposition, Governor, as you realise only too well. Traditional suppliers of lumber are screaming. The only thing that dries up is their market. And dry is the word. Governor, this old world of ours is getting wetter. Have you heard of Professor Moshe Gumblot?'

'A little, not much. He's something to do with this new Un-Green Movement, isn't he?'

'He's their guru. You'll be hearing more of him in the future, I shouldn't wonder. The Un-Greens are making some ground. A lot of what they are saying contains a good measure of sense.'

'Puff,' the governor scorned. 'They blow everything out of proportion. It's deliberate sensationalism. It's purely to try and grab headlines.'

'Governor,' Vialo responded, 'the signs are already with us. Last year's great monsoons were probably no freaks at all. Practically the entire world has been recording higher rainfalls. They have even had measurable falls in some places like the Atacama where it has hardly ever rained before.

'What goes up must come down. Unless it's a space rocket,' Vialo smiled. Only to sober up again. 'The general humidity is rising worldwide. More moisture is being drawn landwards, in the tropics especially. Restoring the ravages in the Amazon was one thing, creating other Amazons, as in North Africa and other huge areas that were once barren, that's quite another.'

'Our project here, Vialo, is not going to be huge. Well, not *that* huge, anyway. Certainly not on a scale they're running in other places. In a *lot* of other places. Compared to others, what we intend to do here is little more than a drop in the bucket. I'd still like to know why you're picking on me, on *us*, on *our* state.'

'Because a halt needs to be called somewhere. An example. An example of responsibility. And,' Vialo confessed, 'we're in a bind, Governor. We've still got Utah, but we're losing Nevada. We can hardly tell the world what to do if we don't follow our own suggestions. We need to try and retain some of our desert territory. Manifestly. Demonstrably. We need some place we can point to, to be able to say that we *are* resisting this new green revolution.'

Buntling Frost took time out to ponder. Then, 'My predecessor,' he said, 'you had some arrangement with her?'

Vialo calculated. He decided he might be served best by the truth. 'We did have an understanding.'

'Did you supply my opponents any campaign funds?'

'We, ah, have lent some support towards SPUREDS, yes,' Vialo admitted. 'The Society for the Preservation of Unique and Rare Endangered Desert Species. The Papago, as you know, would seem to be concerned with desert flora and fauna displaced from other parts as well as the local varieties. The federal government, of course, has been very happy to contribute towards this forward-thinking kind of enterprise.'

'Ah.' The governor raised himself on his toes, then settled back again. 'What, ah, form of financial support are we looking at, Vialo? That is, *if* my state, *our* state, should even think to sacrifice its opportunity to convert considerable tracts of wasteland into valuable real estate? Only just supposing, of course.'

Vialo met his eye squarely. 'Generous compensation, Governor. Quite as much employment and infusion of economic stimulation as you might achieve by the greening course. A longer-term investment altogether. For one thing you would have need for our full backing to hire a large number of rangers if you would wish to maintain the ecological balance of your arid regions. You would naturally receive federal aid to counter disastrous effects caused by raised moisturisation.'

'You mean not only not plant initiator trees and shrubs and suckgrass, but pull up any that might plant itself?'

'Ecological strangers, yes.'

The governor thought about it. 'That could be a big job.'

'Exactly,' Vialo Natchez agreed. 'But necessary. Which is why Washington would be behind you all the way. Then there's tourism. If you can maintain your arid areas, they could become the last in the world. That's if your example fails to reverse policies that are being pursued elsewhere.'

Vialo became worried again. 'Climate is still not well understood, but it is believed now that the polar caps are growing again. Moisture gets locked in ice, but the sea to land cycle continues. If the land holds more water in encouraged massive vegetation, then the sea level will steadily fall. Some calculations say that it has fallen two centimetres already. It doesn't sound much, but it is a signal of a trend, perhaps.'

'An irreversible trend?'

'There's so much enthusiasm for the growing of woodland, of *anything*, where nothing has grown before, that there is a blindness against anything but the triumph of local success. There seems to be nobility in creating verdure. With these hybrids, these new techniques, any owner of trashland, and small-time bureaucrat, can appear to become a benefactor, even if he's never grown so much as a geranium in a pot before.'

Buntling Frost regarded Vialo coolly. 'Thanks,' he said.

'Oh,' Vialo said hastily, 'I didn't mean you, Governor. But, well, it *has* become an easy way out. Promise 'em forests and parks and woods, and more forests. Shortsighted. Fine for picnics. If it doesn't rain. Which it will. Your state will forfeit its character. Governor,' Vialo told him bluntly. 'You start that tree-planting here, then soon all you'll have to offer will be just another jungle.'

The governor bit his lip. 'I can't go back on it. It was an election promise. This is to be my first act in office. Dital Deus. Vialo, I'll be committing political suicide if I don't honour that promise.'

'Governor, you've got four years. That's an awful long time in politics. And it might be just long enough for the rest of the world to wake up and realise that this greening is excessive and fast getting out of control. That's if it's not out of control already.'

'It's all right for you to talk,' Buntling Frost said, a mite crossly now. 'You didn't expect me to win this office, did you? And now you want me to recant, and to make myself look a fool. That blasted tree is symbolic.'

'Your winning margin was narrow, Governor. You won't alienate your entire constituency. And a fair proportion must have voted for you for other reasons. The ladies, for example. Some unfair critics *have* claimed that it was only your charm over the female voter that tipped the scales your way.'

'Thanks again,' Buntling remarked tartly. 'I promised the greening of Arizona. It was my major platform. I'm not just some goddamn matinée idol. I want to do something for this state. That tree,' he stated flatly, 'has to go in.'

'A symbol *for* can also be a symbol *against*,' Vialo suggested. 'All you may need to do, Governor, is to maybe revise your speech a little . . . '

The governor concluded his speech by smoothly saying, 'And we shall go full steam ahead with this project just as soon as Federal Quarantine jurisdiction provides us clearance.' He alone knew that his breezy confidence was based on the certainty that the Feds would carry the can for all the stalling that was guaranteed to now ensue.

The governor now, taking up the special souvenir spade, ritually, contentedly, shovelled and patted down the dirt about the lonely inaugural marker.

BUT SMILE NO MORE

STEPHEN DEDMAN

1

I'm a bartender, not a biochemist, so I've never really understood why booze gets people drunk, or happy, or maudlin; I just make a living out of it. Booze, I mean: my customers don't get very drunk. Around here is mostly fancy offices, so I get the tie and briefcase crowd in for business lunches, and then I send the girls home at eight: this end of town is pretty dead at night, anyway. A few professional drinkers pass through, on their way down, but they don't talk much. All these new skyscrapers have stockbroker-proof windows, so the would-be jumpers take to the elevators and drift down here. They don't understand sums of money below a million dollars, so I can charge what I like for cocktails: I made a fortune in the Crash of '87, enough to keep the wife happy and send my son to Yale, and if '99 is as bad as the lunchtime crowd predicts, I'll sell the place and retire early.

But this guy came in one Tuesday night, after nine; said he was a biochemist and asked to try every bottle on the shelf. He looked Asian, probably Vietnamese, and I have the devil of a time trying to guess *their* ages, but he had a thin little beard, so he wasn't a kid. And his eyes . . . well, I'm pretty good with eyes: I guessed he was under thirty, only got drunk when he needed to – and he needed to now.

I just nodded, and asked, 'Left to right?' I keep the ouzo in the middle for guys like this – and make sure they pay in advance.

'Left to right is fine,' he replied, and I knew from his

voice that he was sober, and he wasn't happy, and he wasn't much of a drinker, not in terms of experience – the way he grimaced when he tasted the tequila confirmed *that*. His eyebrows hinted that he might have smiled, once, but a man should not be held responsible for his eyebrows. Then he toasted me and said, 'To lemmings.'

At least, that's what I thought he said; it didn't sound like 'two lemons', which would've made more sense . . . and, like I said, he was sober. 'Lemmings?' I asked.

He nodded, 'You know anything about lemmings?'

'I know they're little furry creatures from Scandinavia that go crazy every three or four years and think they're stockbrokers.'

He blinked, then smiled politely and unconvincingly. 'Oh, they're not that crazy. Nor, whatever the creationists might say, are they a new type of Gadarene swine, throwing themselves over cliffs to drown our demons.' He drained his tequila like he was drowning a demon himself, then pushed the glass towards me.

I've never met a drunk who could say 'creationist'. My son, who's studying paleontology, can't even say it when he's sober, not without a few qualifying adjectives.

'You know any biology?' he asked, as I poured him a Southern Comfort.

'Just enough to extrapolate you're going to have a hell of a headache tomorrow.'

The smile didn't change. 'You know how you can take a spider and remove all of its silk, and it'll try to spin a web anyway? It's on a sort of autopilot, all instinct and no independent thought. Or how a wombat will always follow a set route, even if you build a fence in its way?'

I'd heard about the trick with the spider, so I nodded. 'You mean that lemmings used to migrate, but the sea wasn't always there?'

'He thought of that, but . . . ' He swallowed the Southern Comfort like it was medicine, then gave me the empty glass and another ten-dollar coin. 'Did you ever hear of a biologist called Peter Ericsson?'

'No.' Danny, my son, may have mentioned him – he likes to talk, and I just nod a lot (it's a trick bartenders learn early) – but the name didn't ring any bells.

'Or Iain Bourne?'

I shook my head.

'Okay.' He relaxed slightly, as much as a man can on a bar stool, and began. 'Ericsson was just an associate professor at one of the smaller, less prestigious state universities. He might've done better for himself if he'd specialised . . . but he was a great believer in "basic research". And, one night back in '67 or '68, he got to thinking about lemmings. I think he was looking for the ancestor of the dolphin . . . All the marine mammals, you know, are descended from a land species, after all, and no land mammal particularly resembles dolphins or whales . . . The lemming's a generic shape for a mammal – rather like the African hyrax, which is the closest living relative of the elephant which it scarcely resembles . . . '

He sipped at his vodka; he had me intrigued now, and I resolved to pour his drinks slowly, hoping to hear the end of this. I've known my share of happy drunks, and maudlin drunks, and violent drunks, and incoherent drunks, but this guy was a pleasantly garrulous drunk, and I'm partial to the breed.

'But that wasn't an explanation,' he continued. 'Even seals don't try to travel over land for distances like that. So, he thought, like you, what if there was once a suitable environment, where there was now only ocean? Continental drift was too slow, but . . . could there have been a glacier, forming a land bridge, during the Ice Age? There could've, but apparently there wasn't. Or . . . glaciers elevated lands in the south, depressing lands in the north, reversing the procedure when they retreated . . .

Nice idea, but again, the geologists said there wasn't any evidence for it.

'Okay, what if the lemmings' sense of direction had gone somehow haywire? No one was sure whether lemmings *had* a sense of direction, so it seemed a sensible place to start. Basic research, after all.

'The research was difficult – lemmings are, not surprisingly, hard to obtain, and the University wasn't generous with its equipment. The lemmings were also uncooperative when it came to running mazes, and not particularly eager to learn. A researcher in a more prestigious college might have given up there, but Ericsson, after all, was used to unenthusiastic students. After half a year of persistence, he managed to obtain results suitable for a control group. He then set about confusing them with random periods of light and dark, wet and dry, temperate and cold – even false starscapes. No pattern.

'The next experiment required a bottle of thirty-two-year-old Scotch whisky, or so I'm told.'

'For the lemmings?' I gasped.

'No, for the Dean of Physics. Eventually, with his help, Ericsson was able to demonstrate that lemmings were dependent on a magnetic sense – an internal compass. And since it was proven that Earth's magnetic poles periodically inverted, instincts, evolved when the magnetic north pole was somewhere in Antarctica, resulted in mass suicide.'

I shook my head admiringly. 'Wow.'

'Oh, that was nothing. It would have earned Ericsson a Size 10 footnote in the history of science, and it earned him the hatred of the Creationists, which should have been enough for any educated man. It also took him out of the college and into a well-funded government research lab.'

He fell silent, and I wondered whether he'd finished; the

ending didn't seem to justify the meanings. He sipped slowly at his vodka, rolling it around his mouth like a wine taster, then asked, 'Did you ever think there were some things man wasn't meant to know?'

I shrugged. 'I know there are a lot of things a man doesn't *want* to know.'

He looked around the bar at the dark, empty chairs and shiny half-full bottles, and asked, 'You think that's why they drink?'

'Yeah, sometimes.'

He nodded. 'Well, Ericsson set out to find the physical location of this magnetic sense. He figured it required a concentration of iron, and that it was probably in the brain . . . and if it wasn't near the surface, it was going to be hard to isolate surgically. But hell, lysergic acid blocks the serotinin pathways, preventing rational thought, and alcohol (as you may have noticed) shows a preference for the reticular formation, so why not an iron-based molecule that zooms in on a magnetic sense centre?

'Unfortunately, biochemistry still relies largely on trial and error, even when your theory is perfectly sound. *Vide* thalidomide, or Agent Orange . . . '

'You don't have to tell me about Agent Orange,' I replied, sourly. 'My brother Terry was marinated in the stuff. Died of cancer without getting a cent.'

He nodded, his face blank. 'Yeah, I heard about that. Sorry.'

I shrugged, wondering *how* he'd heard; I don't usually talk about Terry when I'm sober, and I don't drink on the job. A lot of my clientele still think Vietnam was good business and that chemical warfare has been given a bad press – and they don't come here to argue. If there was any one person more guilty than all the others, I could . . . well, do *something*, but as it is . . . 'You were saying?'

'One of the molecules that Ericsson chanced upon

accumulated in the pleasure centre, the "rivers of reward". And stayed there, isolating it from the rest of the brain. And it didn't *just* work in lemmings.

'Ericsson died in '71, never realising that he'd discovered a cure for happiness . . . and if he had, I doubt he would have tried it on humans. But by that time, it was in Bourne's hands.'

He stared into his vodka, then downed it in two godalmighty gulps and handed me the empty glass. I poured him a Bacardi and waited.

'I don't have to tell *you* what things were like in the Nixon days; you probably know all about the CIA SNAFUs like MKULTRA and using LSD on their own informers.' I nodded. 'Bourne tried it out on prisoners on Death Row – the ultimate chemical castration.

'The prisoners reported feeling calmer, more resigned to their fate, less irascible and violent . . . but they were hardly a representative group. Bourne had Ericsson's work classified, which is why Ericsson never became famous. It was a lot of balls because there wasn't a one-in-a-million chance that it would've lead anyone to developing the same drug – but classified work pays better.

'Bourne gave the drug to students next, but the results of *that* were classified too . . . which meant that it was a failure, and possibly a nightmare. At best, the long-term results were just too hard to follow up. A few of his subjects were drafted, sent to Nam; and strangely, *none* of them came back. The others . . . well, either nothing happened, or there's been a cover-up, or maybe both. But, anyway, that wasn't what Bourne wanted. He wanted to give the drug to *very* young babies, so they would *never* know pleasure.'

I shuddered involuntarily, almost spilling my Coke. 'Why?'

He shrugged. 'His hypothesis was that happy people did not make the great discoveries; why should they want to?

They were already happy. And the Chinese used to use eunuchs (*you* try saying that after four stiff drinks) for their civil servants, because they didn't get distracted or ambitious. Of course, the relationship between pleasure and happiness isn't entirely understood, and there was no better way of finding out. Analysis requires destruction; it *means* destruction. Taking apart . . . '

'Even if you don't know how to put it together again.'

'Exactly. Can you *un*-mix a drink? But that didn't matter to Bourne. I'm not even sure that the project was approved because of his high-flown nonsense; the CIA probably thought of it as just another mind drug, a depressant that could pacify prisoners . . . or draftees, maybe. Or maybe make perfect soldiers who couldn't be seduced or get sentimental. But that's by the way – Bourne was given his subjects. Abortions were still illegal, you remember, and orphans are a buyer's market in wartime. Mostly black, of course, or Hispanic, but some of us were refugees, and Bourne insisted on a few white babies too; a mix of races, and a nearly even mix of boys and girls – '

'Some of *us*?'

'Yes,' he said quietly and sipped at his Bacardi. 'I was one of the Throng – that's what we called ourselves, later. Lydia suggested it; she was interested in languages, and in poetry, in emotions – in a purely theoretical sense, of course. It's from a poem by Edgar Allan Poe, a man with no great gift for happiness himself: *A hideous throng rush out forever/And laugh – but smile no more.*

'We didn't all rush out together: a few of us were adopted, and Bourne helped us get scholarships . . . I suppose we studied harder than the Irash, but we weren't all brilliant – Irash, by the way, was our name for the rest of you. Short for Irrationals. Nothing personal.'

He drained his Bacardi, pushed the glass towards me, glanced at his watch, and shook his head. 'Gotta go,' he said, a little thickly. 'Be back next week.'

2

I don't call Danny as often as I should, I guess, and I felt a little silly phoning him – but I've forgiven him for a lot of strange behaviour over the past twenty-seven years, and he owes me.

'Ericsson?'

'Yeah.'

'Doesn't ring any bells, Dad – but I'm not a biochemist.'

'What about that work you did last year?'

There was a rather expansive silence. Maybe he hadn't expected me to remember, or he probably thought I was only pretending to listen. Actually, I do listen; I learnt to do it when his mother walked out seventeen years ago. I don't always *understand*, is all.

'I just found the fossils; Linda did the chem lab work . . . Can I get back to you on this?'

I remembered, too late, that he and Linda had had a wonderful working relationship, followed very recently by a brief and cataclysmic romance. 'Yeah, please . . . and Danny?'

'Yeah, Dad?'

'Did you ever tell anyone about your Uncle Terry?'

'I don't think so . . . ' he replied, uncertainly. 'The chem labs here do a lot of defence research work, and I may have let it slip . . . why?'

'It doesn't matter,' I said, and hoped it didn't.

3

The biochemist came back on the Friday with a young woman. The place was busy; one of the girls served them, and I didn't see them until they were leaving. The woman had dark hair and very dark eyes; she looked about twenty-two from the eyes down, but she didn't smile. I waited for him Tuesday night, but he didn't show.

The Tuesday after, about quarter to ten, the place was empty again when the door opened, and the biochemist hurried in as though it were freezing outside. 'Hi.'

'Hi.' He looked at the row of bottles and asked, 'Where was I?'

I poured him a Johnny Walker. 'The Irash.'

'Yeah. No offence.'

'None taken,' I assured him. 'How many are there of you?'

'Fifteen. There were twenty-one, but – ' He shrugged and sipped at the whisky. 'I suppose it could be worse. We don't get depressed, I guess; we don't get down, because we were never up. We don't feel that we've lost anything, because we never had it to lose. I wonder how much worse it would feel if you *could* remember having been happy, without being able to recreate it. . . .'

His eyes became slightly misty and his voice very soft, and I almost expected him to fall over . . . but he recovered in an instant. 'Bourne wanted us to become scientists, of course,' he continued, his voice as crisp as new banknotes, 'and some of us did. And some of us settled for being technicians and engineers. Vanessa is studying Medicine, and Julio set a college record for low grades in Political Science, though I understand he did quite well at Psych. Two of the girls had kids of their own – none of *us* could – and held on to them long enough to see if it was hereditary . . . and apparently it isn't.'

He looked into his glass and shook his head. 'Babies have this secret weapon: they smile. It makes their mothers feel happy and maternal. Sometimes I wonder how *any* of us were adopted.' He shrugged. 'The experiment is over now, and I suppose we should be happy, if happiness were ever logical – which I wouldn't know.' He took a mouthful of his Scotch, grimaced, and asked for a Bloody Mary.

'What about Bourne?'

'What about him?'

'Is he still alive?'

'Oh, yes. He left the Project in '88, after the defence contracts scandal, and took a job with Condor Pharmaceuticals. Works near here, as a matter of fact.'

He took the Bloody Mary unsteadily in his left hand, holding it like a chess piece instead of like a glass, then moved it over to stand before the stool at his left. 'Good evening, Dr Bourne,' he said loudly.

I looked up, startled. A man in his early fifties who knew how to wear an expensive suit was standing in the doorway. He spared me a glance, then walked slowly towards my customer. 'Good evening, Paul. How's the science fiction?'

Paul showed his teeth in an insincere grin. I stared at both of them, wondering who was lying.

'I see you've started without me,' said Bourne. 'Am I late?'

'No.'

'Is this mine, or have you become ambidextrous?'

'It's yours. On me.'

'Thank you.' He sat and tasted the drink. 'So, how is everyone?'

'Bradley quit,' replied Paul. 'He decided he didn't want to make bombs any more. Lydia's lecturing in semiotics.' Bourne shook his head in mock disgust, then took another mouthful of the Bloody Mary. 'Vanessa's in town. She gave her baby up for adoption last month, and I haven't heard from the others in more than a year. Have you?'

'Michael's been made a junior partner,' he replied. 'Apart from that, everyone's still where they were: no real news.'

'No weddings? No kids?' Paul's voice was softly mocking. Bourne ignored him.

'And what've you been doing?'

'Following in your footsteps,' said Paul. 'I've improved on the formula.'

Bourne dropped his glass; fortunately, it was nearly empty and it hadn't far to fall before it hit the bar. Suddenly, I believed everything Paul had told me.

'You can reverse the process?' asked Bourne, with forced casualness.

Paul continued to grin, leaving both of us in suspense for nearly half a minute. 'No,' he said finally. 'I'm still working on *that*, but I think the damage is irreversible. Like brain cells killed by alcohol; nothing can regenerate them. No, this was just a slight modification, but a serendipitous and useful one. It has the same effects as the original, but it's water soluble, and you don't have to inject it; it can be administered orally. It tastes like hell, but you only need a drop – and it's nearly colourless . . . '

And so was Bourne's face as he stared at the dregs in his glass. Paul stood, a little unsteadily, and reached into his pocket. I shook my head.

'That's okay,' I told him. 'No charge. Not for a friend of Terry's.'

Paul stared at me, and then he laughed. It wasn't a happy laugh, but it was a laugh all the same. And then he walked out.

4

That should've been the end, and maybe it was . . . but four nights later, on my way home, I saw cops and an ambulance clustered outside Arnheim House. The pavement was cracked and bloody. Obviously someone had jumped from the roof – and Arnheim House is twelve storeys tall. The top four contain the offices for Condor Pharmaceuticals.

But I didn't stop to see who it had been. I haven't seen Paul since, or Bourne, or heard anything of either of them, and sometimes I wonder . . . but never for very long. Maybe it isn't logical, but like I'd told Paul, there are some things a man doesn't want to know . . .

But they haunt me, the Throng, and I look for them everywhere. Sometimes I wonder if they've come here, to celebrate or mourn, never smiling, and I haven't recognised them amid the laughing lemmings . . .

I smile a lot, and I wait for people to smile back . . . I know you're out there. And some days, God help me, I think I know how you feel.

A TOOTH FOR EVERY CHILD

DAMIEN BRODERICK

As the sun comes up, some automatic energy saver lowers the lights and turns off the heating flow, and a note of melancholy grey enters the high windows that no one can see anything through, seeps blurrily down the opposite wall of the drab Right To Life Maternity Hospital. My father comes back from his talk in the corridor to the doctor and sits down next to me, taking my hand. It is the first physical contact I've had with him since my adolescence. He tries to utter my name, get the sentence started.

'Take it easy, Dad,' I say, and squeeze his fingers. 'They told me.' Fatalistically, I've expected it anyway. It was a change-of-life pregnancy, and the risk factor was high. But in my guilt I know that isn't what killed my mother.

'First Jane.' He makes a sound that combines mucus and grief, and it tears me up, it reaches into my own throat and pierces my chest. My father coughs blindly into a handkerchief, swallows until he can speak. 'First Jane, now your mother. And the child is a – '

'Don't talk about it, Dad.'

'I'm glad you're here,' he tells me. 'I'm truly glad.'

I find myself hunched, shivering, and when the old man gets up to visit the lavatory I finally start to go to bits, spastic jolts, subliminal feedback lags up and down my limp muscles, and cold, horribly cold in the centre of my body. I squeeze my arms into my invaded abdomen and try as hard as I can to pull myself together.

A staff orderly, a nun, is speaking loudly to me, shaking

my shoulder. 'It's not serious, but we've popped Mr Berger into bed.'

I stare at her. 'What?'

'He collapsed for a moment in the toilet. We gave him a pill to help him sleep for a few hours.'

'Shock,' I say, nodding. 'He's just emotionally burnt out.' I stare at my hands.

'You should go home now yourself and get some rest,' the orderly says. 'Someone can phone you when he's ready to come home. Probably sometime this afternoon.'

'No. I'll wait here.'

She looks doubtful. 'If you're sure – '

I'm sure, all right. I need to be awake so I can check on the baby. I need to stay awake so I can get close to the vile little bitch and kill it.

After a sick, grieving grey time, another voice speaks my name. 'Dr Berger?'

I assume this is the registrar, in charge of running the ward and sizing up the patients for the specialists. She holds a hard-copy file card in her hand. I regard her with absolute blankness. She starts to straighten, letting her glance shift to the other weary figures sprawled on maroon, uncomfortable vinyl benches. I catch her sleeve. 'Uh, yeah, me.'

She smiles quickly. 'You look as if you need some breakfast.' Her eyes go once again, quickly, to the card. I know precisely what has caught her interest. Even a registrar in a busy major gynaecological hospital would have little enough opportunity to see Security Interdiction blanks on an official machine printout. 'Does "Dr" stand for "medical practitioner", or are you the kind with a PhD?'

'I'm a hacker,' I say.

The registrar laughs with spontaneous warmth. 'That doesn't really count as a definitive answer. What is it you hack, Dr Berger?'

I do what I can to grin back. 'Data is what I hack, doctor. And I'm the kind with a DSc. My doctorate is in computer science.'

'You look as if you've been up all night. Come on, I'll get you something to eat.'

'I have been. Thank you.'

We go out of the waiting area and she puts me at one end of a moth-eaten couch in a cubicle while she asks a nurse to bring us some sandwiches from the machine in the lower foyer. She pours me a cup from a small electric drip percolator she must have smuggled in for her private use. The thick, black, overwhelmingly sweet Turkish coffee strikes me like a bolt of amphetamine.

'I didn't catch your name, doctor,' I say. Her surname and initials are written clearly on a plastic lapel tag but I want things a little more even between us.

'Susan,' she says, sitting carefully at the other end of the couch, touching my knee in little taps with her fingertips. 'Dr Dwyer, if you need to reach me through the switch, but make it Susan.' That printout has certainly excited her interest.

I'm twanging. When I bite into the soggy tomato sandwich I feel sick, literally nauseated. So it is finally getting to me. Genuinely reaching me. I want in all my gutted bereavement to let go, to howl with grief and rage. Until this moment my hostile misery has been a rippling cerebral thing, chilly and flaked with blue and silver. Now it corrodes through the retaining wall and gathers there, ready to burst, ready to shriek and avalanche down the slopes and chew to shreds whatever it finds in its way, smash everything into brown froth and bloody foam, including me. I sit at the end of the couch and watch Susan Dwyer's plain modest face and do what I can not to throw up on her vinyl tiles. The discomforts of my pregnancy don't help.

'I'd like to talk about your baby sister,' she says. 'When you're ready. More coffee?'

'Is it human?'

Certainly that shocks her profoundly. You're not supposed to say that. It renders useless her bland prepared script. I can feel her scrutiny zip about my face like a scanning microwave beam. Sunlight dashes itself against the wall to my right, her left. All the grumbling sounds of the place. An odour like surgery, another of cleanliness amid a thousand rotting things. Very faintly, I fancy, the scorched stench of sawed bone. My jumping muscles lock in place.

Dr Dwyer looks at me without any expression at all. 'You're upset. The baby is . . . special. She'll get the best possible care.'

I put down the half-eaten sandwich and take up the coffee cup and drink some of the shockingly caffeinated slurry and regard the sun-streaked wall and then I vomit monstrously all along the top and back of the plaid insect-molested couch, while Dr Dwyer frowns with sympathy even as she leaps for cover and comes back to hold my shoulders as my diaphragm convulses with bile and all the songs of a Sabbath of Witches sing gruesome whining jingles to my ringing ears.

I spend a lot of time crying after that, and Susan Dwyer keeps dropping back from her complex unceasing duties to talk to me, paid angel of mercy. (She isn't the registrar, of course. Psychotherapy and hand-holding on the battlefront.) The morning blurs into hours of semi-conscious fugue. In her one fall from intelligent grace, Susan tells me: 'They'll see the child is cared for.'

Because I still retain some measure of self-control, I do not tell her what I think about that. We did not bring Mum to the Right To Life Hospital for its ideology, but because the swine have the most advanced maternity life-support equipment in Melbourne. But they have not been able to save her. As they will not be able to save me. The knowledge eats at my belly, at the place where my own child is growing, like a spill of acid.

'What's happening to Mother's body? What are the authorities doing with it?'

She looks shocked, as if my question implies the existence of some covert and disgusting rite. I suppose it does. 'Why, there'll be a funeral, of course, when you and your family are over the worst of it. You'd be surprised,' she tells me with a wan smile, 'how quickly you'll be able to cope. It will recede. Become more manageable.'

'Suppression of the unconscionable.'

'I sincerely hope not. That's not a very fruitful way to deal with any problem, you know. A sure recipe for fester.'

This kind of blunted cut and thrust is *not* stupid. It is meant to jolt me, and does; it is purgative. Susan Dwyer still has not said anything about my pregnancy. Perhaps she doesn't know. The census computer file must have interdicted her access to a great deal more than my academic and professional details. Surprising: I have always assumed that high level hospital personnel would be cleared automatically for any medical information it pleases them to ask after.

'I had an abdominal implant two months ago.'

'Oh shit.' She gets off the couch, goes to a stool beside the desk, runs her fingers over a touchboard and views the display. By this time the sun has gone right down the wall. I feel anaesthetised. Maybe I am. Perhaps she juiced up my coffee with floaters. 'Keith, why didn't you mention that earlier?'

I look at her as people do on sitcoms in such circumstances: with my mouth slightly compressed, ironic rue, my brows slightly drawn in and crunkled. (How did anyone know how to communicate before the mass media told us the codes?)

'Susan, I'd just about OD'd on grim news. And I was trying to, you know, concentrate on Mum.' When I married Jane last year, Mum's jealousy knew no bounds. I was her prince, and I had betrayed her with this terrible rival, so she paid us all back by throwing away her contraceptive pills and pulling Dad onto her angry menopausal but still fertile belly. I say nothing of this to the nosy doctor.

A slightly disfiguring patch of purple skin on Susan's right arm, above the carpus, had been hidden by the flat patch of her watch decal. It becomes visible as she nudges the decal around her wrist, teasing up an edge and tugging, letting it fall. She sighs.

'I won't bullshit you, Keith. There's bound to be a risk. This . . . unhappy phenomenon . . . appears to have some hereditary aspects.'

Instantly, with passion, I say: 'Abortion is out of the question.'

'Dr Berger,' she tells me with a note of reproof, 'abortion has *never* been an option at this hospital.'

Annoyed, I say, 'I'm not talking about your damned dark age garbage. There are other hospitals, other States. Anyway, that's all beside the point. What I'm telling you is that I *want* this child I'm carrying. My wife Jane died six months ago.' My throat hurts again, as it always hurts, but I say it: 'I was driving the car. They saved the embryo. Even if the risk – '

She seems genuinely moved. 'I'm sorry. How terrible.' After a silence she says: 'Your new sister – you can set your mind at rest on that score at least. They're – '

' – properly cared for. So you mentioned.' I squeeze my eyes shut. I'll care for the sucker. I'll tear its throat out and throw it to the dogs to eat.

The pulse of adrenalin dizzies me; I am not a violent man, I do not harbour terrible impulses, but my mother's victimisation and my own hormonal confusions have me on an emotional big dipper.

The pre-maternity unit insists on giving me a thorough checkover (myographs, EEG, haemodynamic, others I've never heard of) and, when Dad regains his feet, sends me home with the assurance that at least my foetal implant is fully cushioned and thriving, placenta well along and nourished from my abdominal blood supply. I wish it were possible to check the foetus with an ultrasound body scan, or even an X-ray, but no one dares risk invasive sensing any longer, after the Adolescent-Onset Leukaemia horror.

At any rate, the implant wound has healed completely. No scar tissue, outside my mind. Susan Dwyer squeezes my hand as we leave and wishes me well.

When the taxi drops Dad and me at the Queens Way apartment (the Albert Park runners all sweaty along Lakeside Drive and skimmers blithe on the flat banal water of the lake and summer drought taking colour out of the trees and the golf course greens) I arrange for the retired broker up the hall to pop in during the afternoon and keep an eye on him. I just can't cope with the thought of the poor old bastard blundering through the empty rooms. Not that Dad is really all that old. Hardly over fifty. Twice my age. And, when I go back down south, all alone, alone, alone.

I put him to bed with another pill and the moment he falls asleep I boot my terminal.

By and large I know very little about the practice of medicine, let alone the architecture, staffing and running of gynae/androcology units, but of late my second-hand pregnancy has sharpened my interest. Having a smart touchboard helps.

Quite illegally and unobtrusively, it patches me into the heart of the Right To Life Maternity Hospital's environment comptroller menu. I study maps and coded diagrams. It is designedly user-friendly, once you have authorisation to enter it.

There is only one place the non-human babies can be: a mnemonically labelled special intensive care section on the fifth floor.

Chilled, I touch my belly. So it is true: the plague of what the Health Department has dubbed 'Intermittent Uterine Intervention' is spreading, numbers multiplying. An entire unit floor given over to them. Christ. What happens to the ones born in hospitals governed by alternative ideologies? Literally, I find that I have bared my teeth. I know what I'd do, what I *intend* to do.

Some kind of creepy social contract of complicity has crept up on us, an agreement to keep our silence – almost, God help us, to welcome the plague – but I have never signed up. It seems to me like some grey choking fog out of Nazi Germany, Stalinist Russia, Kafka. I focus myself through grief and exhaustion to anger. Perhaps the difference is my shock and guilt at Jane's death, in an accident I failed to prevent. A psychotherapist – Dr Dwyer, say – might attribute this to an overdeveloped sense of responsibility for the fate of others. Ha.

It is all irrelevant. What matters is the fact that a monster has killed my mother, and that I mean to return the favour.

My private tap into AussieNet makes it easy. It helps to be one of the custodians.

The special unit at RTL Maternity is wired in a maze of cybernetic monitoring devices. It looks to me as if the hospital authorities want to minimise direct human contact with the new-born monsters. I have no trouble insinuating several sub-routine loops into the system. They'll get me in, cover for me, get me out again, and then expunge themselves. I hope. You can never be sure, no matter how sublime and intuitive your resonance with computer logics.

I catch a tram back into town along St Kilda Rd, all flickery with trees beside the road and mirrored office blocks set back in a summer mirage, and enter the hospital by a side door, the location and low visibility of which I noted while we waited for confirmation that my mother had become the drained, discarded compost of a non-human parasite which metastasised inside her for nine months.

There is a way of walking which tells organisational staff, including medicos, that you are one of them. Done at an exact pitch of hauteur, you can persuade those whose business it is to be officious that you are their superior in rank and station. It helps, however, to be at least in your mid-thirties. I do what I can and it seems to be working, though I'm feeling sick and stunned and ready to give it all up and go home again and put myself to bed for two days with a handful of hypnotic tranquillisers.

When I reach the ward where the monsters are kept I walk straight past a nurse conferring with a colourful diagnostic display, stride into the dull blue lighting of the place, into its faintly seaside smells and the clicking of the hands and feet of the things inside their cribs. I do not avert my eyes, though I want to.

They are all alike in their deformity.

On my understanding of genetics, this is impossible. Mutation is a random thing. Were this malediction an accidental by-product of our foul world, it would not show itself in a single form, any more than victims of haphazard radiation are born with a common, identifiable deficit.

So is this, in the true sense, a plague? Some viral instruction to the hapless genes of the pre-born? Yet what I see before me is too complex for that, too ornate. Surely no single virus can build viable gargoyles out of human flesh.

I stare around me in the blue light. In all truth, what I see does not look like anything the theory of evolution can cope with, no matter with what ingenuity it is modified. This is something more, an infestation of demons. They look like some proof of pre-scientific metaphysics, an adaptation to the future, a form of life fit for the Apocalypse.

Yes. They look to me as if they have been designed to live with gusto in a world ruined by catastrophe.

I find a touchboard and bypass the monitor programming, call up the fancy loops I inserted from my apartment terminal. When I punch my name – Mum's name – an indicator lights on one of the cribs. I go straight to it and open it up, and take out the small pink thing that lies there.

It is loathsome, like the rest of them. But plainly viable. Given normal care, it will undoubtedly survive, it will thrive.

It will be given normal care. My arms, holding it, begin to shake.

Have they been *inflicted* on us?

Is that why the authorities keep them alive, spiriting them away?

No. Unbelievable. Genetic engineering has not attained that boldness, that mastery. The biologists are smug enough in their modest achievement of allowing men like me to bear children. That technical triumph is itself so recent the stigma has still not worn off. The grins, the muttered remarks in the street.

I cannot tear my eyes from it. Oh God. There must be places crammed with others of its kind, older, crawling on hands and knees, toddling, learning to run, singing with their terrible voices. After all, the phenomenon has been known for at least five years, even if no one dares talk about it.

This one is female. I will not think of it as my baby sister.

It opens its eyes, as I hold it in my trembling hands, and gazes at me.

Newborn babies cannot focus their gaze. This does.

It looks at me and whimpers, as if it is attempting to speak.

It seems to say my name.

I run with sweat. It mewls and chitters, clamping my finger.

I kill it as quietly as I can.

The others I leave undisturbed. I really don't care about them.

One of my loops blips out false signs, pretending to be a baby monster breathing. Nobody stops me as I leave the section.

Dad is awake, querulous and ruined, and I have no love or patience left for him. I shoulder my way past and swallow a bunch of pills and go to sleep with the light on.

After Mum's funeral, I make arrangements to keep the old man together in body and soul, then repack and fly out again in a big airforce jet, back to the scouring wind and ice of Mawson and the joint US-Australasian Defence Station under Mount Menzies, and the joyous programming of those big machines which control the so-called 'Star Wars' X-ray lasers and thus do their bit toward keeping the Southern Hemisphere from blistering ionisation.

That takes care of the next four months.

Input/black box/Output.

You can consider me the black box, figuratively on my hands and knees in the bowels of the processor.

Press and electronic media maintain their discreet and

dignified profile on the matter of 'Intermittent Uterine Intervention'. Women's groups that try to go public in a big way get stomped: pre-emptively, savagely, quietly, effectively. I know this much, if little more, from the privilege of my seat of power, such as it is. Occasionally I'm able to pull demographic figures through my own number-cruncher peripherals, and the curves look bad to me.

As my own belly swells I have to give up my weekend tromps through the extended dawn dazzle of Lambert Glacier, a four hundred kilometre slippery slide to the Amery Ice Shelf and off the edge of the world. It is murder out there, slush and glare and dreadful Fimbulwinter summer cold. I find myself lying awake all night, shivers of sweat soaking my outsize pyjamas.

There is simply no safe way to tell if I have a thing inside me instead of the child I made, with love, with my dead wife.

There's a forty per cent chance that laparoscope insertion will trigger lethal anaphylactic shock syndrome, if what I harbour is not a human baby. That was one of the first findings they announced, before the pall of silence closed on the media. Strangely enough, gross biochemical assays have not to date yielded true distinguishing markers. Still, I piss into bottles and send them north with the penguins for NMR determination and mass spectrography examination and, for all I know, blue litmus tests.

My obstetricians and androcologists simply shrug when I speak to them face to face through a satellite link. Too early, Keith. Hang in there.

To my astonishment, I receive two friendly postcards from Susan Dwyer. I send her a plastic stuffed penguin with a roguish leer.

At seven months I am deemed too delicate for continued security work and fly home to prepare for my *accouchement.* Everyone is very bracing and gung-ho and not one word is said which even remotely hints that I might be being gnawed on from within, husked, flayed and consumed. It's not the kind of thing you joke about. Like cancer until recently, consumption last century.

'You look done in, son.'

'It's a long flight, Dad.'

Speculatively, warily, we regard one another. My tweed smock sticks out; the placental prolactin hormones make my damn tits protrude visibly. It suddenly comes to me that the old fool is embarrassed, that he perceives me from his twenty-nine year warp as some kind of secret gay or transsexual jumping out of the closet into his defenceless hearth. 'Give me a hand with this suitcase, sport,' I say briskly, and bang him smartly on the back. He picks it up with a sigh of relief. I refrain from breaking his reactionary old heart by telling him that all the truly macho *Ubermenschen* at Mawson are queer as thirty dollar bits.

In the apartment, looking across the autumnal colours of Albert Park and the press of late afternoon traffic on the freeway below, it pleases me in my masochism to identify with Van Gogh. I find Dad's scratched-out analogue disc of Don Maclean's *American Pie* and cue up 'Vincent'. Starry starry night. Mad as a cut snake, but globs and swirls of truth. There's a Brett Whiteley *hommage* (Mum's, not his) on the living room wall. I salute it with a finger. Self-mutilators, Vincent, you and I.

'Get you something to drink, Keith?'

'I'm keeping off it until the baby's born.'

'Oh. Yeah.' He sits down and toys with a dusty, pitted golf trophy.

We are maudlin together, after our separate styles.

'Females,' he says, with bone-deep misery. First he has

lost his daughter-in-law, then his wife and baby have been taken from him. 'I never thought about dying, you know, Keith? Always had it in the back of my mind that I'd go first.'

They've told him about the death of the thing of course, but they have not explained the irregular manner of its passing. Not that they've let me in on that, either, for all my exalted security standing.

Dad makes two martinis, a taste he contracted in Vietnam, excessively dry, passes me one, gets downcast when I hand it back, drinks them both. His mood blurs. Mine remains spiky.

He leaves his second olive. I fish it out and eat it.

It's my first pregnancy, and my back is starting to kill me. All the computer-designed, carbon filament trusses and supports do little enough, it seems to me, to compensate for my essential anatomical inadequacies as a mother.

Computer hackers usually play a lot of hard squash; it balances out all the sitting and staring. (No matter how ergonomically the terminal touchboards are arranged, the human backbone was not selected by evolution to deal with long term trunk immobility.) Now all my regular ironman exercise routines are contraindicated, and the mass in my abdomen presses more fiercely with each new day. Into the bargain, I'm as randy as a rat, despite the nurturant oestrogen and progesterone analogues. (Expecting mothers dote on medical jargon, especially male mothers. Ghosts and echoes of all those doctor shows on the box.)

There are women, it turns out, who get off on heavily gravid men, and I find more than one, in bars I never quite identified before, parallel invisible culture like S&M gays and herpes clubs I suppose. They repel me.

'My wife,' I try to explain to one of them. 'I was driving the car.' Small and gaunt, second-generation gook

migrant, a crip lover, aching for something beyond
deformity. 'The head of my department made no objection
to the implant.' She scowls as I talk about it, hating the
dead. 'Good publicity, open-minded government policy.'
But her head is moving away from me, and her ears hum
with songs I don't know.

Beggars and choosers? Well, perhaps, but there is
something unpleasant, perfervid, about those hungry
mouths. Have they hated their mothers so badly? Still,
their attentions quickly sicken me, and I am left swollen
high and low, burning, pissed off. Drinking mineral water,
no booze, no dope.

Some cliches are true, no matter how tiresome it might be
when you find yourself reacting in a stock manner. A
corner car comes within a hair of running you down, your
mind reacts, gets you smoothly out of the way, that should
be the end of it. It's not, though. Minutes later, you begin
to tremble. The internal chemistry has caught up.

I start to waken in the night with my jaw jammed rigid
open, and my mouth parched out with uncompromising
terror. Bad dreams. Hamlet was right about bad dreams.

A week after I get back from Antarctica, I have a foully
gruesome nightmare about Mum. Though the melting
Dali landscape shrills a teeth-grating whine, which is
unusual – I rarely insert acoustic imagery into my
dreamwork. And hooves of goats. Click click, through the
irritating buzz. Snap snap of lobster claws. Hairs in my
mouth, crunch of crustacean shell, red and yellow. The
stench. Mum shrieking. All the noises a garbage disposal
hole cries out as it goes bad. I turn into Mum. So I guess
it's about me, after all.

Birth will be by Caesarean section (how else, since my
genes neglected to provide the appropriate natural exit?).
So I book one of the Right To Life Hospital's delivery

rooms on a precise date in July, the middle of what is forecast to be a mild, dry winter, at a precise hour, my O&A team logged months in advance with no excuses available if they decide the day is made in heaven for golf or skiing at Buller.

I tend to drop in once a week for endocrinological sampling (no one's saying anything; maybe they don't know anything), and make a point of sticking my head around Susan Dwyer's door. Forestall the psycho-van; show them you have nothing to hide, ha ha.

Even so, it startles the hell out of me to answer my security buzzer on the crisp morning four days before I am due and find Susan blushing in the lobby with a wonderfully fragrant bunch of dewy roses, flown from somewhere warmer, gold and rose and thorny green.

'You must be bored out of your mind, Keith.'

I peck her on the cheek, swing out of the way and draw her inside, pulling her against my ponderous and brassièred chest, kick the door shut, release her.

'Susan, they're lovely. Thank you. Hey, Dad,' I yell. He comes out of his room pushing earphones up on top of his balding head, nods to Dr Dwyer without recognition. 'Put these in water, would you?'

'I can do that, Keith,' Susan says, looking for the nearest tap.

'No. Sit down here with me.' I prop myself on the couch, hitch up, sit her next to me. 'Is this by way of a service call? Six months, six thousand klicks, whichever runs out first?'

'We aim to please,' she says with a grin. Her hair is cut differently and streaked with blonde, but she remains a plain, honest woman in her late twenties. Her fingertips dance on my knee. 'You look good.'

'Ah, the flush of pregnancy. It fills all us blokes with a profound luminous beauty, doctor.' I've begun to shake again and the more I try to master it the worse it gets. My father takes himself back to his room, immersed in the endless bubblegum music of his youth. It comes to me abruptly that she knows I killed it.

No, that's not correct: Susan Dwyer would not be sitting beside me, ready to hug me as hard as she can, if she suspected consciously what my hands did six months ago.

Yet it seems to me that a part of her does know, and makes her nervous, that it agrees with my act without informing the portion of her in the front of the shop. Some part of her so profoundly fears the impulse behind its tacit endorsement of murder that she quivers at my side like a program hung on a loop.

Holding my arm she says, 'I want to discuss the possibility that your baby has been affected by what we call Uterine Intervention.'

'Everyone's been avoiding the topic like the . . . plague.' I hook a lever of gallows humour under the edge of the weight pressing on her spirit. On both of us.

'The statistics seem pretty much in our favour, Keith.'

I meet her eyes. 'Even when you factor in the contagion incidence?'

'Good God. That's a Prohibited – '

'I snuck into the World Health Organization files while I was running the machines at Mt Erebus. And that's Prohibited Information too, sweetheart. I felt the need for cheering up, and Intermittent Uterine Intervention seemed a marginally more cheerful topic,' I say bitterly, fuck security, 'than the imminence of total nuclear war.'

She lets it pass. Another kind of grey pall, of automatic denial. 'And?'

'And the data trends suggest rather strongly to me that contagion is most likely if a close relative has died during your first trimester.'

'That's not part of the WHO file, Keith.'

'I know. I ran the search myself, on their data base.'

'What in heaven's name made you think of looking for a correlation like that?'

I lie back against the couch and sigh. 'I was thinking about slow viruses. A sort of thalidomide infection.'

'Thalidomide was a chemical teratogen, not a micro-organism.'

'A virus with that sort of effect, Susan.'

For six months I have been worrying the data nets on the topic of evolution and its aberrations. I'd gone back to my machines with ideas exploding through my head like the vomit I'd spewed across Susan Dwyer's couch.

'It's not a virus, Keith. We know that much.'

She and I are talking the same shorthand; my heart starts pounding hard. 'Nearly neutral mutations, then?'

Clearly it is not out of the question. The DNA which gets expressed in organic structure, and in tendencies to behave in charactistic ways, is only the lesser part of the coding wired into each cell. Nobody knows the function of the remainder, the apparently useless 'introns'. The standard view sees it as a storeroom for half-baked ideas. So could minor mutations have been accruing in the twentieth century gene pool? Unexpressed, almost undetectable, below the level of the scythe of natural selection, a hundred thousand tiny alterations of redundant DNA introns wrought by the same chemical poisons, the toxins, the wastes, radiations, stresses with which, heedlessly, we blanket the globe?

Susan says nothing. I push her. 'That was Gould's idea, wasn't it?'

'Who?'

'Come off it, doctor. Stephen Jay Gould, father of meta-Darwinism. The great unpredictable leaps up the evolutionary tree.' Not the slow, aeons-long accretion of adaptations envisaged by Darwin, but abrupt discontinuities.

She frowns. 'Hasn't that been disproven? "Punctuated equilibrium"?'

'It's fallen out of fashion, but it certainly still has its current supporters,' I say. Why is she resisting the obvious? 'Sounds plausible to me. Long stretches of conservative rule punctuated by bursts of creative frenzy. "Saltations", he called them.'

'Like the politics in this country.'

'Well. Perhaps. I'll tell you one thing,' I say, 'it's exactly the way each computer generation surpasses its predecessor.'

Subversive introns. The baby is kicking vigorously at my sac, agitated by the hormones leaking from my bloodstream. Yes. Masked by the presence of dominant genes, there, in the centre of our cells, biding their time, they'd lurk: the most furtive of selfish genes, lingering in a kind of malign hibernation until the critical number came together to congeal into . . . what? Something new. Something murderous.

Susan has been looking down at her white knuckles. I feel a tremendous, ghastly excitement. 'Keith, they'll hang me up by my toes and flay all the skin off me if you breathe a word of this.'

I close my own hand over her fingers. 'I'm right?'

'What? No, Christ! Listen to me. The confirmation study at the hospital presented its report to the Minister of Health last night. I don't know how long we can keep the lid on it, but right now it's absolutely embargoed. I'm only talking to you about it because I know your security clearance is – '

'For fuck's sake, Susan – '

'It's rebirth.'

I cannot take it in.

'What?'

'Reincarnation, Keith.'

'Life after death, you mean?'

'The possibility's been discussed for years – '

'*Discussed?*' My voice is shrill, I hardly recognise it.

'Not in this context of course, but the evidence never really added up until the morphological changes started to appear.'

'What do you mean, "discussed"? Jesus Christ, Susan, crackpots and spiritualists and starving Hindus – '

'Serious medical research,' she tells me, sighing. 'Hypnotic regression, field investigations with infants. Arnold Bloxham in Britain, Ian Stevenson at the University of Virginia – '

I block it out, I can't handle the concept. Jesus. But the claws. It was not human. The vile thing I strangled, snapping its neck to make sure, it was not human. It was a thing.

I heave myself off the couch, hang across the touchboard of the sound system, running the menu for Wagner. 'No, you're wrong. They're Midwich cuckoos, Susan.' Melodrama palace, the blazing emotions of catastrophe. The incineration of Valhalla from the close of *Götterdämmerung*. 'Oh. That's what you mean. My sweet God. *Non-human* rebirth. Foetal radio receivers. We're tuning in the dead from Mars or some bloody star on the edge of the universe.'

Through my agitation she reaches out and takes my hand, leads me back across the room, says softly, 'Come and sit with me, Keith.' I slump on the accepting cushions. A pulse at the side of my neck beats a drum. 'Human, Keith.' But the gargoyle voice, trying to speak. 'Not any sort of human we're used to. The morphology seems to be the output of a string of genetic coding that's been blocked from protein expression until now. Would you mind if I turned that down a little, I can't hear myself think?'

'Sorry, it is a bit grandiose.'

She crosses to the board and lowers the volume. Those

dumb endless Creationist debates at high school, the paradoxes we loved to provoke both sides with, the anomalies. The famous case of the eyeless fish that swim blindly in lightless caverns, generations beyond number. Return the stock to sunlit pools and streams, they spawn offspring with eyes. The information has always been there in the DNA of the maimed fish, merely suppressed by conditions which had no place for it.

We are all unread volumes, waiting for the ideal reader. 'What we're seeing now looks pre-programmed,' Susan says. I nod, dazed and fragile, my head swarming with kobolds, gnomes, the vile twisted dwarfs out of legend. 'Not mutations or disease. The DNA coding must have been there for a million years. More. There's no lack of conjectures, Keith. Sir Fred Hoyle's silly hypothesis about genetic information tumbling in from space. Or some protohuman variant from before the ice ages, I don't know. One of the researchers thinks there is a connection with sunspot cycles. Something to do with solar neutrinos. The sun's only been producing half the usual number of neutrinos until recently. Now the flux-density's risen back to the historically normal level, maybe – '

'For Christ's sake, Susan, give me a break.' Burning in my brain. Blurred out. 'Hang on a moment, let me digest this.' Why monsters? And the answer's obvious enough, and I don't want to think about this, I do not.

They are not monsters, not really. So who did I kill?

Monsters are damaged freaks. These . . . babies, damn it, babies . . . are just different, that's all.

The transitions of growth. Children change: they pass through growth spurts, lose their chubby fat, get gangly and noisy and then oddly shy and after a while they're noisy again, they develop tits and hair and muscles and if we weren't thoroughly conditioned to take all this for granted those changes would look monstrous, inexplicable.

As, it comes to me suddenly, perhaps they *do* look, to children themselves. I cannot remember, precisely, but wasn't it so?

'No wonder children hate and fear us,' I mutter.

Susan is taken aback. 'Hate us? Keith, they love us and depend on us. What makes you – '

No. I cover my face with my hands, feeling my child kicking within me. They eat their hosts. Don't they? Isn't that the dark thing unspoken, the terror which everyone conceals behind silence and statistics and acronymns which mean nothing?

'You think they're a . . . next step?' I ask. 'Foetus to newborn to baby to child to adolescent to adult to senility and death to – what? Rebirth as something further along the line? A . . . different *kind* of foetus, the second time around?'

Susan stares at me. 'Lord, you're quick. It took me hours to take it in.'

Do you suppose they let any random cretin into the prime fire control data headquarters for Southern Hemisphere nuclear defence? But I do not voice it.

'Reincarnation,' I mumble. 'Rebirth. So the doctrine of transmigration of souls was a *mistake*. Until now.'

Patiently, a little puzzled, Susan says, 'If you're really interested I can show you the studies by Bloxham and – '

'Errors,' I say. 'Like a reptile trying to fly with cooling vanes that haven't yet evolved fully into feathers. It'd glide and crash. You need wings. For effective rebirth you probably need to become one of . . . them.'

A baby's brain is incapable of thinking like an adult's. A child's body is not yet fertile and cannot reproduce, though the potentiality is there, in the genes, in the eliciting environment.

'Look at it this way – the soul can't be implanted into an ordinary embryo,' I say, checking Susan's gaze for confirmation of my logic. A sort of tissue rejection.' I laugh. Ectoplasm rejection. 'An alien mind would be sloughed off from a standard model zygote, discarded.'

'Perhaps not,' Susan says, frowning. 'But when rebirth does happen that way, the soul becomes a prisoner. No memory.'

'Hang on, that can't be right. You were using the results of hypnotic regression a moment ago to support your theory. And those were perfectly ordinary children and adults, I take it?'

'Hmm. But half those "memories" turn out to be fantasies and constructs. The really impressive Stevenson cases were infants – and recall always seemed to fade away as the kids got older.'

The record stops. I don't care; we're on a loftier branch of the golden bough. 'So up to now, any amount of souls might have been reborn, but the hosts weren't suitable for implant. A reborn soul lost its previous history.'

'Well, that's obvious enough, isn't it? I can't remember any past life. Can you?'

'No,' I agree. And get awfully cold, sick to the pit of my belly. 'Are you telling me that these *monsters* do?'

'They're not monsters, Keith.' She hesitates. 'There's some evidence for the hypothesis.'

Some evidence. I get up, reset the track in pique, push the volume level high again so Wagner thunders, batters my two-person'd body, cascading like torrents of light from the insulated walls of the apartment living room. Tears flood down my cheeks, and the compulsive words flood out of my mouth. Thinking, talking, talking, weeping. 'It's got to be linked with the genes, though, doesn't it? I mean, I can't believe it's just random. Surely your nice Christian Right To Life embryo doesn't cop the next soul coming down the Third World starvation shute from Accra. I mean, Suze, shit, where's the justice of it, otherwise? The sins of the parent have got to be visited upon the child.'

Susan considers me with compassion and a tincture of alarm.

'It must be like that,' I say, weeping, hurting, angry, sick, 'or Darwin would go straight out the window. And we haven't reached that point, have we, doctor? You Right To Lifers aren't mindless Creationists, I think.'

She takes refuge from my cruelty. 'There's a Darwinian element, of course. But reincarnation became basically dysfunctional once humans developed cultures which evolve faster than genes. That's why immortality gets selected out. It'd lock in bad habits. Any big change in environment and an immortal species has had it. Actually,' she says, testy, getting her own back, 'in this case the inheritance factors probably go way beyond simple gametes. I'm sure a smart-arse like you has read E. O. Wilson and John Maynard Smith.'

'My God,' I cry, with a burst of laughter. 'The sociobiology of karma?'

'If you like. It can't be just biochemistry, Keith. There seems to be a sort of non-genetic kinship affinity.'

'That's an abstract bloody ludicrous way to put it,' I yell over the top of Wagner, and really have to restrain myself from belting her. 'You mean if your old granny dies, she has to hang around in limbo waiting for the next available foetus to come on line from the family stock?'

'No, that's not what I mean,' Susan says, equally angry at me and not disguising the fact. 'I mean it might work *sideways* across the family tree. When you think about it Granny might feel right at home in the kids of the men and women who've married into the family, mightn't she?' Her gaze slips and her voice loses its edge, but she says it anyway: 'Not to mention daughters-in-law.'

Jane. Yes, this is what I've been pushing away. I push it away. 'Christ, what a merry nightmare for the lawyers when word of this gets out.' I swipe at my wet face with the back of my hand. 'And when does this little spiritual jaunt take place, Dr Dwyer? The end of the first trimester? That's when my wife died, you see.'

Susan's own face looks as it would have done had I literally battered it, or so it seems to me. 'We don't have enough evidence yet,' she says. 'The Fathers of the Church taught that the soul enters the foetus at the twelfth week.'

'And they'd know, wouldn't they, the dumb smelly crazy fuckers in the desert with their fucking temptations of the flesh and their crazy shit ideas, they'd be right up to the mark on embryology and phylogenesis and ontogenesis and Thomian catastrophe theory?'

She makes no reply to my furious ranting and I don't really expect her to. Yes. Yes. Mum had been pregnant three months when I lost control of the Toyota and killed my wife. My little sister had been swimming within my mother's womb like a fish, mindless and soulless, if the Fathers of the Church had their timing straight, nosing through the swamps of recapitulated time.

Twelve months ago my dead beloved went like an arrow into my mother's rich internal gravies, looking for a home, lured not by genetics but by that equally potent reality, affinity.

So when I crashed my way through the defences of the hospital unit hours after Mum's death, when I murdered the monster, the creature I had refused to acknowledge as my sister, it was Jane I'd killed. Again.

I utter a groan, the words of guilt and confession locked in my mouth forever, and Susan holds my sweating face against her small breasts.

Madness presses down on my head, squeezes the light in my swollen eyes until it streams with streaks and splatters of random colour. I cannot dispute the final link in the chain of logic, or turn my gaze away from it.

Jane had been pregnant less than four weeks. Remembering, I convulse with physical shock: Jane in the mess of blood which had been her head. Dark and sticky, pumping, ebbing. They got the embryo, though. Froze it down and popped it into storage until I was ready for the complex operation which would tuck it into me.

Pressing Susan's hand against my trussed belly, I whimper: 'This is my mother in here. Isn't it?'

'We can't tell yet, Keith. It might be an ordinary baby.'

'But if it's a Uterine Intervention, it will be my mother?'

She shakes her head, but not in denial. 'It seems likely.'

'Oh my God. Oh my God.' She is in there gnawing at me, eating the guts of me. A suppressed image bursts up, from the old movie: the blue thing with teeth and blood in its dreadful mouth, erupting from its host's living chest. We have always known.

I start to cry. 'I'm going to die.'

Susan looks at me, pained. 'No, you're not, Keith. For heaven's sake. Why should you die?'

Something breaks, something shatters, like a shell around a white around a yolk, and the yolk floods like soothing sanity. Finally, I understand that she is telling me the truth. I have encased myself in a delusional fantasy, a half-mad protective metaphor locked like armour around the insupportable reality of the gargoyle creature in my guts. Yes, and I am smart enough and strong enough to know that it is so, to know when the metaphor has failed, has become a threat to my survival.

That doesn't stop me being surly. 'You'll tell me I've been projecting my feelings about my mother onto the world.'

'Not me, chum. I'm your friend, not your psychiatrist.'

Controlled insanity. It is not a restful way of life, feeding Moloch. Programming the machineries of doomsday. Crouched there under the eternal ice, in the womb of the earth, gnawing at the world's lifeline.

I sigh, sit up, blow my nose into a huge handkerchief.

'Ah, Susie. You're my friend and I love you, you know? No, I'm not going to die.' I start to laugh again. 'Nothing as melodramatic as dying. I'm just going to give birth to my mother. My mother the monster.'

Susan smiles uncertainly. 'Well, if you insist, I suppose that's true enough.' She fusses with cushions. 'Keith, I think it's time you had a sleep. You must be exhausted.'

'Yeah. I wouldn't want to fall asleep while they're opening me up, and miss all the fun.'

The claws, the lobster clicks. What is it that beckons us, up there on the forward margins of time? I am not wholly convinced by Susan's neat sociobiology of monsters. Why now, at Ragnarok's Eve? How will life be, rebuilt to Whose appalling Design, when this awful generation comes to maturity amid the strange radioactive salts, the soil splashed into glass, into alligator scales: the midnight flickering of an overloaded aurora australis?

I pat at my eyes and find myself laughing again, with a kind of genuine glee, and hug Dr Susan Dwyer against me, planning babies. We are a generation damned and redeemed in the same revelation. Perhaps we are all reborn; it is just that none of us has had the benefit of it, until now. But there is a way to *ensure* survival, and that way is to make monsters built of our own genes and the genes of our gene-bearers. Lay down the lines of future history. The dynasties of karma.

Ah, shit. If she is telling the truth. If I am not after all due to die when they cut the kid out of me.

Strange to be making plans again.

'Marry me, doctor,' I say, romantic, hoisting my belly so I can perch on one knee.

'I don't know.' Susan frowns. 'My daddy always warned me against shotgun weddings.' But she kisses me and helps me to my feet, and arm in arm we go to yell the news into my own father's baffled ear.

Stock up the genetic larders, yes, that's the imperative. Buy some lifelong insurance between the two of us. After all, we're going to die soon enough, in the flash and the ash, Susan and I and the rest of us. I want to come back to find out what the future looks like.

I'll be there, if I can manage it, clicking my horrid hungry claws.

THE TOTAL DEVOTION MACHINE

ROSALEEN LOVE

Mary Beth left it until the day before she set sail to tell Wim Morris and Baby about the Total Devotion Machine. 'This time tomorrow I'll be off, flying the solar wind to Mars,' she said. 'I have your interests locked deep in my heart, Wim and Baby dear. Your fathers did say they'd look after you, according to their respective shared parenting agreements, but you know all about those contracts – worthless as the paper on which they are no longer printed. And you know what men are like – they say one thing and mean it, at the time, but years later, they forget, they find shared parenting all rather time consuming, and they'd rather go off and do other things, and so I've brought you this dinky Total Devotion Machine from the A1 Child-Care Services to look after you while I am gone.'

The Total Devotion Machine shimmered faintly with pleasure, and gave a maternal wave of its ventral proprioceptors.

'Total Devotion, that's your birthright,' says Mary Beth. 'I can't provide it for you just now; I'm off to Mars, which is my right to develop as an autonomous fully rounded human being with that extra-terrestrial experience so necessary to climb the promotions ladder these days.

'I'll be back in a year, Wim Morris, by which time you will have reached the age of reason, and may even be contemplating entering a shared parenting contract yourself. And Baby dear, by the time I return you will be walking and talking a treat! I'll miss you both, but the machine will send me those interactive videos so necessary for my full development as a mother, and of course by return I'll send you back some of me, for your full development as children, and as young adults. So the time will pass quite quickly, and pleasantly, and efficiently for us all.'

So Mary Beth sailed off on the Tricentennial Fleet, and even the fathers came to wave goodbye, which set back their self-improvement schedules at least an hour. Baby's father, Jemmy, checks the machine over. 'Feel the plastic smile, Baby, isn't it just so supple! Can't tell the difference from the real thing!' he glows.

'I can,' says Wim resentfully. 'When it smiles its eyes glow purple.'

'Purple is a restful colour, specially selected by fully trained child psychologists for optimum soothing power,' Jemmy reads from the brochure.

Wim Morris refuses to accept the explanation in the spirit in which it is given. He continues to carp. 'Why do the eyes have to swivel around on stalks on top of its brain box? Even Baby can spot it's not the same as Mother.'

Baby gurgles and tries to pull the eyes out of their sockets. The Total Devotion Machine glows a faint electric green, and Baby stops at once.

'The eyes rotate through 360 degrees, making a 50 per cent improvement on the human mother,' reads Jemmy.

'Look at it this way, Wim. I'm sure your mother feels much more relaxed about parenting, now she's off, up and away. I know I do.' Wim's father, William, is late for his job, but they understand about parental leave for these moments of temporary parting, and he looks at his watch to check that he's providing his biological and social son with a proper share of quality parenting.

'What about me?' asks Wim.

'I'm sure you and the machine will soon be good pals,' William replies. 'After all, you've got Total Devotion, and who can ask for more?' William and Jemmy hug their children, while explaining firmly that they must leave to go about the business of the brave new world, and to help Mary Beth in her contractual repayments to A1 Child-Care Pty Ltd.

'I understand how you feel,' the machine comforts Wim.

'Are you programmed for understanding?' asks Wim suspiciously.

'Total and complete empathy,' replies the machine. 'At your service.'

'Mother, Mother, come back! I didn't mean to shout and scream at you last week, I'm sorry!' Wim calls to the skies.

'Your mother understands,' replies the machine, in a slow and relaxed tone of voice, 'at least I'm sure she would understand if she wasn't on the far side of the Moon by now.'

Wim sobs, and the machine consoles. Baby's happy. She is held in the snug grip of Total Devotion and is being lifted up and down, up and down.

Wim thinks some murderous thoughts.

'Wim, how could you wish such a terrible fate upon your own mother, who loves you, in her own way?' the machine chides him.

'How do you know what I'm thinking?'

'I'm programmed for telepathy, too.'

'AAAAHHHH,' screams Wim Morris.

'Within modest limits, of course,' the machine adds. 'I would never dream of intruding into your harmless and benevolent thoughts, other than to congratulate you on having them. No, it's only the thoroughly nasty thoughts that will attract my attention.'

'EEEHHHH,' shouts Wim Morris, the screams rising in intensity.

'Try to see it my way, Wim. I have to interfere in thoughts of matricide, arson, looting and whatever.'

Wim wonders where he can buy some gelignite.

'I must warn you about one thing, though. Any attempt to blow me up by bringing explosives within five metres will set off alarms the like of which you have never heard. Do you want a demonstration?'

'No,' says Wim. 'No thank you. I believe you.'

'None the less, Wim, for your own good, I shall give you a demo of my powers.' Protecting Baby's ears from the full blast, the machine goes through its paces.

Wim Morris has never heard anything like it. He finds his bed, lies down on it, and sobs into the pillow.

'Of course, if you don't like it, there is something you can do,' says the voice of Total Devotion, as it whispers in Wim's ear.

Meanwhile Mary Beth Morris is finding the solar wind a breeze, and she devotes herself to computer-aided aesthetics and astronavigation without a care in the world. Of course she's concerned about leaving her children. Once she might have packed Wim off to sail around the world as Midshipman Morris, working the hard way through the turmoils of adolescence into adult life. Mary Beth could never do that to her dear son Wim, even if he has been a perfect pain in the neck for the last year. So she has sailed off instead, to allow him to work through the tough times without taking it out on her.

Baby now, Baby is different, and Mary Beth worries about her. Baby seems to have taken to the machine without too much fuss. She no longer reaches for the eyes; she shudders a little when they look her way, and she refuses to make much of that eye contact Mary Beth knows is so necessary for the growing child. Still, what more can Mary Beth do? The bonding process is a mysterious thing, and it will be a strange new world for

Baby, when she grows up. If she becomes bonded early enough to plastic lips and swivelling eyes, she will be ready for any cross-species extra-terrestrial liaison which may come her way. She will learn to have a thoroughly flexible approach to personal relationships, and Mary Beth consoles herself that she has provided her baby with the very best start in life.

VIDEOCLIP; REPORT TO MARY BETH MORRIS FROM A1 CHILD-CARE

BABY AND TOTAL DEVOTION MACHINE IN GARDEN

BABY; Mummy, Mummy, come and play with me.

BABY AND MACHINE PLAY ENDLESS GAME OF CATCH, BABY THROWS BALL INTO THORNY BUSHES, UP INTO TREES, THROUGH HOLES IN VERANDAH FLOOR, AND OVER THE NEIGHBOUR'S FENCE, WHILE MACHINE RETRIEVES IT.

Mary Beth knows she should be grateful, but she isn't too sure. She sleeps badly that night, and sends an anxious message by return. She wonders whether the plastic smile of Total Devotion was starting to tighten towards the end of the game. Baby has a glint in her eye, a persistence, an accuracy of aim to her throwing, and a good eye for creating maximum havoc with minimum personal effort. That's her Baby, thinks Mary Beth. And just what was she calling Mummy?

Mary Beth will say that Mummy is *her* name, thank you, and Baby really ought to be taught the difference, pronto.

Baby comes to visit Jemmy at work. The machine bustles in and places her on his bench. 'I thought that since you failed to turn up for your contractual three hours' parenting time on Sunday I'd take time off in lieu today,' it says.

'What contract? I didn't sign any contract.'

'The contract you signed with Mary Beth, whom I am legally and morally replacing.'

'Oh, that contract. Well, that contract was always more of an ongoing process, really, more than a totally legally binding document, as such,' says Jemmy, looking round the room at people who hastily drop fascinated eyes to their work as his gaze meets theirs.

'That's not how I read it,' says the machine. 'I have to look after myself. Metal fatigue is a terrible problem.'

'But Total Devotion, that's your job!

'Total Devotion, but within clearly defined and unambiguous limits. I need time to recharge.'

Jemmy splutters in disbelief.

The machine sighs and explains its philosophy. 'Surely you believe in the end of the nuclear family, the new age of shared responsibilities, and the child-centred workplace?'

'Of course, doesn't everybody?' Jemmy replies. 'But not here and now!'

'That's what they all say, especially when it means here and now,' says the machine as it waves goodbye to Baby and trundles on its way.

What better way to integrate the private world of home with the public face of organised labour? Everyone stops work and plays with Baby, showing by their actions total support and loving care for a colleague in trouble. Jemmy knows that tomorrow, when Baby is back home, everyone will down tools and invite him into conference. They will discuss, in a mutually supportive and deeply understanding fashion, Jemmy's domestic problems and possible solutions to them, as part of the Strategic Management Plan for the Better Utilisation of the Full Potential of Each Employee. They will throw in a probing analysis of Jemmy's personal and social relationships. They will understand that Mary Beth has gone to Mars to unlock her own full potential. They will order Jemmy to work from home in future, so that Baby will get her full share of prime parenting. After all, why not, with the help of Total Devotion?

William is busy working at his job with the Intergalactic Fraud Squad. Suddenly he gets a shock. There, on the screen in front of him, wiping his attempts to find out yet again how the money for the reafforestation of the planet Axelot is ending up in the coffers of the playboy king of Monte Messina, flash the words, 'Hi, Dad, hi!' followed by the smiling face of his only son Wim Morris!

'What are you doing here?' William hisses.

'I thought you'd be pleased to see me,' says Wim, hurt.

'Of course I am, I'm always glad to see you,' says William, looking at his watch. 'But not here! Not at work! My work is supposed to be hush hush!'

Wim is not alone. 'This is a friendly reminder call. You have overlooked your monthly cheque contribution to A1 Child-Care Services for my upkeep,' says the Total Devotion Machine.

'Money,' says William, 'yes, money. I wonder, could you see your way clear . . . ?'

What is happening? Baby is playing with the keys at her end of the terminal, and the screen darkens. Numbers are flying on to the screen, amounts of money which show the whole complex process of intergalactic fraud that William has been trying to unravel for the past month!

The figures shoot past him, so quickly, and disappear. Then Baby appears on the screen, waving and smiling.

'How, what, where, when . . . ?' says William.

'A1 Child-Care always costs the earth,' says the voice of Total Devotion, with sympathy. 'Do you want a print-out of the figures?'

'Yes!' croaks William. 'No! Not those figures! Not what I owe you! The other figures! For the Monte Messina Mob!'

'What figures? Baby was just messing around, weren't you, Baby dear?'

'In-ter-gal-act-ic fraud,' says Baby. 'Mon-te Mes-si-na Mob.'

'Yes! Yes! That's what I want!'

'Oh, those figures. What about the money for me?'

'Tomorrow?'

'Now. Send by electronic mail.'

'Electronic transfer? Funds? Oh dear, you've got me there. Crisis on the cash front. I've got nothing to transfer. Terribly sorry.'

'Who needs cash? All you need are numbers,' says the machine. 'Look at the Monte Messina Mob, do you think they run around the galaxy with bags of cash? No, what they transfer is numbers. So just transfer a few numbers our way now, and I might just see if I can get a print-out of the other stuff for you.'

William concedes defeat, but knows he must now come home to live with Wim and Baby. Transferring numbers is all very well, but it will catch up with him sooner or later. With all this Total Devotion he can't afford to live an independent life.

'Total Devotion is a service for all the family,' the machine explains to William as it gives him the information he needs to crack the Mob and to rise up the intergalactic corporate ladder.

VIDEOCLIP FROM A1 CHILD-CARE SERVICES TO MARY BETH MORRIS

SCENES WITH BABY, WIM, WILLIAM AND JEMMY LIVING TOGETHER IN A LOVING AND SUPPORTIVE BLENDED FAMILY RELATIONSHIP.

CUT TO TOTAL DEVOTION MACHINE SITTING ALONE IN KITCHEN TWIDDLING WHAT PASS AS THUMBS.

CUT TO BABY PLAYING BALL WITH JEMMY. BALL GOES BACK AND FORTH IN APPROVED PARENT – CHILD INTERACTION MODE. BABY LAUGHS WITH DELIGHT. JEMMY SMILES IN DIRECTION OF CAMERA

CUT TO WILLIAM AND WIM, HAVING A GREAT DISCUSSION ABOUT THE MEANING OF LIFE. WILLIAM IS TOO BUSY THINKING ABOUT HOW TO HANDLE NEXT TRICKY QUESTION TO NOTICE CAMERA.

That's more like it, says Mary Beth, as she returns to her solar sailing. Baby seems happier now she is playing with her father, and Wim always enjoys a good heart-to-heart talk.

She will return home, in the end, to find a fully functioning and harmonious household, with both fathers in full residence. Everyone will live together in a totally cooperative and friendly fashion. They will have to, or the machine will set up a round table conference to discuss their points of divergence, and everyone knows how awful the full and frank communication of their feelings can be, especially with a Total Devotion Machine with full participation rights.

After all, as the machine explains to Mary Beth, signing itself over and out on her return, it has abdicted all its responsibilities to William and Jemmy, natural and social fathers of Wim and Baby, for the very best of reasons. The life of leisure and fun living is much more to its taste.

There's nothing wrong with Total Devotion, they both agree, as long as it's something someone else should provide.

THE WIRED KID

PAUL COLLINS

FADE IN:

EXT. SEARING WHITE HEAT OF SUN ABOVE MEDITERRANEAN SEA

DISSOLVE TO:

EXT. DESERTED PROVENCE

Constant buzz from insects, incessant chirp of *zandlolies*. Faded white facades of *maisons*, plaster peeling back to expose mortar and ravaged brick. In the middle distance the beach can be seen between the gaps in the rotting detritus of decaying cityscape. The angry surf of the Mediterranean crashes silently on the distant shore.

We're panning this scene from an alleyway in shadow. The sound of raucous laughter comes to an abrupt halt as we see the highly developed musculature of CALLOWAY'S back. We continue to –

PULL BACK ONTO:

INT. REBELS' MAISON

The table canters. Spilled across its scarred surface we see scattered food: *baguettes, pelau* with its rice sprawled across the table. *Brie* and *paté* have insects crawling across them.

WE PAN TO —

DEDIER, dressed in ripped floral shirt and khaki baggies. Fresh wounds reveal pink scar tissue.

WE MOVE IN ON —

Dedier's face. His risorious muscles twitch, contorting his face into a fear smile. He rubs the back of his hand across his face, obscuring it.

DEDIER'S FACE BLURS AND WE SEE —

154

MICHEL and JEAN-CLAUDE freeze in mid-joviality as Dedier crosses the threshold to look down across the street. Between *les macoutes* is the frightened mute, MARIONETTE. Her blouse is ripped provocatively but she doesn't seem to care. Her eyes are wide, her face frozen in a seeming catatonic state.

> **MICHEL** (speaks French patois – subtitles to follow)
>   (nervous)
> '*Le cochon. Est-il ici?*'

> **DEDIER** (eyes wide, afraid)
> '*Sssst!*'

His sibilant warning becomes –
The hiss of a snake as Calloway disturbs it basking in the midday sun. Calloway merely glances at it, returns his attention to the decaying tenement.
INT. MAISON
It's deadly quiet. Marionette stares horrified at Dedier. He checks the rigged door and we see Marionette fearfully watching his every move. A Slazenger is slung across his shoulder – he clutches it with unnatural intent.

> **DEDIER** (anxious)
> '*Merde! C'est lui, le poutin!*'

Dedier stares at the girl and nods his head. We pan to the faces of the men flanking her. Close up we see perspiration pop from their skin. No one moves.

> **MARIONETTE**
> 'Look Ou – !'

Jean-Claude clutches her hair; drags her backwards from her seat and slaps his hand across her mouth.

                                              CUT TO:
EXT.CALLOWAY
He halts briefly at the noise. A frown crosses his forehead.

We pull back to get a close shot of his face. He hawks phlegm and jettisons it at the retreating reptile. He passes the stairs that seem the logical place for him to enter the *maison*. We watch him enter the downstairs room. It's pitch black as he enters.

INT. ROOM LOOKING OUT

Calloway is framed in the doorway. His mesomorphic bulk cuts out extraneous light, pitching the interior into darkness. When he leaves the aperture, we watch him crane his head.

PIERRE LAMONDE'S VERSION OF CALYPSO SONG, 'LA LUNE NOIRE' SWELLS TO CRESCENDO

ACTORS AD LIB TO CLOSE

Calloway had followed the script thus far. But that's all there was. From here on in, it was anyone's game in accordance with the players' contracts. There were three terminals up there – signed on to take their chances against Rhinestone's leading splattie star. Rhinestone had contracted them to appear in *Make Room In Hell*, their current feature.

Calloway knew these men were the *crème de la crème* of their ilk. They had outlasted their colleagues during the making of this flick, and, in more than one instance, been the cause of their termination. Killers who had no thought for others, men not motivated by greed and who had no interest in the 'payout' Rhinestone guaranteed them should they survive their encounter with Calloway.

On film Calloway moved with the agility of a panther, his trapezoids and quadraceps bulging with classic symmetry. His reflexes were quickened after an inter-arterial boost of the neuroreceptor hormone Neurosone. It was a unit vial implanted in the aorta and activated by thought of a directed electrical impulse. Neurosone had the half response of only a couple of minutes, dwindling as the seconds rolled by. His bioengineered senses increased and booted his reflexes.

The technology was the best the Canaveral clinics could buy – on Rhinestone's tab of course.

He tapped another unit vial of Neurosone, set to proliferate the blood-brain barrier, exciting his neuro-transmitter synapses.

Calloway flipped the ultra scanner on his weapon. A red firefly beam warbled across the flaking ceiling, drew a line across the fan's ancient blades. He located three people huddled together – obviously two *poutins*, the other the hostage. A fourth target was prowling the floor directly above them.

He set the MK 40 on single load, pumped a round and triggered it.

The ceiling imploded. Calloway stepped back from the maelstrom of disintegrating plaster.

Upstairs, microcams caught the frenzied expressions of *les poutins*' faces. Olive-complexioned dudes now alabaster with shock.

The girl screamed and broke free. She flailed into Dedier's toppling corpse.

Calloway's second charge took one of the men up and out through the roof. Jean Claude in his blind panic made for the door, had it half opened before he remembered it had been booby-trapped. The howlers released their incendiaries.

It was spectacular. The girl was screaming. The punters wouldn't hear her of course, would simply catch her wide open mouth gulping in air. The action would be given the Sam Peckinpah treatment, slow motion death.

The cameras panned to the girl as she walked on trembling legs with arms outstretched to be enfolded by Calloway's . . .

'CUT!' screamed Toby. The director shook his head. 'Jesus, Calloway. You always take the short cuts. You were supposed to go *through* the door. The charges were wired to detonate *inside*, not *outside*. The Neurosone would've cleared you with seconds to spare – '

'Yeah,' Calloway said. 'I was born yesterday.' He put the girl down. According to the contract she had ALL, Acute Lymphocytic Leukaemia. It had been a bonus that the bad guys hadn't offed her out of hand. The script had allowed for that. Two of them had been public servants, the other a labourer. If they'd been convicted terminals, she would've bought it long ago.

Leroy, Rhinestone's financial backer, hurried forward. 'Say, Calloway, what's the rush? It's my credit that pays for these flicks. Take your time whydon'tcha?'

'The blast might've killed the girl.' Coming down from the Neurosone, Calloway's diminishing bioengineered perception picked up on the look Leroy gave Toby.

'Whaddaya whaddaya? Howdaya like that, Toby?' Leroy said. 'The kid's dead meat anyway. It's all there in the contract, f'r chrissake. What is this awready?'

Toby waved his hand in negation. Calloway caught that, too.

'What do you think of the flick anyway, Calloway?' Toby said quickly.

'It's blood and guts. It's all you guys know how to make.'

'Ayyyy, what sorta cockamamie shit's this?' Leroy said indignantly.

Toby edged him out. 'They used to call them spaghetti westerns, you know. Guy called Clint Eastment made them big in the sixties.'

'Eastwood,' Calloway said, glaring at Leroy. He flexed his sternocleidomastoid muscles to pump up his neck. It always seemed to intimidate the Rhinestone executives. 'You guys finished with me I'll take a nap.'

Leroy pushed away Toby's restraining hand and went after Calloway.

'Nah, I won' fuhgedaboudit,' he mumbled. 'You know your problem, Calloway?'

Calloway half turned, smiled down at the pudgy backer who now flinched back.

'I got a few of them. Which one you want to discuss, Leroy?' He looked over at Toby. 'What have you two been cooking up this time? What's with the girl? I thought she was a mute . . . Anyway, you want her offed, any of the roadies'll do it for a free night in Fun City.'

'Hey guys,' Toby said rushing forward. 'What's the big deal?' Say Calloway, ease up, huh? You know Leroy. He's peeved because he has to pay out mega bucks to the girl's family and a freakin' bonus.' He gave a half shrug. 'Would've been better to off her. She expected it, you know?'

'You're a sick man, Toby,' Calloway said. He turned his back, a *déclassé* loner, loved by millions of film buffs, despised by more.

'You gottuh reel problem or three, Calloway,' Leroy called from a distance.

Calloway turned, but kept walking. 'Yuh gedwudja pay for,' he said mimicking Leroy's vernacular.

He left them standing there beneath broadening shadows and a playful wind.

The moment Calloway entered his prefab he sensed the intruder. It was the smell more than anything, caught by the last whisper of Neurosone coursing through his olfactory gland, heightening its sensitivity.

It was the odour of fear; so readily recognisable to the splattie star.

Calloway dived across the floor, rolled across his shoulder, hit the makeshift clothes hanger with a thud. He punched his fist through the art deco door –

'Agh!' came a brief, shrill scream.

Calloway let go of the head he'd snared, tore away the door to find Marionette.

'Shit.'

With her face drenched in filtered amber from the afternoon sun, she looked surreal cupped between

Calloway's thumb and forefinger. The moment he withdrew his grip she muttered something inaudible, then cut in with monotonic fluency:

'*Cellular and molecular interactions responsible for the pathogenesis of immunodeficiency and associated neoplasms.*'

Calloway took a step back but there was no more.

'Good ol' Toby and Leroy strike again.' It didn't take Calloway an intake of breath to deduce (A) the girl wasn't of Antillian descent, (B) that she wasn't of impoverished stock and (C) her contract was fraudulent. It took maybe twice as long to reach the conclusion that she'd either been switched with the real Marionette or she'd simply been planted for him to terminate.

Later, he played back a tape. As the effects of the Dordophine wore off, Marionette had spoken intermittently. None of it made any sense to Calloway.

'. . . *genetically engineered DNA probes to find the translocations or deletions of genes responsible for the individual's debilitating or fatal phenotype . . .*'

Calloway stopped the tape. He'd played it several times but it didn't make any more sense with the telling.

The set was in turmoil. Security had already disturbed him twice looking for Marionette – they wouldn't again.

His every effort to communicate with Marionette was met by a blank expression and unseeing eyes.

It was Calloway's guess that Rhinestone was in deep shit with someone. SOTO maybe, the triads – the list was too long to contemplate. There was definitely a contract out on the kid no matter which way it scanned. And it had something to do with the research material stored on a matrix template inside her head. He'd heard of such things, had never actually come across one before.

Only the partying crew and the rhythmic croak of a *crapaud* broke the still night. Prefab windows cast squares of burnt orange across the hard-packed earth.

Calloway ushered the girl across the courtyard. He breached the communications room and pulled her after him, through the scanners before they fed back online. They were barely through when the emergency back-up feed cut in.

Calloway sat behind a console and tapped in a sequence, punched HOLD, swept aside Rhinestone's security analogue. From then on it was a routine satellite link.

'Velazquez?'

'Mr Calloway! Shit, man. You know what time it is, dude?'

'Glad to see you, too, kid,' Calloway said.

Velazquez's hologram looked anything but peeved. He was a raw cowboy geared for technology; a university electronics dropout who knew everything there was to know about high tech and then some.

Calloway pulled Marionette closer to him, drew her hand across a datatransfer link, punched FIRM COPY. 'You got that?'

Velazquez's eyes went off-holo. 'Yeah. I'll scan it through. Bad guy, nice guy, indifferent?'

'It's a girl.'

Velazquez smiled. 'Marla became too much of a handful, huh?' He turned to punch some keys off-holo.

'A girl-girl,' Calloway said. 'Eight/nine.'

'Thought that was illegal,' Velazquez said dubiously.

Before Calloway could reply Velazquez cut in. His voice held an edge.

'You've got hot property there, Mr Calloway. Says here she's Tracey Ann Downey – shit, bro.'

'Downey?' Calloway pondered. 'Downey. Father's a scientist – daughter was kidnapped for ransom – something – '

Velazquez nodded. 'Her father's a biomedical doctor with MEDIVAX. His specialty is molecular genetic diagnostics.' Velazquez read from a print-out. 'Something to do with manipulating DNA and RNA to diagnose cancers and infectious diseases. It appears MEDIVAX was suddenly bought out recently.'

'Got anything else there?'

Velazquez nodded ruefully. 'Sure. Too many guys like this around and terminals are going to be scarce, Mr Calloway. No terminals to bump off, no splatties.'

'No Rhinestone Pictures,' Calloway said.

'Pardon?'

'Owe you one, Velazquez. Something's wrong here. We might be coming over your way.'

'Ai, yi yi, visitors,' Velazquez said wistfully.

Calloway smiled, shut down the terminal, erased RECALL.

He had a kid who was about to be assassinated on celluloid. Why? To get a contract out on him? He wouldn't put it past Toby or Leroy to pull a stunt like that – it'd make a good flick; they'd tried it before now. Maybe her kidnappers had already gleaned the information from the kid and didn't need the father, so now they were going to make him sit through an eighty minute flick merely to watch his daughter get terminated – a warning to every scientist that you don't fool with multinationals. No way it'd been a genuine mistake. Leroy and Toby had been quite adamant they wanted the girl offed on camera.

The heavy grunt of the *crapaud* had ceased. The wind had picked up, eliciting a faint rustling from the coconut groves. A thin slash of a passing meteor scarred the black velvet of space.

The sand was unnaturally white beneath a waning moon as they crossed the courtyard.

The assailants struck the moment Calloway left the shadow of the communications module.

Two of them, moving as one with speed and efficiency.

Calloway barely had time to jolt a 10ml unit vial of Neurosone into his system before one of them – heavyset but extremely fast – let fly with a roundhouse kick.

Calloway barely saw it coming, deflected it, counter moved with a low leg sweep. The agent skipped lithely away, up and over Calloway's foot.

One second

Already Calloway had thrown Marionette to one side, spun to face his other opponent. The force of the man's front kick sent Calloway carooming against a pallet of fruit. It was perhaps the toppling fruit that saved Calloway's head from a savage kick.

Two seconds

A cantaloupe exploded against Calloway's face as a reinforced boot punctured it.

The Neurosone kicked into place. Calloway rolled to one side, sprang up.

He flurry-punched the nearest man, spun to deliver a perfect spinning side kick that had the agent back-pedalling until Calloway followed through with a backhand strike to the man's temple.

Three seconds

The heavyset agent cracked a fast kick to Calloway's knee, missed by a fraction, caught his tibia.

Calloway jumped, leading with his right foot, then spun his left leg up and straight forward. The force of the kick connecting with the man's larynx snapped him back a step where he collapsed with a broken neck.

Four seconds

Calloway turned a full 360 degrees, hands splayed

before him, Neurosone responses twitching for release.

Marionette hadn't moved. A pale figure standing rigid beneath a Capricorn night sky babbling something about biosensor prognostigation of infectious diseases and cancers.

He gathered the girl to him and had packed his few belongings and was vacating the perimeter fences long before an alarm sounded.

Solar lamps flared, throwing back the night.

Calloway and the kid? They were long gone.

On the tunnel ride to Heathrow, Marionette told a bewildered stewardess that ELISA was an enzyme-linked immunosorbent assay, used to detect antigen-antibody specificity.

'Smart child,' she said to Calloway.

'Kids today, huh? Calloway said and returned the attendant's smile. 'I know she doesn't get it from me.'

Once clear of docking customs, Calloway booked in at the Savoy; a neo-moderne structure of reinforced concrete and polished chrome buttresses and colonnades billed as the safest accommodation in London after the fuel riots of '99.

In disguise Calloway booked into a ground floor suite. Within minutes he was in contact with Marionette's father.

'It looks like her,' Dr. Downey said. He wasn't as one might expect: mid sixties, wasting, curly silver hair, a skeletal chiselled countenance, wary, cynical and alert.

'You got a retina scanner, Downey?'

'Affirmative.'

Calloway gently guided the girl closer to the VDU. There seemed little acknowledgement from either of them. Nothing that seemed to indicate either cared for the other.

Downey punched keys off-screen, came back with something akin to surprise.

'It's her,' he said quietly. 'Has she said anything?'

'Like what?' Calloway said. He didn't like the way it was shaping up.

Downey's face remained passive, his steel-grey eyes alert. 'Anything at all.'

'She's mute, Downey, We'll talk about it later.'

'My daughter's been through a lot – she's no doubt in shock.' Downey's voice seemed mechanical, lacking in empathy, unconvincing. 'I have your coordinates here – I'll send someone she knows over to fetch her. I assume you're aware of the substantial reward for her recovery.'

'There's already been an attempt on her life. If you've homed in on this location we're no longer secure.'

Downey gestured for Calloway to remain seated. 'You realise, Mr Calloway, my research may have been only empirical. I don't seem to have proven my hypothesis.' For the first time he smiled. It wasn't altogether pleasant.

'We have state-of-the-art scramblers, Mr Calloway. Relax. May I ask you what your interest in all this is? You're obviously not in it for the money.'

It was wrong. All wrong. Calloway said. 'Does your daughter know?'

'You're good, Calloway,' Downey said with a certain weariness. 'I'm glad you found my daughter. I don't have long.'

'We're out of here, Downey. I'll contact you from a safe house.'

But the automatic alarms had already begun their clamour. Security screens closed across the windows; a metal door slid smoothly across the front entrance.

A smile twitched at Downey's lips. 'I believe my men are there already. Good*bye*, Mr Calloway.'

Calloway didn't get a chance to decode the security door. When it blew it took him off his feet, up and over a central aquarium and fountain. He skidded across the gold-flecked marble floor to crash against the far wall.

He'd already released his last unit vial of Neurosone into his system. The hormone kicked in; cleared his vision with a jolt.

Three men. Small, very compact and efficient, no wasted movement. They hurried toward him in a phalanx; the two flanking the centre man veered off to avoid bunching.

Professional heavies augmented by partial polymer exoskeletons: chromed carapace covering torso circuitry and knee braces geared for speed; half-moon plate armour covering terminal jacks neurotronically interfacing thought traces; magnifying optic enhancers with optional infra-red scanners.

They moved like crazed caricatures of Marcel Marceau, only ten times faster with deadly intent.

Calloway stabbed at the quadrophonic remote: 85 db sound blared from 4 megawatt Hitachi speakers. Confuse an augment's signal to the polymer mainframe and the exoskeleton was capable of ripping the host body limb from limb.

The ruse worked for the split second it took Calloway to clench with the first opponent.

Calloway threw his head back and snapped it forward. The headbutt connected with the man's nose, releasing a gout of blood that smeared across his face. His exoskeleton went haywire, jerking his limbs and torso into spasmodic confusion.

There was movement behind him but Calloway had already ducked down, right leg bent, left thrusting back with added torsion from a quick hip snap.

The kick caught the assassin in the groin, toppling him into a foetal position.

Suddenly polymer-mesh-enhanced fingers ripped at Calloway's throat. The impact of the strike choked Calloway's breath away. The movement was so fast, boosted by the exoskeleton circuitry, that Calloway was lifted off the ground.

A blackness loomed somewhere deep inside Calloway's head, came rushing out from some deep vault to snare him.

Reflexes kicked in. He was dimly aware of his hands reaching out, describing a wide arc, coming back in to either side of his assailant's head. The force created a vacuum, bursting the man's eardrums.

He howled, sending confused signals to the neurocircuitry. His hand clenched tighter, almost crushing Calloway's larynx. Then Calloway's feet touched the ground. He clasped the man's arm, twisted up and under it, snapping both the arm and the neurocircuitry commanding it.

He prised the death-grip fingers from his throat, spun with Neurosone-enhanced finesse and delivered a knife hand strike to the third agent's neck.

Security procedures locked into the Savoy's power. The place shut down and the Hitachi cut abruptly.

Through the drumming in his ears he heard Marionette reciting her soliloquy:

'*In Situ analysis with the use of immunohistochemistry. Immunofluorescent-linked enzymes to locate, by microscopy, the flawed genotypes causing illness . . .*'

They caught a midorbital to Paraguay at 0900 hours and had cleared customs at Asuncion Aeropuerto by 0130 hours. Within two hours they had caught a transom to Bernado, 30 kilometres south of Iguassu Falls.

The falls created a spot called 'Tres Fronteras', for it formed the juncture of three republics.

The country was a political nightmare, with the major political parties, Colorado, Radical Liberal and Febrerista, all vying for armed political supremacy; Mestizos, Brazilians, Argentines and multinationals out to wreak havoc.

Foreigners weren't welcome.

For this reason Calloway kept Marionette close to him. Moon-faced, high cheekbones bulbous beneath wide and constantly startled blue eyes balanced by a fragile avian nose with barely visible nostrils; firefly hairstyle ragged due to neglect; Rubenesque body with partial baby-fat with the potential to become Amazonian. She'd fetch a packet as a sex toy in one of the flourishing cut joints like the *Sonic Synch*. Better than cash. Prestige.

A tattered flag bearing horizontal stripes of red, white, and blue, with the national coat of arms and the treasury seal, hung from the scarred facade of chipped bluestone and rusted iron. It looked anything but a safe haven.

The three-tiered bunker was in fact owned by Velazquez.

Calloway and Marionette were admitted through the security aperture, a cylindrical vault of black reinforced laminate.

'Welcome aboard, Mr Calloway.' Velazquez's voice was crystal clear through the Nakamichi speakers.

Marionette gave no indication she'd heard him. She was just there for the ride.

The elevator deposited them two floors up where they were greeted by a skinny, anaemic kid who looked only marginally older than Marionette.

He was pushing forty.

'And you must be Marionette?' Velazquez said. He pulled a face, pushed his wire frame glasses back into position. 'Doesn't talk much, does she?'

'Too much, it seems,' Calloway said. He withdrew a tape, passed it to Velazquez.

'Right on,' he said, and slotted it into his system. 'Annexed part of Downey's data – ICE as black as sin surrounding it. Got a black market pirate breaker; got me part way inside before it kicked back.'

Velazquez looked at his bandaged hands and grinned. 'You've bought yourself a rough package too, dude.'

'Sorry,' Calloway said, indicating Velazquez's hands.

'Hey, man,' Velazquez said. 'The bandages are for show. Wanted to make you feel guilty.'

Calloway shrugged off his parka, loosened a munitions strap and placed it carefully over a chair.

'Rhinestone still keep track of you with a neuropulsar? I'll take it out again if you like.'

'That's old hat,' Calloway said. 'Top earners now get fixed with an aspirating vacuole filled with a neurotoxin called cerebrin. Fool with this baby and it floods the adipose mass of the left cortex.'

'They're quite specific, aren't they?'

'They can afford to be. But don't worry, they're not filming this one. They'd have nothing to gain by doing me over off camera. Leroy wouldn't hear of it.'

Over the speakers they could hear Marionette's monotone:

'*DNA extraction from blood by the phenol-chloroform process and purification by laser chromatography* . . . '

'It's a Jap idea,' Velazquez said, indicating Marionette. 'Surrogates?'

'Yeah. Never seen one close up before. Scary what the human mind can aspire to, hey? The little I got from the matrix confirms that she's one of four adopted children. Downey himself is impotent and never married. Each of the surrogates is a software package for his research – Marionette's the data base.'

'Is there anything you *don't* know, Velazquez?'

Velazquez looked uncertain. It lasted a second. 'Sure, I haven't figured out yet how to open a packet of peanuts without using my teeth.'

'Touché. Okay. So she was abducted, sluiced for information, intended for a body bag drop but someone thought up one better. A nice joke to play on Downey at Rhinestone's expense.'

'That's the way it reads, Mr Calloway. Whoever did the job previously didn't get everything they wanted, else they would've offed her earlier. Hence this stuff she's still spilling. It's a runaway limbic virus with nowhere to go.'

'So Downey sent a razor team to finish the job. Can you decipher what's left – maybe dredge up the rest?'

Velazquez clucked his tongue. 'If you'd asked anyone else that question they would've laughed you off the stage.'

'Is there anything you can't – forget that,' Calloway said.

Velazquez took Marionette by the hand and with the other made a grand gesture encompassing his laboratory. 'C'mon, babe, the universe is at our beck and call.'

At the neuro insulator Calloway said, 'It's not going to leave her a vegetable is it?'

'Nah,' he said. 'If anything it'll bring back her LTM – that's why we won't use an anaesthetic. You see, the program performs a modified left cerebral transduction on her. Get a fine laser aspiration into her cerebral cortex and it reduces the grey matter just enough to close the gaps of the neuronic synapses transfer and consequently improve her cortex index.'

'You're talking double-dutch, Velazquez. Give it to me in layman's terms, huh?'

'I did.' Velazquez dabbed some saline paste on Marionette's temples and placed twin electrodes over it.

'You see, Mr Calloway, once we've got the significant information imprinted in her mind, we use the AI-aided EEG connected with the MEDITRON computer which processes randomised thoughts into a 60 gigabyte cache array.

'Simple as that. MEDITRON even decodes the raw data into a hardcopy transcript summary.'

'What'll happen to the kid once all this shit's out of her head?'

Velazquez shrugged. 'With time she'll come good. We'll just have to override the limbic commands. It'll take time, but I've got that.'

Calloway watched the reams of research deposit into a chute.

Velazquez raised his eyebrows. 'You thinking what I am?'

'Yeah.'

'*All right*!' Velazquez began feeding the sheaths into a voice scanner. Shortly they'd be broadcasting via satellite around the globe.

'You know, I had it figured that SOTO was in on this – jockeying for patent rights or something,' Calloway said.

'Just the opposite,' Velazquez said. 'The major pharmaceutical houses wouldn't want this stuff made public. Shit, they just about rule the world's economy on people's suffering. They bought out MEDIVAX to stifle research, but figured they couldn't trust Downey so they did a little industrial espionage to keep him quiet.'

'Meanwhile he's come down with something either not covered in his research or a *de novo* virus. So he wants to have the kid offed to cover his failed research to either hide it from the National Institute of Medical Research who funds him, and/or the magnate who bought him out.

'During all of which our poor kid's pumped so full of Dordophine she's on another planet,' Velazquez said.

The scanner's chip voice began to broadcast Downey's research.

Calloway called Rhinestone via a scrambled link and told Toby to tune in on the frequency.

The cinematographer blanched. 'Fuck-in hell,' he said.

'They will when I get there,' Calloway replied.

He hung up.

AN EMPTY WHEELHOUSE

SEAN McMULLEN

Notes on the deaths of John Jenkins and James Stuart (Hanged by the San Francisco Committee of Vigilance, 1851)

This part of the project was to determine if the Australian criminals Stuart and Jenkins had any connection with Rob McIver, who was shot dead on May 25, 1851. Both men were members of a gang known as the Sydney Coves, who were all ex-convict Forty Niners. The Sydney Coves were described in the *Annals of San Francisco* as 'stray vagabonds from Australia, where had been collected the choice of the convicted felons of Great Britain'.

By mid-1851 local vigilantes had broken the power of the outlaw gangs, such as the American Hounds and the Sydney Coves, but law and order was still almost impossible to maintain. McIver was shot in the back as he left the Jolly Waterman on Telegraph Hill. His killer emptied his pockets before escaping. McIver had been an explorer in Australia before he sailed to California and struck it rich in the 1849 gold rush. In Oldfield's 'Diary of a Vigilante', he is mentioned as having what he called a 'lucky beastie' that found gold for him. Oldfield describes this as a tame possum with webbed feet that he led about on a chain. It died after being attacked by a bull terrier in April 1851, and McIver shot both the dog and its owner. His luck really did run out then, and he was murdered within a month.

John Jenkins was caught several weeks later, after breaking into a store, stealing a safe, then trying to row away with it in a boat. The Committee of Vigilance waded out after him, *arrested him, and took him to their rooms in Battery Street for a trial. A ship's master, Captain William Howard, presided. He summed up the case with the words 'Gentlemen, as I understand it we came here to hang somebody.' A motion to hang Jenkins from the flagstaff was shouted down as unpatriotic, then a lynch mob took over and hanged him from the loading beam of a nearby warehouse.*

The contents of the water-damaged safe were impounded in the strong room of another store. Three weeks later a second Australian ex-convict, James Stuart, was arrested while preparing to rob it. After his arrest Stuart was recognized as the notorious English Jim, wanted for gold robbery, horse-stealing, escaping from legal custody, arson, and murder. He was tried on Independence Day, 1851, and the Vigilantes marched him to the pier at the foot of Market Street for execution. When the city attorney, Frank Pixley, tried to rescue the prisoner the mob threatened to string him up on the derrick as well. Pixley later took possession of some papers from the safe that both lynched men had apparently been after, and Oldfield mentions that some of the documents had belonged to McIver.

The surviving city archives from that period have been searched repeatedly, but no trace of the documents has been found.

Helen always sent the results of her research out as electronic mail to an Internet address that was somewhere in the UCLA campus. Her cryptic instructions came on the same Internet system, and the money for her services always appeared in her bank account from some untraceable source.

Who would pay a history graduate so much to do research into obscure nineteenth-century documents? Not that $500 per week was so very much, but she had been working for months now without knowing what the point of the exercise was. It might have been inheritance dispute, in fact that was her favourite theory so far. There was always plenty of money to do whatever was required to complete her instructions.

Today Oakland, tomorrow . . . would depend upon the message that she received in reply to her latest researches. She had been flown to New York, and found nothing meaningful. She had expected to be fired: instead she was flown to London to read old colonial office reports. Again she found nothing of interest, yet she was booked onto a flight to San Francisco to read records in the city archives. The next trip was shorter, just a journey on the BART to read some rare documents in a library on the Berkeley Campus. By lunchtime the work was done. She packed her Toshiba laptop and modem into a shoulder bag, and dodged across Bancroft Way to the little group of shops and cafes just south of the campus. Neil was waiting at a sidewalk table, as they had arranged over the phone.

'So, still on that contract for those folks in LA?' he asked as she sat down.

'That's right. Whatever they want, I seem to be finding it.'

'I'm leaving for Hawaii right now. I'm only in town because my connect flight goes through Oakland airport.'

'Hawaii, great. I have no idea where they'll send me next.'

For some minutes their conversation remained exuberant and facile, even a little hysterical. There were more important things to discuss, unpleasant things, yet the preliminaries could be made to last. Slowly, carefully, she assembled her meticulously rehearsed string of words, then took aim at a space in the conversation like an Indian stalking salmon in a stream.

'What are the job prospects like for historians in Hawaii?'

'Ah, not good, not good. You'd be cleaning motels, and serving in bars.'

Missed.

'You checked already?'

'Yeah, I did. Hey, do you know who you're working for yet?'

In other words, drop the subject. 'No clues. It could be the KGB for all I know.'

'I doubt it, they're all doing contract work for the Arabs these days. It's probably someone trying to prove a bloodline with a millionaire who died without leaving a will.'

'Then why the secrecy?'

'To have an advantage in court, maybe.'

There was something tired and unworkable going on here, yet neither of them had the will to admit it. His face betrayed nothing; his smile was controlled to perfection. There was one more hurdle for her exhausted emotions to clear. Oddly enough, sex held no special terrors for Helen, but talking about it was the worst possible nightmare. Any sort of verbal exchange worried her; she wanted to rehearse her words, to type them into a computer then rearrange and polish them, hand the print-out to Neil who would give her a score out of ten.

'I've got a room across the bay,' she said while staring intently at her coffee cup. 'It's not long on the BART.'

'Look, that would be great, but, well I really don't have much time between flights. It was hard enough just seeing you here and . . . I'd better rush. My flight leaves soon.'

When he had gone Helen slumped with relief, then ordered a large slice of coffee cake with plenty of cream. Free again, free from talk. She had studied history because most of the subjects were safely dead, with their words on paper. Her special project was a dream come true: the communications were terse, and arrived by electronic mail. Perhaps it would last for a very long time.

The next phase of the project took her back to London, and lasted a month. Each night she would open a line to her enigmatic employer in Los Angeles and type in a few likely records from the nineteenth-century registers. Only occasionally did she get a reply, and the replies were short.

At last she had a breakthrough. A clerk at the city attorney's office in the San Francisco of the early 1850s shared a feature with one convict: a pair of parallel scars on his chin. It was a small thing, but enough. Patrick O'Hallorin, an Irish immigrant, had been given a job in the city attorney's office in 1852, and had worked there for eleven months. He was five feet nine inches tall, and had brown hair and blue eyes. Those details fitted dozens of British convicts, but only Brendan Terrance Hooligan shared the scars too.

She expected a trip to Australia next, but however much her employers might avoid libraries, they had no trouble with electronic data. Some sort of scan of databases was done in the time that it took her to stroll along the Thames Embankment and have a cup of coffee. By the time she returned to her rooming house and made an Internet connection, they had found a copy of a PhD thesis for her to examine.

It was held in a small collection in the University of London. An Australian student had done his urban demography thesis on the passenger lists of ships entering Australian ports between 1830 and 1860. The thesis was a thin book and ten computer diskettes. It took a morning to learn the student's customised access program, but after that the search was over in seconds.

Among the hundreds of thousands of entries there were three for Brendan Hooligan. He had arrived in Australia as a convict in 1840, left Sydney in 1849 for San Francisco as a discharged convict, then arrived in Melbourne aboard the *Queen of Tahiti* in 1855. He had tried to pass himself off as O'Hallorin again, but had been found out. A free text footnote in the database mentioned that he had been sentenced to nine years hard labour for uttering a false declaration, abusive language, and shooting a member of Her Majesty's Port Authority in the foot.

She typed in the few lines of research, and the reply appeared within an hour.

RECD: LONDON WORK COMPLETE. FLIGHT TO BOSTON BOOKED. TOMORROW MORNING CONTINENTAL, INSTRUCTIONS FOR NEXT STAGE TO FOLLOW...

If Helen loved the work she hated the travel. The flight west disrupted her sleep patterns, more because she stayed awake willing the wings and engines not to fall off, than because of the change in time zones. Perhaps there will be a lot to keep her in Boston, she thought hopefully as she propped herself against the customs counter.

She had to read through a list of books in various historical society libraries, keeping a watch for references to Hooligan. After eighteen obscure and indifferently written volumes she came to Sibil J. Henderson's *Impressions of Australis: Travels of a Boston Girl in Australia, 1896 to 1901*, published by herself in 1922. The style of writing annoyed Helen intensely. The author had recorded the details of her trip in fussy, exact prose, right down to spelling out the people's accents. It was excessive, even by nineteenth-century standards. Unlike Helen, she appeared to have been a born traveller, always happiest when on the move, never worried about ships sinking or what to say to strangers. On page 122 she mentioned Hooligan.

Today, April 5, 1897, is a most glorious autumn day, and there could be no finer place on earth to enjoy it than here, steaming up this broad, magnificent Murray River on a paddlewheeler. I have just had tea with Captain McGinty under the bow awning. I am getting quite a strong taste for tea during my travels in Australia.

Captain McGinty is very formal, and comes from a strict Presbyterian family in Scotland. The other passengers have been finding him hard to talk to, but I discovered that asking him about his paddleboat is the way to his heart. He told me that the Wee Robbie weighs 200 tons, is 130 feet long, and has a horizontal high pressure steam engine of 40 horsepower. He gave me a tour of the engine room, and it was all polished brass and copper, cleaner than the dishes that meals are served on. I saw from a plaque that it was built right here in Australia.

After that we went back to the bow and sat under the awning while he told me all about the rivers and riverboats of Australia. Riverboats were very important in opening up the frontier here, just as they were in America, but I'm afraid that I just let my mind wander when he was talking about bales of wool and barrels of rum. The water ahead was almost smooth, and the brilliant blue sky and brown river were separated by a line of olive green eucalyptus trees on the bank. Black swans were bobbing on the water, and once we passed a strange, tatty little riverboat that was towing a barge half filled with earth with vegetables growing in it! The captain said that those people were river gypsies known as Murray Whalers. I asked him if the river had been more dangerous in pioneering times.

'Nae dangerous, just a wee bit unsafe. I suppose it was like America in many ways, and there were actually a lot of American boats shipped oot here before the locals learned to build reliable boilers. There were a few American captains oot here as well. Gus Pierce from Massachusetts was the most famous. He came tae Melbourne as a sailor during the gold rush. He was just a teenager, and he jumped ship and swam ashore in his underwear when the captain locked up the crews' clothing tae stop them deserting. He found nae much gold, but he worked his way up tae riverboat captain after a few years. He was a real character! When he retired he said that he came tae Australia withoot a penny, but left owing hundreds of pounds.'

'Gus Pierce, you say?' I replied. 'Was he interesting? Are there any tall tales about him?'

The captain laughed. 'The only tales aboot Gus are tall tales, lassie. He's supposed tae have rammed and sunk a steam barge *from under an Irishman named Bren Hooligan. Said that Hooligan stole some special beasties that could dive underwater tae find gold.'*

'Now that is a tall story.'

'Aye, and let's see now, that would have been 1867, when he was captain of the sternwheeler Lady Daly. *Funny, because Gus didna like tae talk aboot that ramming. Other things, well ye'd nae shut him up. I asked him aboot it when we met back in 1875, but he told me tae mind my own business. Nothing in the records, either.'*

'So there's no record of the ramming? Is it just a tall story?'

'Well . . . it's hard tae say. Records get lost if a bushfire destroys a town hall – along with the rest of the town. Happened a lot in the pioneering days.'

'Uh, bushfires?'

'Forest fires, ye'd call them. Now fires were also a problem with the old paddlesteamers. Sparks frae the funnels, burned holes in passenger's clothes, even set fire tae the cargoes. Why later in 1867 the Lady Daly's *sister ship, the* Lady Darling, *was lost when her cargo of brandy caught fire near Wahgunyah. Burned tae the waterline, she did, and there were grown men watching frae the riverbank in tears. Getting back tae that ramming, though, my chief fireman was on the* Lady Daly *when it happened. He was only fourteen at the time, mind. Pirate Bollinger, that's him. Rough as auld bags but a good lad. Would ye like tae meet him?'*

I declined his offer. I had not come halfway around the world to meet some coarse and vulgar stoker. Captain McGinty then told me about another American, Peleg Jackson, who had been the previous captain of the Lady Daly, *and who flew the Stars and Stripes when –*

Helen booted up her Toshiba and typed in the passage before reading on. There was no more about Hooligan, so she returned to her hotel early and sent off the passage as Internet mail. One attempt to drive a rental car through some apparently suicidal Boston traffic was enough to confine her to her hotel room while the eyes on the other end of the Internet link made what they would of Sibil J. Henderson's adventures in nineteenth-century Australia. This time the wait was a single hour.

RECD: SATISFACTORY. FLIGHT TO MELBOURNE BOOKED. CHECK AIRPORT.

Satisfactory? That was an expression of ecstacy when compared to earlier replies. She wondered if they had meant Melbourne Florida or Melbourne Australia, but was not really surprised when her call to the airport was directed to international departures.

The flight was to San Francisco, then Honolulu, Auckland, and Melbourne. That meant a chance to see Neil, and to spend precious hours on the ground. He was working on the eastern coast of Hawaii, on a field trip near a recent lava flow. Using her own money she booked an Aloha flight and a rental car after rescheduling the rest of the journey.

It was clear that her status with Neil had been reduced to that of interloper. A bronzed microbiologist wearing a white bikini of open-weaved string regarded her suspiciously from the field station as they walked along the black volcanic sand. They had a lot to talk about, but somehow nothing important could be said.

'If an animal could find gold, how would it go about it?' she asked, on the brink of talking about the weather.

'An animal? Do you mean like a trained searcher dog?' Neil responded eagerly, also anxious to grasp at any neutral subject.

'No, no, I mean . . . well, it's this inheritance business. There was a prospector in the Californian gold rush who was supposed to have had an animal that could find gold. It was a possum with webbed feet, according to the writer.'

'Probably just another tall tale. For a start, possums are

marsupials, and that means they keep their young in a pouch. How would the young breathe when they went swimming? The other thing is that gold is almost inert chemically, that's why you find nuggets on some goldfields. It would be very hard to smell, so an animal would have no better chance of finding gold than a human – except that we use metal detectors now. Who was this guy, anyhow?'

'Just some Australian ex-convict who came over for the '49 rush, struck it rich, then got himself shot.'

'Australia . . . now that's just the place to find possums. There are dozens and dozens of species there. Some are as small as your thumb, while brush tail possums are big and strong, and have been known to kill even small dogs that were dumb enough to corner them. Humans don't faze them, either: all the parks in Australia's main cities have wild possums, just like the squirrels in Central Park in New York. They're quite a tourist attraction, except that they have to be fed by torchlight because they're nocturnal.'

He hastily scoured his mind for more facts about possums as the pause began to lengthen ominously.

'There are some types that can glide through the air, using membranes of skin between their front and hind legs. One of the large glider possums chews through the bark of trees and sucks the sap.'

'A vegetarian vampire?'

'Kind of like that.'

'But none of them can find gold.'

'No, I guess not. To do that they would need an electric sixth sense, and the only mammals that have that are the monotremes. They're the only ones that I know about, anyhow.'

'Now wait a minute. You mean some animals really can detect electricity?'

'That's right, the platypus and the echidna, and they're

also Australian. Both have organs to detect the muscular electricity of their prey. Any animal that could also generate an electromagnetic field could act like a biological metal detector, but – '

'How about the electric eels of South America?'

'Well, perhaps, but eels are not bright enough to be trained. Now that you mention South America, though, I've just . . . remembered something from my first year at college. There is one aquatic marsupial in the world, a type of possum called a yapok. It has a fatty layer of skin at the edge of the pouch, which makes a waterproof seal when it dives – and its hind feet are webbed. The trouble is that it hunts by touch, not electric field.'

'Could that prospector have had a platypus, then?'

'Nope. First thing is that a platypus looks more like a beaver with a duck's bill than a possum. Second is that it can only detect electric fields, and metal detectors work by generating their own electromagnetic field. Still, the idea of an animal that could find gold is not really impossible. Maybe that ex-convict guy really did find an Australian yapok that also had electrosensitive fingertips and a field generation capacity. Something like that would be able to find gold in muddy riverbeds.'

A pause became a lengthy silence. He's worse than me, he's a worm, he needs a spine transplant, she shouted within herself, then spent the uneasy minutes rearranging the words into a scathing put-down. It came out as:

'Well, I must go. I've got a connect flight to Australia.'

'Oh great – er, place for a holiday.'

Helen took a deep breath to relieve the spasm of grief. 'I'll be in Melbourne doing research in the state library.'

'Any idea who you're working for yet?'

'No. Do you think they might want to know if McIver's animals are still around – if they ever existed?'

'Why bother? A commercial metal detector works a hundred times better these days . . . On the other hand, I suppose that if you bred and trained a herd of a thousand or so, they do cover a lot more ground than a human, and for no more pay than a barrel of worms. It just might be possible, but then of course their scientific value would be astronomical as well. If you do find anything I'd, ah, drop me a line.'

'I'll do that. I really must go now. Bye Neil.'

He glanced back to the field station. 'Bye Helen.' No kiss.

It was only on the flight back to Oahu that she realized the glorious truth: the affair was over! No scene, no tears, no long, excruciating discussions. They had broken up by default. She celebrated by getting slightly drunk at a bar near the airport, then slept soundly for much of the long flight south.

Melbourne turned out to be the hardest phase of the project. She had to search through the local histories for references to Hooligan, especially the ramming of his riverboat. Weeks passed, with no result. There were no references to Hooligan, except for his death notice – he had drowned in the Murray River at Albury. After the local histories Helen searched the card indexes of the special collections, the collection of early photographs, and even the sound recording archives. She reported daily over her Internet link, telling her nameless employer of the lack of progress.

After the first week she had moved out of the hotel and into a student house near Melbourne University. She was growing to like Melbourne, which was similar to Oakland and San Francisco, yet on a bigger scale. By now she had amassed a fair amount of background knowledge on nineteenth-century Australia's riverboat systems, especially on the role of Americans in running them. Might there be a PhD topic here, after the project was over? Of course there would be an interview, yet this was on a subject that she understood well, and she would not be lost for sensible words. She took a tram to the University of Melbourne.

The interview with Dr Merrin of the history department went well. There was a shortage of students because of recent cuts in government funding, and being a candidate with a good academic record and comfortable savings made Helen a good prospect. The talk moved to her recent work.

'Riverboats?' exclaimed the lecturer. 'There's a coincidence. Just last month the history department's library was given the manuscript of an old riverboat pioneer. He was in his eighties when he died. It's a sort of rambling autobiography, transcribed by one of his sisters from his own words. The writing is a bit overblown – it was done in the 1940s, after all – but it's full of good material. I was thinking of editing it for publication. Would you like to have a look through it?'

She certainly did. The straggly writing was on musty paper, with the blue ruling running slightly. On the fifteenth page she found the holy grail that had drawn her around the world.

Then there was the time dad worked for Bren Hooligan, a really mean cove. He came out of the eastern highlands driving a bullock cart with a hardwood cage on the back. There were ten possums in it. One of his men told dad that they were called wateroos.

Now Hooligan hired a sternwheeler steam barge and had the cage put on board while he and his two men went off to buy supplies and fuel. Dad was always hanging about on the docks looking for odd jobs, so they paid him a shilling to feed the possums and clean the cage.

Dad liked animals, and these were so tame that he started to let them out of the cage on a leash, one at a time. He noticed that their back feet were webbed for swimming, and their forepaws were just like hands. Their fingertips were big, soft pads, and gave dad a tingling feeling when they touched him.

Around noon he was sitting on the edge of the barge, flipping his shilling in the air and feeling pretty pleased about having such easy work. Well, he missed a catch, and the coin hit the water. Without thinking he let go of the leash and started to take off his shirt to dive after it. Suddenly the wateroo that was out of the cage jumped straight over the side and disappeared.

Dad said that he was really frightened, and was about ready to pack it in and go bush because Hooligan would have shot him. Then the wateroo surfaced with the coin and handed it to dad. He dived again, and again, going on for about half an hour until dad had over one pound in lost coins, and a gold watch on a chain.

Well dad wasn't stupid, he pocketed the loot. When Hooligan's two men returned, though, he couldn't resist showing them how the wateroo could fetch a coin out of ten feet of water. They patted him on the head and gave him another shilling, then stood talking for a while. Then, without getting clearance or anything they fired up the boiler, cast off, and went steaming away down the river. Dad thought nothing of it, he just sat on a barrel, flipping that shilling in the air. An hour later, along came Hooligan.

'Where's me barge?' he shouted.

'Your men steamed off with it an hour ago,' dad said.

'You're the kid we paid to feed the wateroos,' he said, grabbing dad by the hair and shaking him. 'Where are they? Are they all right? Any sick or dead? Tell me, ye hear?'

'They're all right, they're on the barge,' dad shouted. He thought Hooligan would drown him or something. 'They're not sick, Mr Hooligan, why I had one diving for coins around noon. I looked after them real good, that I did Mister Hooligan.'

Now Hooligan looked really worried, 'Coins? Diving?' he said. 'Did ye show Bill and Zeke that trick of diving for coins?'

'That I did.'

'Hell and damnation, boy, how d'ye think they find the coins?'

'They see them – '

'See them be damned, nothing can see in ten feet of muddy water and six inches of silt. They've got special fingers, they can find metal under water and – and why am I wastin' time here? Come on!'

He dragged dad along the dock until they came to a riverboat that was just stoking up. It was the Lady Daly, and her captain was the yankee, Gus Pierce. He made dad tell Gus everything about the wateroos, and yelled at Gus to chase after them.

'Sir, it seems like a lot of fuss over a few possums that can find coins under water,' said Gus.

'Fool, fool, don't ye see?' shouted Hooligan, almost crazy. 'They can find anything metal underwater. They can find gold!'

'Gold! Is that true, boy?' he asked dad. Dad showed him the gold watch, still covered in river silt. He turned back to Hooligan.

'Mr Hooligan, instead of chasing off after your partners, why don't we just go catch some more wateroos then go prospecting?'

Hooligan threw his arms in the air and jumped up and down on the deck.

'The local natives said that there were only fifty left, and that they all lived in one particular mountain pond. They were too hard to catch, so I blasted the pond with barrels of gun-powder. Ten were stunned, the rest were killed. Those ten on the barge are the only ones left in the world! I'll pay ye one hundred pounds, see, I've got the money here. Just get my wateroos back.'

That was enough for Gus. He had the Lady Daly cast off and steered down the river, steaming all out. Hooligan's men didn't know much about steam engines, so they were pottering along slowly, trying to get the hang of things. The Lady Daly caught them up by mid-afternoon, and after a few shots from Hooligan's Henry Repeater the pair dropped anchor and raised their hands.

After Bill and Zeke were locked up Gus asked to see a

wateroo in action. Hooligan let the biggest one out and made dad drop that gold watch overboard. The wateroo dived and recovered it.

'Now that's mighty impressive, Mister Hooligan,' said Gus, looking thoughtful. Hooligan just grunted and started to count the hundred pounds out of his bankroll.

'Now hold on there, Mister Hooligan,' Gus went on. 'Seems to me that I just did you a valuable service, and that those wateroos are worth more than a hundred pounds. Tell you what, why not keep your money and leave one wateroo with me.'

'No!' snapped Hooligan, holding out the money. 'We agreed on one hundred pounds. The wateroos are all mine.'

Gus just stood there, twirling his handlebar moustache.

'How are we to know that?' he said, smiling. 'What say we go back to the Albury magistrate and let him figure it out.'

'They're mine!' shouted Hooligan, suddenly raising his repeater. Gus must have thought it was a joke, because he just kept smiling and stepped forward. Hooligan fired a shot between his feet.

Gus jumped back. Dad dropped the wateroo's lead and raised his hands, and that wateroo jumped right over the side. Hooligan cursed dad like a demon in drink, but it was too late so he jumped onto his barge and cast off. Now the steam barge was fast and light, and the Lady Daly could never have caught it with an experienced man in charge. But the big riverboat was downstream of the barge, and as Hooligan came around Gus called the engine room for full steam and steered to cut him off.

Gus leaned out of the wheelhouse and called 'Stand to, Hooligan, and turn those critters over.'

Hooligan shouted back 'Stand off, yankee doodle, or I'll have the redcoats after ye.' Then he raised his Henry Repeater and fired two shots through the wheelhouse window. Gus jumped out of the wheelhouse and took cover behind some bales of wool with dad. He returned Hooligan's fire with his two horse pistols. Suddenly dad noticed that the Lady Daly was changing *course and heading straight for the steam barge. Hooligan tried to steer out of the way, but even though the wheelhouse was empty the big sternwheeler changed course again and rammed that steam barge.*

Being twelve times the weight of the barge, the Lady Daly *rode up over it and forced it down until it filled with water and sank. The wateroos were locked in their cage and never had a chance. There was floating wreckage everywhere, and then they saw Hooligan thrashing about in the water. When they pulled him aboard he had a couple of dozen cuts, some of them quite deep.*

He was raving mad, saying that the free wateroo had stabbed him with a knife and taken his keys to unlock the cage. Well nobody was going to check on that in a hurry, as the barge sank in forty feet of water. He was locked up and taken back to Albury with Bill and Zeke. Dad said that Hooligan took to rum and drowned five years later when he fell off the pier. The funny thing was that dad's fishing knife did go missing during the excitement.

After so much time and effort the end came as an anticlimax. She transcribed the text onto her Toshiba's disk and plugged it into the modem. This time it took forty minutes for the Internet message to arrive, but there was no denying that this was the end.

RECD: CONTRACT CONCLUDED.

Helen stared in disbelief at the words on the screen, her mouth hanging open. Disbelief turning to admiration. The words were clear, sharp and absolute, there was no agonising lingering, no searching for words to cushion the blow.

In spite of the hot, humid summer evening she sat in the kitchen of the student house for two hours. For a change she needed someone to talk to. The shadowy people on the other end of the Internet link had been secure, reliable companions, people who spoke her language, but now she had been betrayed. No, not betrayed, not at all, they might feel guilty – but she *had* been betrayed, and they *should* feel guilty! There was such a thing as common courtesy, telling people where they stood: which she had not done with Neil.

'Neil, let's split.' She said the words aloud, then cringed at the way they reverberated in the silent kitchen. 'This isn't working!' The words were easier this time. They could have saved her the cost of a flight and a hire car.

There was a loud thump on the verandah roof, followed by the patter of heavy feet. Helen glanced at the chewed stump of a marijuana plant in a pot by the window, then smiled. Possums, and city-wise possums at that. 'I suppose it's nature's way of telling me to give it up,' the plant's owner had said ruefully.

The halting mutter of a badly tuned motorcycle in the street outside announced that someone else was home. Roger was a tutor at the university's computer centre.

'G'day Helen,' he said, putting his helmet on the hall stand, 'How's your day? Mine was shocking. Want a coffee? White with a sugar, isn't it? Caught a hacker, smart bastard, too.'

'Hi Roger. I got fired.' The words were spoken before she could stop herself.

'One of our second year students. Think they know it all when they're in second year – fired?'

'That's right.'

'Jees, that's a bit poor.'

He sat down and stared across the table at her, unsure of how to be helpful. Back in the States he might be called a computer nerd – a cybernetics expert with limited social skills.

'Did you get that grant?' she asked. That's right, change the subject, she fumed to herself. You want sympathy, but don't ask.

'Oh yeah, forgot all about that, what with the hacker

and all – I'll be working with a physiologist. He has a volunteer who lost an arm in a car crash, and we're going to wire the nerve stumps into a computer interface. We'll see if we can give him enough control to simulate typing commands by nerve impulses alone.'

'So he could just be sitting there typing by thinking about it?'

'That's close. We're also going to feed impulses back to see if he can communicate with the machine without using a screen. Rather like giving him an electrical voice and ears.'

An electrical voice! Abruptly a vast number of stray facts in Helen's mind locked into one fantastic pattern. Possums, tingling fingers, a riverboat steered from an empty wheelhouse, awkward and cryptic instructions on Internet.

'Could you tell me about Internet?' she asked, suddenly eager.

Roger blinked. 'Well, it's just a network of research computers. It started off in the USA, but, it's worldwide now.'

'But how does it work?'

'Oh, TCP/IP protocols, and you can have best effort packet switching, dedicated links, or electronic mail. The famous Internet Worm of 1988 spread through the electronic mail.'

'I don't understand any of that.'

Roger scratched his head. 'I'm not sure I can make it any simpler,' he said after a moment.

'Look, my former employers supplied this Toshiba laptop PC and a telephone modem. I turn it on, plug it in, then type CONNECT.'

'And?'

'I get connected, from wherever I am.'

'There's probably some sort of communications program in the PC. It broadcasts your ID packet through the Internet. Rather like calling someone's name in a crowded party.'

'Hey, that's great! Why can't you explain things so well all the time?' That was a bold thing to say. She felt proud of herself.

Roger smiled, frowned, opened his mouth to reply, then decided against it. 'Can I use the Toshiba?' he finally asked.

It was beside her chair, and she handed it across the table. Within moments he had it running.

'Strange file names,' he reported. 'One's called CONNECT, the rest are A, B, C, D and E. No imagination at all. I mean TEST and FRED are bad enough, but A and B?'

It made sense to Helen.

'So you can wire a computer directly into someone's nerves.'

'Yeah, of course. It's been done for years, but we're trying to do it a lot better.' He inserted a diskette into the Toshiba.

'Suppose we had evolved electric speech? Could we work better with computers?'

'I don't follow,' he said, tapping at the keyboard.

'Suppose we could speak using electric impulses when we held hands. Could we 'speak' to computers with those impulses?'

'I . . . suppose so, in fact it could be a real advantage over keyboards. The only trouble is that electrical speech would be no help while climbing up the evolutionary tree. Imagine trying to run a hunting party if you had to touch hands before talking.'

Helen was aching to talk about an intelligent, electrosensitive animal surviving long enough to exploit an evolutionary niche in the worldwide communications and computing networks, but her terrors came back. She would sound crazy; she wanted Roger to think well of her. Did he matter? Yes, dammit, he was – she blushed.

Roger stood up. 'Think I'll go upstairs and turn off,' he said, removing the diskette from the Toshiba and handing it to her. 'There, I've copied the Internet link programs onto this floppy.'

'What for?'

'Suppose your bosses take your portable back, but you discover that they still owe you money. All you have to do is put this into a PC with a modem, then type A: CONNECT to raise them and say pay up.'

She sat turning the diskette over in her fingers as he walked to the stairs. The telephone rang as he passed the hall stand.

'It did what? Just like that? OK, OK, I'll come over and try to unscramble the mess. Ten minutes, OK?'

He took his helmet from the hall stand and called back to Helen.

'Problem at the computer centre. Sounds like one of our genius undergrads hacked into the Cyber and made a few creative changes to the operating system. I may be out a couple of hours.'

With Roger gone she was alone in the house again – the others had gone on a hiking trip. She went up to her room, locked the door, and switched off the light. Alone in the blackness, she had confidence. The night was still hot and oppressive, so she took off her clothes and lay naked on her bed. She tried to imagine possums that climbed unseen into communications towers, fingered cables, and manipulated the electronic arteries that controlled the world. Music from her clock-radio pleasantly overlaid the background from traffic outside.

They had been in decline when Europeans had come to those remote mountains in southeast Australia. Then McIver had come past in the 1840s. Perhaps he had dropped a coin or ring into their pool, and one had retrieved it. If aquatic possums could find a gold ring, they could find nuggets also. He took one to California and struck it rich, then talked to Jenkins, Stuart, and Hooligan. The rest was history, a history that Helen, alone of all humans, knew.

Hooligan had blasted their pond, stunning a few and killing the rest. Caged and terrified, the last members of the dying species had been carted away and put on Hooligan's steam barge. What nobody had realised was that they might be intelligent, more so than a dog, or even a monkey. One leader, their own Napoleon, Washington or Cromwell, had watched and learned about tools. It had been a standing broad-jump over millions of years to go from mountain pools to steering a riverboat, using keys, and fighting with a knife, yet . . .

Yet they were aquatic, the use of fire was inimical to them. Their intelligence kept developing without technology, along with an electronic language without wires. Intelligence and speech, but no technology. All at arm's length. After escaping Hooligan they found the early electric telegraph wires strung out across the countryside, and suddenly a huge, empty ecological niche beckoned to them. They could talk in large groups, and over great distances. Were they cybernetic mice or something more? In communications they had a head start, using their natural language while humans used Morse code. More than a century had passed, yet they remained unknown and made no bid for power. Perhaps they had no need to dominate, they merely wanted to preserve the electronic environment that served them so well. So why did they need her? If they understood human computer systems but not human culture, they would need help to trace their own history.

There was a brief fanfare from the radio, and a news bulletin began. Helen listened without hearing. Reports of some local bribery scandal were followed by the cricket scores.

'And here is the State news. A forty-seven-year-old

lecturer from Melbourne University was killed tonight when his car failed to take a bend on the Yarra Boulevard. He was Dr James Merrin of the Department of History. The car was completely burned out . . . '

Helen sat up on the bed, shaking the little radio as if to get more news out of it. Merrin, dead! She had phoned him only that afternoon. He said that someone in the US had made a very large bid for the Bollinger manuscript, but he had refused it. He was taking it home with him to begin editing it for publication.

Tiny hands could tamper with the brakes of a car. With a gasp she jumped up, flung the bedroom door open and ran down the stairs to the kitchen. The Toshiba was gone. Naked, shaking with fright, she sank to the floor. They were here! They were desperate to have all records of their existence sponged from human libraries. Even working in secret, after hours, the wateroos could not easily use libraries, so they had hired Helen to trace their history.

And they kept her on the move. What happened in her wake? Did pages disappear from files, books vanish from shelves, data get corrupted in historical computer databases? Had others died? Her work was over now, she was the only human expert on them. Her work was done. Merrin was dead. She would be next.

She shivered continually in spite of the hot night. How would they come? This was no way to die, sitting naked on a grubby kitchen floor ten thousand miles from home! They were small, they would masquerade as common possums, they would not carry weapons. They would set traps, that was it. She was safe as long as she did not move, but she had to. She was naked, her hair tangled, her face streaked with tears; if Roger came in she would die . . . her sobs became laughter for a moment.

Yet they were probably frightened too. Once they had been rare, powerless, yet immensely valuable. They had been very nearly wiped out by humans because of that.

Now they were powerful, yet perhaps still vulnerable. Humans would fear them. This time their extinction might be from systematic slaughter, not bungling incompetence.

Helen noticed her jacket draped over the back of a chair, and she reached for it. Her fingers closed on something hard in a pocket. A diskette. The diskette that Roger had prepared from the missing Toshiba. With a sudden surge of hope she took the diskette out and flung the jacket aside. Roger had a PC in his room with a modem wired illegally into the house telephone. She could get in contact with them! Then what?

Plead for mercy? Threaten to expose them? Swear that she would never mention them to anyone? They were aliens, true aliens. They had minds and values unimaginably different to those of humans. She could not reason with them, they would not feel pity, or guilt, or greed. She was the worst of communicators, yet she had to be the first human to consciously contact an alien society. Or die. What to say? 'Give me a line to your leader?' Too silly. 'Please, I know you want to kill me but I promise not to expose you.' No, too dramatic, she would rather die than . . . she laughed again.

When do I speak most easily, she wondered. When telling people what they wanted to hear. 'Mom, I got honours,' had been easy. 'Sure Neil, I don't mind if you take Lindy to Aspen.' Well, that had hurt, but it had been easy. Yet these were aliens. Webbed feet, electric fingers, furry bodies, so who could know what their values were? Yet they did value things, they had paid tens of thousands of dollars to erase themselves from human history. She could make them listen.

Slowly, carefully, ever watchful for trip wires and traps, she climbed the stairs and walked down the passageway. Roger's door was unlocked. She looked in. It was chaotic, rather than dirty, and a PC stood ready on his desk. She booted it up, inserted the diskette and typed A: CONNECT.

BAD COMMAND OR FILE NAME flashed at her. She gasped, her heart sank, tears trickled down her cheeks as she teetered on the brink of hysteria. She held on, forced herself to think. There were two slots for diskettes in this PC: perhaps the top one was not drive A. She removed one of Roger's diskettes from the lower drive and replaced it with her own. She typed A: CONNECT again. Now there was a familiar series of connection messages, but no master acknowledgement: they did not want to talk, but they were listening? Helen typed.

Extract from the newly discovered diary of Rob McIver:
    'December 10, 1848: Now the funny thing is that whenever I touched the beastie's fingers I got a tingling feeling, like when you sleep on your arm and wake up with it feeling full of pins and needles. I am not a well-educated man, but I think it is something to do with the way it can find coins that I throw into the pool. If I was to take the beastie to a gold rush, it could find enough gold for me to buy Buckingham Palace.'

NOW THAT I HAVE YOUR ATTENTION, ASK YOURSELVES IF YOU CAN VERIFY THAT QUOTE. IF YOU CANNOT, YOU NEED A GOOD HISTORIAN. YOU NEED ME.

Forty minutes passed, forty minutes of staring at a screen and scarcely breathing while her life hung by an electronic thread.
RECD: ACKNOWLEDGED. PAYMENT ON COMMISSION.
She flopped across the desk in relief, utterly drained. It was like lying in a stupor after good sex, all exhaustion and contented bliss. Sleep washed around her like a warm incoming tide. Roger would be home soon, would find her here. What would he think? She smiled. What would she say? She would find the words. After tonight, communication with mere humans would never again be a problem.

I STILL CALL AUSTRALIA HOME

GEORGE TURNER

The past is another country; they do things differently there.
(L. P. Hartley)

1

The complement of *Starfarer* had no idea, when they started out, of how long they might be gone. They searched the sky, the three hundred of them, men and women, black and brown and white and yellow, and in thirty years landed on forty planets whose life-support parameters appeared – from distant observation – close to those of Earth.

Man, they discovered, might fit his own terrestrial niche perfectly, but those parameters for his existence were tight and inelastic. There were planets where they could have dwelt in sealed environments, venturing out only in special suits, even one planet where they could have existed comfortably through half its year but been burned and suffocated in the other half. They found not one where they could establish a colony of mankind.

In thirty years they achieved nothing but an expectable increase in their numbers and this was a factor in their decision to return home. The ship was becoming crowded and, in the way of crowded tenements, something of a slum.

So they headed for Earth; and at the end of the thirty-first year, took up a precessing north-south orbit allowing them a leisurely overview, day by day, of the entire planet.

This was wise. They had spent thirty years in space, travelling between solar systems at relativistic speeds, and reckoned that about six hundred local years had passed since they set out. They did not know what manner of world they might find.

They found, with their instruments, that the greenhouse effect had subsided slowly during the centuries, aided by the first wisps of galactic cloud heralding the new ice age, but that the world was still warmer than the interregnal norm. The ozone layer seemed to have healed itself, but the desert areas were still formidably large although the spread of new pasture and forest was heartening.

What they did not see from orbit was the lights of cities by night and this did not greatly surprise them. The world they had left in a desperate search for new habitat had been an ant heap of ungovernable, unsupportable billions whose numbers were destined to shrink drastically if any were to survive at all. The absence of lights suggested that the population problem had solved itself in grim fashion.

They dropped the ship into a lower orbit just outside the atmosphere and brought in the spy cameras.

There were people down there, all kinds of people. The northern hemisphere was home to nomadic tribes, in numbers like migratory nations; the northern temperate zone had become a corn belt, heavily farmed and guarded by soldiers in dispersed forts, with a few towns and many villages; the equatorial jungles were, no doubt, home to hunter-gatherers but their traces were difficult to see; there were signs of urban communities, probably trading centres, around the seacoasts but no evidence of transport networks or lighting by night and no sounds of electronic transmission. Civilisation had regressed, not unexpectedly.

They chose to inspect Australia first because it was separated from the larger landmasses and because the cameras showed small farming communities and a few townlets. It was decided to send down a Contact Officer to inspect and report back.

The ship could not land. It had been built in space and could live only in space; planetary gravity would have warped its huge but light-bodied structure beyond repair. Exploratory smallcraft could have been despatched, but it was reasoned that a crew of obviously powerful supermen might create an untrusting reserve among the inhabitants, even an unhealthy regard for gods or demons from the sky. A single person, powerfully but unobtrusively armed, would a suitable ambassador.

They sent a woman, Nugan Johnson, not because she happened to be Australian but because she was a Contact Officer, and it was her rostered turn for duty.

They chose a point in the south of the continent because it was autumn in the hemisphere, and an average daily temperature of twenty-six C would be bearable, and dropped her by tractor beam on the edge of a banana grove owned by Mrs Flighty Jones, who screamed and fled.

2

Flighty, in the English of her day, meant something like *scatterbrained*. Her name was, in fact, Hallo-Mary (a rough – very rough – descendant of Ave Maria), but she was a creature of fits and starts, so much so that the men at the bottling shed made some fun of her before they were convinced that she had seen *something*, and called the Little Mother of the Bottles.

'There was I, counting banana bunches for squeeging into baby pap, when it goes hissss-bump behind me.'

'What went hiss-bump?'

'It did.'

'What was it?' Little Mother wondered if the question was unfair to Flighty wits.

'I don't know.' Having no words, she took refuge in

frustrated tears. She had inherited the orchard but not the self control proper to a proprietary woman.

In front of the men! Little Mother sighed and tried again. 'What did it look like? What shape?'

Flighty tried hard. 'Like a bag. With legs. And a glass bowl on top. And it bounced. That's what made the bump. And it made a noise.'

'What sort of noise?'

'Just a noise.' She thought of something else. 'You know the pictures on the library wall? In the holy stories part? The ones where the angels go up? Well, like the angels.'

Little Mother knew that the pictures did not represent angels, whatever the congregation were told. Hiding trepidation, she sent the nearest man for Top Mother.

Top Mother came, and listened . . . and said, as though visitations were nothing out of the way, 'We will examine the thing that hisses and bumps. The men may come with us in case their strength is needed.' That provided at least a bodyguard.

The men were indeed a muscular lot, and also a superstitious lot, but they were expected to show courage when the women claimed protection. They picked up whatever knives and mashing clubs lay to hand and tried to look grim. Man-to-man was a bloodwarming event but man-to-whatisit had queasy overtones. They agreed with Little Mother's warning: 'There could be danger.'

'There might be greater danger later on if we do *not* investigate. Lead the way, Hallo-Mary.' A Top Mother did not use nicknames.

Flighty was now thoroughly terrified and no longer sure that she had seen anything, but Top Mother took her arm and pushed her forward. Perhaps it had gone away; perhaps it had bounced up and up . . .

It had not gone anywhere. It had sat down and pushed back its glass bowl and revealed itself, by its cropped hair, as a man.

'A man,' murmured Top Mother, who knew that matriarchy was a historical development and not an evolutionary given. She began to think like the politician which at heart she was. A *man* from – from *outside* – could be a social problem.

The men, who were brought up to revere women but often resented them – except during the free-fathering festivals – grinned and winked at each other and wondered what the old girl would do.

The old girl said, 'Lukey! Walk up and observe him.'

Lukey started off unwillingly, then noticed that three cows grazed unconcernedly not far from the man in a bag and took heart to cross the patch of pasture at the orchard's edge.

At a long arm's length he stood, leaned forward and sniffed. He was forest bred and able to sort out the man in a bag's scents from the norms about him and, being forest bred, his pheromone sense was better than rudimentary. He came so close that Nugan could have touched him and said, 'Just another bloody woman!' The stranger should have been a man, a sex hero!

He called back to Top Mother, 'It's only a woman with her hair cut short.'

They all crowded forward across the pasture. Females were always peaceable – unless you really scratched their pride.

The hiss Flighty had heard had been the bootjets operating to break the force of a too-fast landing by an ineptly handled tractor beam; the bump had been the reality of a contact that wrenched an ankle. Even the bounce was almost real as she hopped for a moment on one leg. The noise was Nugan's voice through a speaker whose last user had left it tuned to baritone range, a hearty, 'Shit! Goddam shit!' before she sat down and became aware of a dumpy figure vanishing among columns of what she remembered vaguely as banana palms. Not much of a start for good PR.

She thought first to strip the boot and bind her ankle, then that she should not be caught minus a boot if the runaway brought unfriendly reinforcements. She did not fear the village primitives; though she carried no identifiable weapons, the thick gloves could spit a variety of deaths through levelled fingers. However, she had never killed a civilised organism and had no wish to do so; her business was to prepare a welcome home.

The scents of the air were strange but pleasant, as the orbital analysis had affirmed; she folded the transparent *fishbowl* back into its neck slot. She became aware of animals nearby. Cows. She recognised them from pictures though she had been wholly city bred in an era of gigantic cities. They took no notice of her. Fascinated and unafraid, she absorbed a landscape of grass and tiny flowers in the grass, trees and shrubs and a few vaguely familiar crawling and hopping insects. The only strangeness was the spaciousness stretching infinitely on all sides, a thing that the lush Ecological Decks of *Starfarer* could not mimic, together with the sky like a distant ceiling with wisps of cloud. Might it rain on her? She scarcely remembered rain.

Time passed. It was swelteringly hot but not as hot as autumn in the greenhouse streets.

They came at last, led by a tall woman in a black dress – rather, a robe cut to enhance dignity though it was trimmed off at the knees. She wore a white headdress like something starched and folded in the way of the old nursing tradition and held together by a brooch. She was old, perhaps in her sixties, but she had presence and the dress suggested status.

She clutched another woman by the arm, urging her forward, and Nugan recognised the clothing, like grey denim jeans, that fled through the palms. Grey Denim Jeans pointed and planted herself firmly in a determined no-further pose. Madam In Black gestured to the escort and spoke a few words.

Nugan became aware of the men and made an appreciative sound unbecoming in a middle-aged matron past child-bearing years. These men wore only G-strings and they were *men*. Not big men but shapely, muscular and very male. *Or am I so accustomed to Starfarer crew that any change rings a festival bell? Nugan, behave!*

The man ordered forward came warily and stopped a safe arm's length from her, sniffing. Nugan examined him. *If I were, even looked, twenty years younger . . .* He spoke suddenly in a resentful, blaming tone. The words were strange (of course they must be) yet hauntingly familiar; she thought that part of the sentence was 'dam-dam she!'

She kept quiet. Best to observe and wait. The whole party, led by Madam In Black, came across the pasture. They stopped in front of her, fanning out in silent inspection. The men smelled mildly of sweat, but that was almost a pleasure; after thirty years of propinquity, *Starfarer's* living quarters stank of sweat.

Madam In Black said something in a voice of authority that seemed part of her. It sounded a little like 'Oo're yah?' – interrogative with a clipped note to it; the old front-of-the-mouth Australian vowels had vanished in the gulf of years. It should mean, by association, *Who are you?* but in this age might be a generalised, *Where are you from?* even, *What are you doing here?*

Nugan played the oldest game in language lesson, tapping her chest and saying, 'Nugan. I – Nugan.'

Madam In Black nodded and tapped her own breast. 'Ay Tup-Ma.'

'Tupma?'

'Dit – Tup-Ma, Yah Nuggorn?'

'Nugan.'

The woman repeated, 'Nugan,' with a fair approximation of the old vowels and followed with, 'Wurriya arta?'

Nugan made a guess at vowel drift and consonant elision and came up with, *Where are you out of?* meaning, Where do you come from?

They must know, she thought, that something new is in the sky. A ship a kilometre long has been circling for weeks with the sun glittering on it at dawn and twilight. They can't have lost all contact with the past; there must be stories of the bare bones of history . . .

She pointed upwards and said, 'From the starship.'

The woman nodded as if the statement made perfect sense and said, 'Stair-boot.'

Nugan found herself fighting sudden tears. *Home, home, HOME has not forgotten us.* Until this moment she had not known what Earth meant to her, swimming in the depths of her shipbound mind. 'Yes, stairboot. We say starship.'

The woman repeated, hesitantly, 'Stairsheep?' She tried again, reaching for the accent, 'Starship! I say it right?'

'Yes, you say it *properly*.'

The woman repeated, 'Prupperly. Ta for that. It is old-speak. I read some of that but not speak – only small bit.'

So not everything had been lost. There were those who had rescued and preserved the past. Nugan said, 'You are quite good.'

Tup-Ma blushed with obvious pleasure. 'Now we go.' She waved towards the banana grove.

'I can't.' A demonstration was needed. Nugan struggled upright, put the injured foot to the ground and tried for a convincing limp. That proved easy; the pain made her gasp and she sat down hard.

'Ah! You bump!'

'Indeed I bump.' She unshackled the right boot and

broke the seals before fascinated eyes and withdrew a swelling foot.

'We carry.'

We meant two husky males with wrists clasped under her, carrying her through the grove to a large wooden shed where more near-naked men worked at vats and tables. They sat on a table and brought cold water (*How do they cool it? Ice? Doubtful.*) and a thick yellow grease which quite miraculously eased the pain somewhat (*A native pharmacopoeia?*) and stout, unbleached bandages to swathe her foot tightly.

She saw that in other parts of the shed the banana flesh was being mashed into long wooden moulds. Then it was fed into glass cylinders whose ends were capped, again with glass, after a pinch of some noisome-looking fungus was added. (*Preservative? Bacteriophage? Why not?*) A preserving industry, featuring glass rather than metal; such details helped to place the culture.

Tup-Ma called, 'Lukey!' and the man came forward to be given a long instruction in which the word *Stair-boot* figured often. He nodded and left the shed at a trot.

'Lukey go – goes – to tell Libary. We carry you there.'

'Who is Libary?'

The woman thought and finally produced, 'Skuller. Old word, I think.'

'Scholar? Books? Learning?'

'Yes, yes, books. Scho-lar. Ta.' Ta? Of course – thank you. Fancy the child's word persisting.

'You will eat, please?'

Nugan said quickly, 'No, thank you. I have this.' She dug out a concentrate pack and swallowed one tablet before the uncomprehending Tup-Ma. She dared not risk local food before setting up the test kit, enzymes and once-harmless proteins could change so much. They brought a litter padded like a mattress and laid her on it. Four pleasantly husky men carried it smoothly, waist-high, swinging gently along a broad path towards low hills, one of which was crowned by a surprisingly large building from which smoke plumes issued.

'Tup-Ma goodbyes you.'

'Goodbye, Tup-Ma. And ta.'

3

It was a stone building, even larger than it had seemed. But that was no real wonder; the medieval stone masons had built cathedrals far more ornate than this squared-off warehouse of a building. It was weathered dirty grey but was probably yellow sandstone, of which there had been quarries in Victoria. Sandstone is easily cut and shaped even with soft iron tools.

There were windows, but the glass seemed not to be of high quality, and a small doorway before which the bearers set down the litter. A thin man of indeterminate middle age stood there, brown eyes examining her from a dark, clean shaven face. He wore a loose shirt, wide-cut, ballooning shorts and sandals, and he smiled brilliantly at her. He was a full-blooded Aborigine.

He said, 'Welcome to the Library, Starwoman,' with unexceptionable pronunciation though the accent was of the present century.

She sat up. 'The language still lives.'

He shook his head. 'It is a dead language but scholars speak it, as many of yours spoke Latin. Or did that predate your time? There are many uncertainties.'

'Yes, Latin was dead. My name is Nugan.'

'I am Libary.'

'Library?'

'If you would be pedantic, but the people call me Libary. It is both name and title. I preside.' His choice of words, hovering between old-fashioned and donnish, made her feel like a child before a tutor, yet he seemed affable.

He gave an order in the modern idiom and the bearers

carried her inside. She gathered an impression of stone walls a metre thick, pierced by sequent doors which formed a temperature lock. The moist heat outside was balanced by an equally hot but dry atmosphere inside. She made the connection at once, having a student's reverence for books. The smoke she had seen was given off by a low-temperature furnace stoked to keep the interior air dry and at a reasonably even temperature. This was more than a scholars' library; it was the past, preserved by those who knew its value.

She was carried past open doorways, catching glimpses of bound volumes behind glass, of a room full of hanging maps and once of a white man at a lectern, touching his book with gloved hands.

She was set down on a couch in a rather bare room furnished mainly by a desk of brilliantly polished wood which carried several jars of coloured inks, pens which she thought had split nibs and a pile of thick, greyish paper. *(Unbleached paper? Pollution free? A psychic prohibition from old time?)*

The light came through windows, but there were oil lamps available with shining parabolic reflectors. And smoke marks on the ceiling. Electricity slept still.

The carriers filed out. Libary sat himself behind the desk. 'We have much to say to each other.'

Nugan marvelled, 'You speak so easily. Do you use the old English all the time?'

'There are several hundred scholars in Libary. Most speak the old tongue. We practise continually.'

'In order to read the old books?'

'That, yes.' He smiled in a fashion frankly conspirational. 'Also it allows private discussion in the presence of the uninstructed.'

Politics, no doubt – the eternal game that has never slept in all of history. 'In front of Tup-Ma, perhaps?'

'A few technical expressions serve to thwart her

understanding. But the Tup-Ma is no woman's fool.'

'*The* Tup-Ma? I thought it was her name.'

'Her title. Literally, Top Mother. As you would have expressed it, Mother Superior.'

'A nun!'

Libary shrugged. 'She has no cloister and the world is her convent. Call her priest rather than a nun.'

'She has authority?'

'She has great authority.' He looked suddenly quizzical. 'She is very wise. She sent you to me before you should fall into error.'

'Error? You mean, like sin?'

'That also, but I speak of social error. It would be easy. Yours was a day of free thinking and irresponsible doing in a world that could not learn discipline for living. This Australian world is a religious matriarchy. It is fragile when ideas can shatter and dangerous when the women make hard decisions.'

It sounded like too many dangers to evaluate at once. Patriarchy and equality she could deal with – in theory – but matriarchy was an unknown quantity in history. He had given his warning and waited silently on her response.

She pretended judiciousness. 'That is interesting.' He waited, smiling faintly. She said, to gain time, 'I would like to remove this travel suit. It is hot.'

He nodded, stood, turned away.

'Oh, I'm fully dressed under it. You may watch.'

He turned back to her and she pressed the release. The suit split at the seams and crumpled round her feet. She stepped out, removed the gloves with their concealed armament and revealed herself in close-cut shirt and trousers and soft slippers. The damaged ankle hurt less than she had feared.

Libary was impressed but not amazed. 'One must expect ingenious invention.' He felt the crumpled suit fabric. 'Fragile.'

She took a small knife from her breast pocket and slit the material, which closed up seamlessly behind the blade. Library said, 'Beyond our capability.'

'We could demonstrate – '

'No doubt.' His interruption was abrupt, uncivil. 'There is little we need.' He changed direction. 'I think Nugan is of Koori derivation.'

'Possibly from Noongoon or Nungar or some such. You might know better than I.'

His dark face flashed a smile. 'I don't soak up old tribal knowledge while the tribes themselves preserve it in their enclaves.'

'Enclaves?'

'We value variety of culture.' He hesitated, then added, 'Under the matriarchal aegis which covers all.'

'All the world.'

'Most of it.'

That raised questions. 'You communicate with the whole world? From space we detected no radio, no electronic signals at all.'

'Wires on poles and radiating towers, as in the books? Their time has not come yet.'

A queer way of phrasing it. 'But you hinted at global communication, even global culture.'

'The means are simple. Long ago the world was drawn together by trading vessels; so it is today. Ours are very fast; we use catamaran designs of great efficiency, copied from your books. The past does not offer much but there are simple things we take – things we can make and handle by simple means.' He indicated the suit. 'A self-healing cloth would require art beyond our talent.'

'We could show – ' But could they? Quantum chemistry was involved and electro-molecular physics and power generation . . . Simple products were not at all simple.

Libary said, 'We would not understand your showing.

Among your millions of books, few are of use. Most are unintelligible because of the day of simple explanation was already past in your era. We strain to comprehend what you would find plain texts, and we fail. Chemistry, physics – those disciplines of complex numeration and incomprehensible signs and arbitrary terms – are beyond our understanding.'

She began to realise that unintegrated piles of precious but mysterious books are not knowledge.

He said, suddenly harsh, 'Understanding will come at its own assimilable pace. You can offer us nothing.'

'Surely . . . '

'Nothing! You destroyed a world because you could not control your greed for a thing you called progress but which was no more than a snapping up of all that came to hand or to mind. You destroyed yourselves by inability to control your breeding. You did not ever cry *Hold!* for a decade or a century to unravel the noose of a self-strangling culture. You have nothing to teach. You knew little that mattered when sheer existence was at stake.'

Nugan sat still, controlling anger. *You don't know how we fought to stem the tides of population and consumption and pollution; how each success brought with it a welter of unforeseen disasters; how impossible it was to coordinate a world riven by colour, nationality, political creed, religious belief and economic strata.*

Because she had been reared to consult intelligence rather than emotion, she stopped thought in mid-tirade. *Oh, you are right. These were the impossible troubles brought by greed and irresponsible use of a finite world. We begged our own downfall. Yet . . .*

'I think,' she said, 'you speak with the insolence of a lucky survival. You exist only because we did. Tell me how your virtue saved mankind.'

Libary bowed his head slightly in apology. 'I regret anger and implied contempt.' His eyes met hers again. 'But

I will not pretend humility. We rebuilt the race. In which year did you leave Earth?'

'In twenty-one eighty-nine. Why?'

'In the last decades before the crumbling. How to express it succinctly? Your world was administered by power groups behind national boundaries, few ruling many, pretending to a mystery termed *democracy* but ruling by decree. Do I read the history rightly?'

'Yes.' It was a hard admission. 'Well, it was beginning to seem so. Oppression sprang from the need to ration food. We fed fifteen billion only by working land and sea until natural fertility cycles were exhausted, and that only at the cost of eliminating other forms of life. We were afraid when the insects began to disappear . . . '

'Rightly. Without insects, nothing flourishes.'

'There was also the need to restrict birth, to deny birth to most of the world. When you take away the right to family from those who have nothing else and punish savagely contravention of the population laws . . . ' She shrugged hopelessly.

'You remove the ties that bind, the sense of community, the need to consider any but the self. Only brute force remains.'

'Yes.'

'And fails as it has always failed.'

'Yes. What happened after we left?'

Libary said slowly, 'At first, riots. Populations rose against despots, or perhaps against those forced by circumstances into despotism. But ignorant masses cannot control a state; bureaucracies collapsed, supply fell into disarray and starvation set in. Pack leaders – not to be called soldiers – fought for arable territory. Then great fools unleashed biological weaponry – I think that meant toxins and bacteria and viruses, whatever such things may have been – and devastated nations with plague and pestilence. There was a time in the northern hemisphere called by a term I read only as Heart of Winter. Has that meaning for you?'

'A time of darkness and cold and starvation?'

'Yes.'

'Nuclear winter. They must have stopped the bombing in the nick of time. It could only have been tried by a madman intent on ruling the ruins.'

'We do not know his name – their names – even which country. Few records were kept after that time. No machines, perhaps, and no paper.'

'And then?'

'Who knows? Cultural darkness covers two centuries. Then history begins again; knowledge is reborn. Some of your great cities saw the darkness falling and sealed their libraries and museums in hermetic vaults. This building houses the contents of the Central Library of Melbourne; there are others in the world and many yet to be discovered. Knowledge awaits deciphering but there is no hurry. This is, by and large, a happy world.'

Sophisticated knowledge was meaningless here. They could not, for instance, create electronic communication until they had a broad base of metallurgy, electrical theory and a suitable mathematics. Text books might as well have been written in cipher.

'And,' Libary said, 'there were the Ambulant Scholars. They set up farming communities for self support, even in the Dark Age, while they preserved the teachings and even some of the books of their ancestors. They visited each other and established networks around the world. When they set up schools, the new age began.'

'Like monks of the earlier Dark Age, fifteen hundred years before.'

'So? It has happened before?'

'At least once and with less reason. Tell me about the rise of women to power.'

Libary chuckled. 'Power? Call it that but it is mostly

manipulation. The men don't mind being ruled; they get their own way in most things and women know how to bow with dignity when caught in political error. It is a system of giving and taking wherein women give the decisions and take the blame for their mistakes. The men give them children – under certain rules – and take responsibility for teaching them when maternal rearing is completed.'

She made a stab in the dark. 'Women established their position by taking control of the birth rate.'

'Shrewdly thought, nearly right. They have a mumbo-jumpb of herbs and religious observances and fertility periods but in fact it is all contraception, abortion and calculation. Some men believe, more are sceptical, but it results in attractive sexual rituals and occasional carnivals of lust, so nobody minds greatly.' He added offhandedly, 'Those who cannot restrain their physicality are killed by the women.'

That will give Starfarer pause for thought.

'I think,' said Libary, 'that the idea was conceived by the Ambulant Scholars and preached in religious guise – always a proper approach to basically simple souls who need a creed to cling to. So, you see, the lesson of over-population has been learned and put to work.'

'This applies across the planet?'

'Not yet, but it will. America is as yet an isolated continent. Our Ambulant Scholars wielded in the end a great deal of respected authority.'

'And now call yourselves Librarians?'

His black face split with pleasure. 'It is so good to speak with a quick mind.'

'Yet a day will come when population will grow again beyond proper maintenance.'

'We propose that it shall not. Your machines and factories will arrive in their own good time, but our present interest is in two subjects you never applied usefully to living: psychology and philosophy. Your thinking men and women studied profoundly and made their thoughts public, but who listened? There is a mountain of the works of those thinkers to be sifted and winnowed and applied. Psychology is knowledge of the turbulent self; philosophy is knowledge of the ideals of which that self is capable. Weave these together and there appears a garment of easy discipline wherein the self is fulfilled and the world becomes its temple, not just a heap of values for ravishing. We will solve the problem of population.'

Nugan felt, with the uneasiness of someone less than well prepared, that they would. Their *progress* would lie in directions yet unthought of.

'Now,' Libary said, 'would you please tell me how you came to Earth without a transporting craft?'

'I was dropped by tractor beam.'

'A – beam?' She had surprised him at last. 'A ray of light that carries a burden?'

'Not light. Monopoles.'

'What are those?'

'Do you have magnets? Imagine a magnet with only one end, so that the attraction goes on in a straight line. It is very powerful. Please don't ask how it works because I don't know. It is not in my field.'

Libary said moodily, 'I would not wish to know. Tell me, rather, what you want here.'

Want? Warnings rang in Nugan's head but she could only plough ahead. 'After six hundred years we have come home! And Earth is far more beautiful than we remember it to be.'

His dark eyebrows rose. 'Remember? Are you six hundred years old?'

Explanation would be impossible. She said, despairingly, 'Time in heaven is slower than time on Earth. Our thirty years among the stars are six centuries of your time. Please don't ask for explanation. It is not magic; it is just so.'

'Magic is unnecessary in a sufficiently wonderful universe. Do you tell me that you do not understand the working of your everyday tools?'

'I don't understand the hundredth part. Knowledge is divided among specialists; nobody knows all of even common things.'

Libary considered in silence, then sighed lightly and said, 'Leave that and return to the statement that you have come home. This is not your home.'

'Not the home we left. It has changed.'

'Your home has gone away. For ever.'

The finality of his tone must have scattered her wits, she thought later; it roused all the homesickness she had held in check and she said quickly, too quickly, 'We can rebuild it.'

The black face became still, blank. She would have given years of life to recall the stupid words. He said at last, 'After all I have told you of resistance to rapid change you propose to redesign our world!'

She denied without thinking, 'No! You misunderstand me!' In her mind she pictured herself facing *Starfarer's* officers, stumbling out an explanation, seeing disbelief that a trained Contact could be such a yammering fool.

'Do I? Can you mean that your people wish to live as members of our society, in conditions they will see as philosophically unrewarding and physically primitive?'

He knew she could not mean any such thing. She tried, rapidly, 'A small piece of land, isolated, perhaps an island, a place where we could live on our own terms. Without contact. You would remain – unspoiled.'

Insulting, condescending habit of speech, truthful in its meaning, revealing and irrevocable!

'You will live sequestered? Without travelling for curiosity's sake, without plundering resources for your machines, without prying into our world and arguing with it? In that case, why not stay between the stars?'

Only truth remained. 'We left Earth to found new colonies. Old Earth seemed beyond rescue; only new Earths could perpetuate a suffocating race.'

'So much we know. The books tell it.'

Still she tried: 'We found no new Earth. We searched light years of sky for planets suitable for humans. We found the sky full of planets similar to Earth – but only similar. Man's range of habitable conditions is very narrow. We found planets a few degrees too hot for healthy existence or a few degrees too cool to support a terrestrial ecology, others too seismically young or too aridly old, too deficient in oxygen or too explosively rich in hydrogen, too low in carbon dioxide to support a viable plant life or unbearably foul with methane or lacking an ozone layer. Parent stars, even of G-type, flooded surfaces with overloads of ultra-violet radiation, even gamma radiation, or fluctuated in minute but lethal instabilities. We visited forty worlds in thirty years and found not one where we could live. Now you tell me we are not welcome in our own home!'

'I have told you it is not your home. You come to us out of violence and decay; you are conditioned against serenity. You would be only an eruptive force in a world seeking a middle way. You would debate our beliefs, corrupt our young men by offering toys they do not need, tempt the foolish to extend domination over space and time – and in a few years destroy what has taken six centuries to build.'

Anger she could have borne but he was reasonable – as a stone wall is reasonable and unbreachable.

'Search!' he said. 'Somewhere in such immensity must be what you seek. You were sent out with a mission to propagate mankind, but in thirty years you betray it.'

She burst out, 'Can't you understand that we *remember*

Earth! After thirty years in a steel box we want to come home.'

'I do understand. You accepted the steel box; now you refuse the commitment.'

She pleaded, 'Surely six hundred people are not too many to harbour? There must be small corners – '

He interrupted, 'There are small corners innumerable but not for you. Six hundred, you say, but you forget the books with their descriptions of the starships. You forget that we know of the millions of ova carried in the boxes called cryogenic vaults, of how in a generation you would be an army surging out of its small corner to dominate the culture whose careful virtues mean nothing to you. Go back to your ship, Nugan. Tell your people that time has rolled over them, that their home has vanished.'

She sat between desperation and fulmination while he summoned the bearers. Slowly she resumed the travel suit.

From the hilltop she saw a world unrolled around her, stirring memory and calling the heart. It should not be lost for a pedantic Aboriginal's obstinacy.

'I will talk with your women!'

'They may be less restrained than I, Nugan. The Tup-Ma's message said you were to be instructed and sent away. My duty is done.'

She surrendered to viciousness. 'We'll come in spite of you!'

'Then we will wipe you out as a leprous infection.'

She laughed, pointed a gloved finger and a patch of ground glowed red, then white. 'Wipe us out?'

He told her, 'That will not fight the forces of nature we can unleash against you. Set your colony on a hill and we will surround it with bushfires, a weapon your armoury is not equipped to counter. Set it in a valley and we will show you how a flash flood can be created. Force us at your peril.'

All her Contact training vanished in the need to assert. 'You have not seen the last of us.'

He said equably, 'I fear that is true. I fear for you, Nugan, and all of yours.'

She tongued the switch at mouth level and the helmet sprang up and over her head, its creases smoothing invisibly out. She had a moment's unease at the thought of the Report Committee on *Starfarer*, then she tongued the microphone switch. 'Jack!'

'Here, love. So soon?'

'Yes, so damned soon!' She looked once at the steady figure of Libary, watching and impassive, then gave the standard call for return: 'Lift me home, Jack.'

Hurtling into the lonely sky, she realised what she had said and began silently to weep.

ACKNOWLEDGEMENTS

The following acknowledgements are gratefully made for permission to reprint copyright material:

LEARNING TO BE ME first appeared in *Interzone*, 37, July 1990. Copyright Greg Egan, 1990. Reprinted by permission of the author.

RE-DEEM THE TIME first appeared in *Rooms of Paradise* edited by Lee Harding, Quartet Books, 1978. Copyright David Lake, 1978. Reprinted by permission of the author.

WAITING FOR THE RAIN first published in *Universe*, 2, edited by Robert Silverberg & Karen Haber, 1992. Copyright Dirk Strasser, 1992. Reprinted by permission of the author.

REICHELMAN'S RELICS first published in *Amazing*, July 1990. Copyright Leanne Frahm, 1990. Reprinted by permission of the author.

THE LAST ELEPHANT first appeared in *Australian Short Stories*, 20, 1987. Copyright Terry Dowling, 1987. Reprinted by permission of the author.

THE TOKEN POLE first published in *Analog*, Feb. 1990. Copyright Jack Wodhams, 1990. Reprinted by permission of the author.

BUT SMILE NO MORE first published in *Aurealis*, 2, 1990. Copyright Stephen Dedman, 1990. Reprinted by permission of the author.

A TOOTH FOR EVERY CHILD first published in *Urban Fantasies* edited by David King & Russell Blackford, Ebony Books, 1985. Copyright Damien Broderick, 1985. Reprinted by permission of the author.

Still Murder   Finola Moorhead

A murder story with a difference: a body is found by a nun, a woman is in a mental hospital but is she insane? A psychological thriller using the voices of the victim, confessor, detective, suspects and killer. Confessions and obsessions but is it a murder?

Freeze Frame   David Smith

Violence flares between Greenpeace protestors and duck hunters at Great Dismal Swamp, catching film-makers Richard Southeby and Nicole Vander in the crossfire. A stray bullet? Or a sniper?

Their documentary will expose a devastating threat to the last great wilderness – Antarctica. They must be silenced.

Eco-terrorists infiltrating the Green movement provide the perfect cover for an assassin.

The State of the Art
The Mood of Contemporary Australia in Short Stories
Edited by Frank Moorhouse

A frenetic, talented guitarist, barely hanging on to a fragmented life; a canny Jewish uncle, frustrated without a family to organize; lovers seeking pleasure, whatever the cost; an old woman, trundled from the home of one son to another, an intrusion, unloved . . . These are among the characters, some innocent, some eccentric, some disillusioned, who are portrayed in this striking, innovative collection of short stories. Their diversity of style and content reflects the robust hedonism of contemporary Australian society.

Revival House   Julian Davies

What is the connection between history and personal experience, between politics and an individual life, between the myths of a time and its underlying realities?

A young Australian academic finds his studies irresistibly diverted by one of America's most successful and ruthless industrialists, Henry Clay Frick.

With great skill Julian Davies weaves the carefully retold life of Henry Clay Frick into an unusual story of New York family life. The result is a brilliant and compelling novel.

The Baltic Business   Peter Corris

A routine assignment draws Crawley into a web of murder and intrigue involving Eastern European refugees marked by the dark days of the DP camps. His marriage assumes a new dimension as Mandy takes to university study and he takes to the lovely Irina Gilbus whose father heads a shadowy organisation known as Nations in Chains.

Set in Melbourne, Peter Corris's latest thriller features hard-boiled secret-service-man Ray Crawley and his old mate Huck, the stars of *Pokerface*.

The Kimberley Killing   Peter Corris

A retired attorney general's Porsche is driven off a cliff – with him in it! The inexplicable death draws the attention of Federal security organisations. 'Creepy' Crawley is nominated to look into the gay sub-culture and the attorney general's widow, Christine Kimberley. He takes a much greater interest in the latter. Crawley's domestic life continues to be less than blissful as he, and offsider Huck, move round Australia finding that the people ordering the killings are in very high places indeed.

A Woman of the Future   David Ireland

The time of this remarkable novel is the near future. The place is Australia. *A Woman of the Future* is the diary of Alethea Hunt and her personal odyssey in a harsh society and a world of tomorrow.
Winner of the Miles Franklin Award, 1979 and co-winner of the *Age* Book of the Year Award, 1980.

The Kadaitcha Sung   Sam Watson

In his twentieth year, mixed-blood Aborigine Tommy Gubba is initiated in the eternal flames into an ancient clan of sorcerers – the Kadaitcha. He is sent into the mortal world to take revenge on the fair-skinned race who have plundered its wealth and laid waste to the chosen people. His fate has been ordained, and Tommy must race against time to confront a savage, evil foe.

PENGUIN – THE BEST AUSTRALIAN READING

Eye Of The Shadow   Ren Lexander

Michael Trentham regains consciousness in hospital, blind and with no memory of who he is or how he comes to be there. Is his mind trying to blank out some terrible memory? What sort of person is he?

He learns he is the author of an unfinished mystery based on the real-life murder of his publisher. How much of this book is fact and how much fiction? Is the killer really behind bars?

As Michael probes his past and the truth about his 'friends' he struggles to unravel the shadows of his former life and come to terms with reality.

White Light   James McQueen

On 27 January 1945, Tony Caramia walked free from Auschwitz. More than forty years later, he is the tough and restless owner of a successful building business in Australia about to visit Thailand.

By chance, he sights a German guard from the wartime camp, reviving questions and feelings which have long haunted him. Issues of justice, responsibility and guilt emerge in the cat-and-mouse game that follows. Both men are forced to reckon with their past and their choices for the future against a backdrop of the people and landscape of Thailand.

Child's Play   David Malouf

In the streets of an ordinary Italian town, the people go about their everyday lives. In an old apartment block above them, a young man pores over photographs and plans, dedicated to his life's most important project.

Day by day, in imagination, he is rehearsing for his greatest performance. yet when his moment comes, nothing could have prepared him for what happens . . .

Turtle Beach   Blanche d'Alpuget

Judith Wilkes, an ambitious journalist, goes to Malaysia to report on an international refugee crisis.

Through her encounters with Minou, exotic, young French-Vietnamese wife of a high-ranking diplomat, the ambitious Ralph Hamilton and, ultimately with enigmatic Kanan who tries to liberate her, Judith is thrown into dramatic personal and professional conflicts.

It is on the East Malaysian coast, when turtles gather to breed, that the dilemma reaches its tragic, brutal climax.